Praise for *Sunday's Child*

"The feelings run deep and it speaks sensibly, amusingly and passionately." – Marian Engel

"A witty, wonderfully poised, poignant, self-pityless book."
– *Montreal Gazette*

"Written with exquisite style, perfect pace and unusual elegance . . . always engaging, it is a genuine tour de force."
– *Hamilton Spectator*

Praise for *Working on Sunday*

"[Phillips] offers diversion, good humour, some entertaining scenes, a few pungent *aperçus* and a sideways glance at the human condition." – Carol Shields, *Globe and Mail*

Praise for *The Mice Will Play*

"The writing flows wonderfully . . . . All in all, quite a lovely read – a pleasure to the eye, the mind, the heart."
– Merilyn Simonds

"A pleasing, light romp reminiscent of an Oscar Wilde parlour play, with hard truths veiled in happy façades . . . . Phillips has managed to give his work his own stamp while reviving a genre – the parlour farce – that's been dormant for too long." – *Globe and Mail*

"A treat from start to finish . . . . Phillips continues to mine his rich vein of Wildean wit." – *Quill & Quire*

Sunday Best

by Edward O. Phillips

Edward O. Phillips

Sunday Best

A Geoffry Chadwick novel

The Riverbank Press

Copyright © 1990, 2000 by Edward O. Phillips

First published in Seal hardcover by McClelland & Stewart, 1990
Second publication in Seal paperback by McClelland & Stewart, 1991
Third publication in paperback by The Riverbank Press, 2000

Cover and text design: John Terauds

THE CANADA COUNCIL | LE CONSEIL DES ARTS
FOR THE ARTS | DU CANADA
SINCE 1957 | DEPUIS 1957

We acknowledge the support of the Canada Council for the Arts for our publishing program.

Canadian Cataloguing in Publication Data

Phillips, Edward, 1931-
    Sunday best

A Geoffry Chadwick novel.
ISBN 1-896332-14-5

I. Title.

PS8581.H567S94 2000   C813'.54   C00-930938-1
PR9199.3.P44S94 2000

The Riverbank Press
P.O. Box 456, 31 Adelaide St. East, Toronto, Ontario, Canada M5C 2J5

Printed and bound in Canada

for K.S.W.

"Experience, though noon auctoritee
Were in this world, is right ynogh for me
To speke of wo that is in marriage."
                    – Chaucer, "The Wife of Bath's Prologue",
                                        The Canterbury Tales

I

I have always detested shopping malls. Even though the underground plaza has been hailed by city planners as the solution to life in a cold climate, these subterranean caves of commerce are at their worst in winter. The dry, over-heated air imposes two choices: either one continues to wear the heavy overcoat imposed by the cold and suffocates, or else one drapes the garment over an arm, as cumbersome carapace. Should one also be carrying an attaché case, as I frequently do, then both hands are occupied, hardly an asset when upending merchandise to check out the price.

I never enter an underground mall without thinking enviously of that Indian deity, Shiva perhaps, who sports at least three pairs of arms. I could tackle any shopping plaza with six hands: one for the overcoat, one for the briefcase, two for manipulating the merchandise, with two still free for a little discreet shoplifting, should the occasion arise. The big draw-back, of course, would be trying to keep track of six gloves, when I am sorely pressed hanging on to two. I know it must be January because I have already lost my December gloves.

However, one does not really need free hands in most mall boutiques. The salesperson, often the owner, is so greedy to make a sale that he is making a lunge before you are fully through the door. With face fixed in a barracuda smile, the clerk, male or female, asks the same, predictable question,

"Can I help you, sir?" as if I were having some sort of seizure. Just as predictably I fasten my eyes on a point above his right shoulder and reply, "No thanks, just browsing."

The question might legitimately be asked as to why I found myself in one of these underground emporiums at half-past five on a Friday afternoon in mid-January. I was on my way to the liquor store. My bar was out of Scotch, and there remained enough vodka for one strong, two weak, drinks. I discount those other things like brandy and sherry and Campari, which I keep only for other people. Still, there was a time when I drank Campari, along with equal parts of red vermouth and gin, in a lethal concoction known as a Negroni, a mind-altering liquid that brought on some bizarre behaviour. Adieu, Ten Commandments. But that was then. Now, whatever I drink is well diluted with water.

I made my way across the travertine floor, ignoring the hand-lettered signs in boutique windows offering reductions of up to 50 percent. Experience has taught me that any merchandise I might want to purchase has slipped through the sale, or is reduced a scant 10 percent. Furthermore, I have reached the age when one begins to shed possessions, not acquire them. I remembered, not without some amusement, when underground shopping malls were still a novelty and young gay blades cruised in them. But AIDS, age, and apathy have put an end to that formerly energizing pastime, for me at least. Especially age. A curious thing happens to people sometime around fifty-five. They become sexually invisible. Young and attractive men look at you, but there is no recognition in their glance, no more of that brief but knowing eye contact that generates its own electricity. Even young women, far more liberated today than when I was a young man, glance at me and then away, as if they understood I have scaled my walls, slain my dragons, made my treaties, and retired from the battlefield.

I entered the liquor store and made my way to the rear, where the Scotch was secreted as if contraband. The readily accessible shelves near the cashier's counter feature local wines with terrifying names like Cold Duck, Snowdrop (Perce-Neige), Vat of Patriots (Cuvée des Patriotes), or White Orpheus (Orphée Blanc), nothing you would ever want to drink, not even during the biannual liquor board strike, when Saturday morning means driving to Ontario to stock up. I collected forty ounces of Scotch, forty of vodka, and took them to the cashier. I was about to leave the mall, so I buttoned on my overcoat before paying. The spotty young man who took my money slid the two bottles into a large paper bag.

"May I have a shopping bag, please?"

He looked crestfallen. "The manager says we can only give shopping bags to customers who buy three bottles or more."

"You mean to say that if I buy three six-dollar bottles of wine I get a shopping bag, but not with two twenty-five-dollar bottles of liquor?"

I could see what I suspected to be a limited intelligence grappling with the subtleties of my argument. What the hell! The cashier was not at fault, but the tight-assed manager, with whom I had recently jousted over a grown-up bottle of wine whose cork had disintegrated.

At the end of the counter stood rows of those doll-house-sized bottles of liquor served on airplanes. I reached for a teeny-weeny Cointreau, which would get lost in a fruit salad, and set it down beside my Scotch and vodka.

"You did say three bottles?"

Cornered, the young man capitulated and slid my pur-chases into a white plastic bag emblazoned with the words "Sélection, Acceuil, Qualité."

My liquor in one hand, my briefcase in the other, I headed for the door leading into the street. Already anticipating that first cold refreshing blast of carbon monoxide, I heard a voice call my name.

"Geoffry? Geoffry Chadwick! Halt!"

I am not yet old enough to plead deafness, and I turned to see Audrey Crawford in full sail skimming over the travertine in a billow of natural mink. Even before she coasted to a stop in front of me I knew she would comment on the liquor I was car-rying. Many Canadians still think drinking is the stuff of comedy.

"We've been doing a bit of shopping?"

"Just picked up a little something for dinner."

She laughed without merriment, laughter meant to convey that she came in peace. "You're looking well, Geoffry. We sur-vived Christmas, I see."

"We did." Of late, Audrey Crawford (Audrey McMaster when I first knew her) has taken to using the royal we, like one of those grimly cheerful nurses who tell quadriplegics that we are going to wash our face and hands. "It's an exhausting time. So terribly compressed. All those people we have to see in the space of a week. Well, it's done for another year. Let me buy you a drink. I just had my hair done."

This was all too evident. A blond in her youth, Audrey Crawford had tried to maintain the status quo by chemical means, with limited success.

"I'd love to," I fibbed, "but I have a dinner date."

Years ago, during our first year at university, Audrey and I once spent what used to be called a dirty weekend. Her father was in Europe, and her mother had left town for a few days. We had to take advantage of the empty house. There was no passion and very little pleasure. My principal satisfaction came from knowing that I was finally doing what all boys were supposed to do – lay girls. (When I grew to know myself better, I took a cue from Alexander Pope and decided that "The proper study of makind is man.") Audrey's real motive for going "all the way" under the parental roof was to shaft Mummy. A messy divorce subsequently revealed to her that Mummy had been doing precisely the same thing in Toronto.

Audrey married well, meaning money. I sometimes wondered whether her trip down the aisle to marry Hartland Crawford had been occasioned by love or the gravitational pull one blue-chip portfolio feels for another. In any case, Audrey has never relinquished a proprietary air towards me. It was almost as though having once been the cause of a few tame orgasms, she now owned a block of stock in Geoffry Chadwick, Inc.

Over the years Audrey Crawford had become a close friend of my sister, Mildred, now living in Toronto. This tenuous connection, rather than our grand amour, kept us linked for the past three decades.

"Sorry you don't have time for a drink. I thought we'd toast the good news."

"Good news?" Beneath my buttoned overcoat and knotted scarf I was beginning to experience hot flashes, which I hoped were a result of the central heating.

"Wedding bells, of course. Another June bride. You must be pleased."

"For whom?"

"Oh, Geoffry, stop being such an old stick. She is your niece, after all."

"My niece?"

"Yes, dearest, your niece. Jennifer. She is being married in June. Have you forgotten?"

"To be perfectly candid, no. I never knew."

"You're having me on."

"Indeed not." I remembered that Mother had telephoned the office this morning, but I was with a client. When I called back the line was busy. "Now, do you want to tell me, or shall I go home and call Mildred?"

"You've got to be pulling my leg."

A quick sigh of impatience caused a blast of body heat to escape from under my collar. "I'm not pulling your leg, or any other part of your anatomy. Now, are you going to tell me or not?"

Audrey Crawford gave her heavily lacquered curls a slight toss. "Well, Jennifer is to marry Douglas Fullerton, in June. Because the Fullerton boy is from Westmount, and since your mother does not like to travel, the wedding will be held right here, at the church of St. Luke the Apostle."

"I guess it beats holding the ceremony on a sand bar at low tide, with guests throwing handfuls of brown rice. Thanks for telling me. Now off I go, to pencil it in on my calendar and to brush up my Sunday best. I may have to get the tailor to let it out an inch or so around the waist."

"I hope your Sunday best is a morning coat."

"How so?"

"You're to give the bride away."

"Am I, now. 'Well, well, well,' said the old oaken bucket. Is there anything else you think I should know at the moment?"

"I really find it extraordinary Mildred hasn't spoken to you."

"She will, in her own good time. And now, my dear Audrey, before I melt away completely, like the Wicked Witch of Westmount, I must go. We will waltz at the wedding."

I exposed my teeth in what could have passed for a smile, and left. By now tiny trickles of perspiration were running down my back, and once outside I felt instantly chilled. As my car was at the garage, I gestured awkwardly with my briefcase and managed to flag down a cab. I suddenly felt in a great hurry for that first drink.

When I was a small boy, certain friends of my parents still draped the parlour furniture in dust covers whenever they went away. Summer rooms looked haunted, especially at twilight, with the outlines of chairs and sofas still visible beneath spectral sheets.

My own apartment had that same spooky appearance. Some decorating, long overdue, was in progress, with the result that all my living-room furniture had been pushed together in the middle of the floor and covered in drop cloths. The effect was unsettling. I felt a little bit like the child in that Ravel opera who finds himself confronted by objects he has once abused, now suddenly alive: an armchair, a grandfather clock, a teapot. I would not have been in the least surprised had the Charles Eames chair leaped out from under its protective covering and chased me around the room.

I switched on the lights; illusion gave way to the reality of a large room being refurbished. At least the painter was gone. A small, reedy man, his life is a sitcom, although I don't much feel like watching a sitcom at eight in the morning. When he arrives, the light still twinkling on my coffee machine, I feel in all civility that I should offer him a cup. He adds three spoon-fuls of sugar and I marvel at his metabolism. He sighs a deep sigh, then tells me about his pregnant wife, his seven children, and how he has trouble making ends meet. I once suggested he might be well advised to buy a television set, implying he should spend less time fooling around. Ignoring my ham-fisted irony, he replied that he already owned one, and a VCR as well. He will be gone next week, well tipped, and I will breathe a huge sigh of relief.

I poured myself a Scotch and water, which I carried into the bedroom, much compressed by occasional tables, lamps, and *objets d'art* in temporary storage from the rest of the apartment. Mother's line was still busy; quite obviously she was having a high old time telling the world about her granddaughter's im-pending wedding. I toyed with the idea of calling my sister and listening with the smug confidence that springs from being told at length about something you already know. My hand was reaching for the receiver when I pulled it back. If, as Audrey Crawford had just informed me, I was to be conscripted into the wedding, then I was not about to scamper up to the com-manding officer and volunteer.

I am certainly not the first to have observed that nobody brings out your shortcomings more quickly than a member of your own family. My sister, Mildred, shines as a striking ex-ample of this truism. Somewhere, in the recesses of her mind, she has a book, a giant volume with embossed cover set with precious stones, of the sort once chained to a lectern in a medieval library. Inside, on illuminated and rubricated pages, are set out rules governing the conduct of one member of a family towards another. The underlying principles are those of duty and impingement. Put simply, Mildred believes that a member of any family can ask another member of that family to perform difficult and disagreeable tasks merely because they are related. It is a principle I have never endorsed.

To be sure, I was truly sorry when her husband died un-expectedly last year. The sudden void left by the abrupt death of someone who has been part of your landscape for many years is, if nothing else, a mute reminder of your own mutability. Bruce was two years younger than I, a confirmed hypochondriac, and firmly convinced that if he did not drink and ate right and did not smoke and exercised regularly and did not stay up late and took vitamins, then he would live to be ninety. Nobody, least of all Bruce himself, expected he would have a massive stroke while riding his exercycle.

I went to Toronto simply to be present both at the funeral service and at the graveside. The funeral was private, the coffin open. Bruce lay with his eyes closed, heavily made up as though he were about to be interviewed by a local TV station. Rest in peach. Mildred had not even dried her eyes at the cemetery before she began turning the screws. She is too cunning to attack me directly, but she is a true professional when it comes to the oblique observation hinting at my inadequacies. We had hardly climbed into the chauffeured limousine for the drive home from the cemetery when Mildred suggested that it would have been nice had Mother been at the service.

Although I had already performed the routine, I patiently

explained once again that obliging Mother – old, frail, alcoholic – to drag herself up to Toronto just to look at a coffin would be less an expression of family solidarity than a penance. Furthermore, I took full responsibility for the decision. Subjecting an old lady to that ordeal would have done nothing for Bruce and might well have put Mother herself into one of those shiny brown boxes with handles that look like linen-boutique towel racks.

Realizing she had driven herself down a blind alley in her search for the perfect guilt trip, my sister shut up, at least for the time being. For once in my life I blessed the claims of business. The corporate law firm in which I was a partner, Lyall, Pierce, Chadwick, and Dawson, had been retained to fight an important takeover. We were standing up for the small shareholders, those owning nonvoting shares, and I had become genuinely interested in the case. My presence was required in Montreal, and the limousine drove me directly from Mildred's house to the airport.

Not long after the funeral, Mildred came to Montreal to visit Mother, not to play the bereaved daughter, dabbing at the furtive tear with a cambric hankie, but to show how unflinchingly she was taking the whole thing. Mildred boasts that dubious virtue known as character, an ability to suppress the so-called weaker feelings and present to the world an expression of assurance and self-control that would do credit to the Statue of Liberty.

She had packed an exclusively black wardrobe, mix and match, although with black everything already matched. Her rigorously tailored appearance, when I took her to dinner, only reinforced the impression I always had that Mildred was born to wear a uniform. Her shoulders looked incomplete without epaulettes; her bust cried out for brass buttons; her belted waist ought to have been cinched by broad, burnished leather. She inhabited an imperative world. *Ought* and *should* found their frequent way into her conversation.

She resumed her offensive by suggesting it was a shame Bruce and I had not been better friends. I really *ought* to have made more effort to know him. There are two possible responses to such an accusation. The first is a belt in the chops. The second is a clumsy attempt at self-justification. It being the Ritz dining room, I chose the second alternative, explaining that it is difficult to be close friends with someone who lives in another city and whom one sees infrequently.

The explanation failed to satisfy my sister, but then I knew it would. Her rules for family behaviour dictated that the man she married be totally absorbed into our family group. It was not enough that Bruce and I were civil when we met. Mildred wanted, demanded, commitment. Her idea of masculine friendship was the stuff of saga, gashing our palms with a dagger and mingling blood. She would have liked us to swear oaths on a naked sword, exchange talismans, stand shoulder to shoulder against the barbarians.

It is difficult to adopt a heroic stance with a man who has about as much personality as the hole in the doughnut. Bruce Carson was my sister's husband. As such he was entitled to my respect and courtesy. More I did not offer; nor did he expect more. And now that he was dead it seemed pointless, even ghoulish, to subject our relationship to a postmortem. I disapprove of necrophilia, emotional or otherwise, although it has been observed that when having sex with a dead body you don't have to worry about looking your best. I steered the conversation onto problems dealing with the estate, Bruce's will, and what Mildred could reasonably expect to live on, and we got through dinner.

By now I had finished my drink. I returned to the kitchen to top it up and decided to give Mother's number another try. I must have caught her during that split second between calls, because the phone began to bleat. Mother's vision, coordination, and attention span are all sliding rapidly downhill. As a result I gave her a touch telephone for Christmas, one with oversized numbers. She manages to punch the buttons in the correct sequence most of the time. Should she get a wrong number she apologizes and proceeds to explain about her bifocals and the new telephone she still isn't used to. Yes, a Christmas present from her son. He's a lawyer, you know. Yes, they are much nicer than the dial ones, but it's so very easy to make a mistake. You do too? Well, I'm so relieved to learn I'm not the only one. I really hope I didn't disturb you, but it's so nice to chat. I don't get out very much these days, and in winter? Yes, they say snow is on the way. Be very careful when you go out, and don't slip. Just lovely talking with you. And you have a nice day too. She loves it, but the device makes a sound more like a sheep than a bell.

I have to confess it is a bit galling to know that she is having a far better time with her el cheapo, bought-on-special touch telephone than with the VCR I gave her last year. She is terrified to use that very expensive stocking stuffer.

Mother must have been sitting on the phone. Halfway through the second ring she picked it up. "Hello?"

"Mother, it is I, your son and heir."

"Geoffry! I've been trying to reach you all day."

This was totally untrue, but age and alcohol have combined to make Mother's grasp of reality tenuous at best.

"Here I am. I tried to return your call, but the line has been busy."

"Has it really? Well, I do have some exciting news. Jennifer is to be married, to that nice Fullerton boy she has been seeing. And you are going to give her away."

"Am I, now?"

"You have to admit you are the logical person, now that your sister is a widow. Not that you could really fill Bruce's shoes. Poor Bruce."

Coming from anyone else but Mother that last observation could have been taken as a snub. However, I knew hers was not a qualitative observation but a simple statement that Bruce, like all human beings, was unique. In the ensuing pause I heard a slight tinkle coming over the line, as of ice cubes in a glass."

"I disagree with you, Mother. Richard is the bride's brother, and he is the eldest child. Far better he give his sister away than her shop-soiled uncle."

"Richard is to be head usher. And her sister Elizabeth will be maid of honour. Mildred has it all worked out. What a thoughtful girl she is. She knows how much I dislike travel, so she has arranged to hold the wedding right here, in Westmount, at St. Luke the Apostle."

Remembering how Mildred tried to work me over because Mother had not gone to Toronto for the funeral, I suddenly found a lot of very naughty words dancing through my mind, but I refrained from saying them out loud. "At the risk of sounding like one of those boring Greek women who hung out in sacred groves uttering bad news, I strongly suspect that by the time Mildred and company have taken over our apartments, our attention, and our lives, you will wish the two of us had taken the easy way out, like riding to Toronto for the wedding on a tandem bicycle."

"Oh, Geoffry, you are turning into such a – such an irascible old curmudgeon. You really must watch yourself."

That Mother managed to get out those two heavy-duty words without stumbling showed she was really flying. Another faint tinkle came down the Bell Canada wire.

"Don't worry, Mother. Six weeks before the wedding I shall enrol myself for a refresher course in sweetness school."

"A good idea! Just remember: it's always darkest before the silver lining. And Geoffry, when your sister calls, do act surprised. I really should have let her tell you the good news, but I was too excited. Now the fat is out of the bag."

"And the cat's in the fire. Don't worry, Mother. I will greet the news with whistles of surprise and gasps of astonishment. Best actor in a supporting role. Now, I'm sure you have other people to call."

"Jennifer will be coming down soon, next week perhaps, to make preliminary arrangements. She'll stay here, of course. You'll come to dinner?"

"Sure thing, Mother."

"Here comes Madame with my supper tray."

"Bon appétit!" I hung up, grateful to the housekeeper for her timely interruption. It is becoming increasingly difficult to get Mother off the telephone once the conversation has ended. Age and alcohol aside, she has that old-fashioned idea of courtesy as time spent on others. To be civil means giving people your undivided attention, and, it goes without saying, demanding theirs in return. My idea of courtesy is minimalist, to use a fashionable buzzword. I try to leave others alone as much as possible, neither compelling their attention nor allowing them to impinge on mine. In my family that makes me a comfortable majority of one.

Sunday morning was just about to slide into Sunday afternoon when Mildred got around to telephoning. With her impeccable sense of timing, she caught me just as I had finished bundling myself up warmly and was on the point of going out. I use the term *going out* in the tame sense of leaving the apartment. When I was younger, *going out* meant heeding the call of those jungle drums. But nowadays that sound is muffled, even more so when the city lies buried under thirty-seven centimetres of snow, or fifteen inches as I tell my American friends so they can grasp the extent of the inconvenience.

There is something infinitely depressing about four bare walls waiting for the final coat of paint, and I intended to kill the afternoon with lunch and then a movie, perhaps the one about the musical man-eating plant from outer space. I was just thinking that with any luck I might obtain a cutting of this same plant to send to my sister, when the phone rang.

One of the qualities I most dislike in myself is my capacity for being bullied by the telephone. An appliance that began life as a communications convenience has turned into the control centre of any household, even more compelling than the television set. People will tear themselves away from the climactic moment of a favourite TV program to answer the importunate ring. I even had a lover once who interrupted a terrific fuck-in-progress to answer the phone in the next room. By the time he hung up I had dressed and departed, for keeps.

I wanted to leave my apartment, to hear the phone ringing more and more faintly as I headed for the stairwell, which I have taken to using so as not to be obliged to speak to neighbours on the elevator. But I knew two of my partners were at the office today and maybe wanted to reach me. Then there is Mother, a walking accident waiting to happen. Lastly, there was always the chance, remote I must admit, that a grateful client might want to fly me to New York City in a private jet for early dinner at the Four Seasons, followed by a box at the opera.

I gave in and decided to answer the phone.

"Geoffry?" My sister's naturally resonant voice was so amplified by the receiver that my ear buzzed.

"You are listening to a recorded announcement. Geoffry Chadwick is unable to come to the telephone at the moment because he is levitating. At the sound of the dry, hacking cough please leave – "

"Geoffry, I have something important to tell you. Please pay attention!"

I guess it was the "Please pay attention!" that did it, but the promise I had made to Mother about feigning astonishment went up in smoke.

"You telephoned to say that Jennifer is to be married and I am to give her away."

"You've been told!"

"Bad news travels fast."

"Really, Geoffry, I hardly think that word of Jennifer's engagement could be called bad news. But then you have always treated my children as though I bought them on the black market."

"The bad news part is not the engagement. That's Jennifer's affair. If she wants to tie herself down to one man for the rest of her life it's her – " I was going to say "funeral," but remembered my recently interred brother-in-law, "decision. What concerns me is giving her away, like a promotional gift. What happens if I have to take her back?"

"You're just being silly. All you will have to do is walk down the aisle with Jennifer on your arm. It doesn't seem too much to ask, for your own niece."

"Why doesn't Richard give her away? He's more closely related than I, and the male presence in the household."

"Richard will be head usher. And the bride really should be given away by a senior relative."

"Thanks a lot. As far as I'm concerned, senior begins at seventy. Audrey Crawford tells me I have to wear a morning coat."

"Oh, so Audrey told you."

"And Mother."

"How is Audrey? Haven't seen her for months."

"All right, I guess. Her hair is still the colour of ripe corn, and she's beginning to look like a middle-aged kewpie doll. But she wasn't wheezing or gasping or limping or anything. Now about that morning coat: I don't own one."

"You really should, a man in your position."

"And what position is that, pray tell?" I was tempted to make an off-colour observation, but my sister has no sense of humour about sex, or much else for that matter. She knows perfectly well I am homosexual (I don't add "practicing" because I got it right years ago). However, Mildred still carries on as though the right woman were waiting just around the next corner.

"You know perfectly well what I mean. If you don't wish to have one made you could rent, but do so in plenty of time. There is always a shortage of dress clothes in June."

"Rented clothes? Other people's armpits? You've got to be kidding."

"Indeed not."

"Hold on a minute." Heat and irritation were making me prickle; I put down the receiver and took off my overcoat. Reluctantly, I retrieved the receiver.

"Don't be stubborn," said Mildred. "Go to a reputable outfit, where they dry clean clothes between rentals."

"You seriously expect me to put my dainty private parts into a pair of rented trousers that God only knows who may have worn?"

"Your dainty private parts, as you call them, have been in worse places, I venture to say."

"Mildred, don't be coarse."

"Stop being squeamish."

"Have you no other friends, colleagues of Bruce's, equipped with morning coats and anxious to be of service to the Widow Carson?"

"Geoffry, is it really too much to ask you to do this for your own niece? Once in a lifetime?"

"Wrong again! We live in the age of serial monogamy. Jennifer will probably have at least three husbands, not to mention her share of serious shackups."

"You are quite impossible."

"What is the date of this extravaganza? I'll have to consult my horoscope."

A quick sigh of impatience came down the line from Toronto. "June thirteenth. It's a Saturday."

"Doesn't sound very auspicious to me. Not at all. I'll have to have my fortune told before I can give you an answer."

There ensued a slight pause. From experience I knew Mildred was manoeuvring her big guns into position.

"Of course I can't force you to wear a morning coat, or to give Jennifer away, if you refuse to do so. However, I would sooner you broke the news to Mother than I. She will be dreadfully disappointed. The last thing she said to me before she hung up the phone was that looking forward to the wedding will help her get through the winter months. That she couldn't wait to see her youngest granddaughter walk down the aisle on the arm of her only son. And Geoffry is so tall; he will look so handsome and distinguished in a morning coat."

She had me, the bitch. I was the butterfly in the bottle, waiting for the cotton wool soaked in chloroform. I could gladly push Mildred fully dressed off a pier – and did once as a child, to no end of recrimination. But I could not disappoint Mother. The whims of the old and frail carry more weight than edicts chiselled in stone. There was another reason. Even though my father had been dead many years, I still remembered him with the warm glow of affection. He was the first man I ever loved, and now that I look back on my life I realize I probably loved him best of all. He would have expected me to do as Mother wished. And it was for him that I capitulated.

"Very well, dear sister. I can see you take no prisoners. I will give Jennifer away. And I will wear drag, although a bigger drag than having a morning coat made I cannot imagine. You have won your point. I am shot down in flames. And I have had nothing to eat today. I am going out. You are listening to a recorded announcement: this conversation will self-destruct in five seconds. So long, Millie." (She hates being called that.)

I did go to see the movie about the carnivorous plant. Even as it gleefully gobbled down various members of the cast, I couldn't help thinking that Mildred would have given it heart-burn.

II

Monday morning on the dot of ten the red light on my telephone began to flicker. As I had a good deal of work to get through, I had asked my secretary to screen calls.

"A Mrs. Lois Fullerton to speak to you, Mr. Chadwick. Shall I say you're busy?"

"No, Mrs. Patterson, I'll take it." There followed a faint click. "Good morning, Mrs. Fullerton. Geoffry Chadwick here."

"Good morning, Mr. Chadwick, I hope I'm not calling you at an inconvenient time. I could call back, or leave my number."

The voice on the line was the stuff of adolescent erotic fantasies, low, vibrant, melodious. Her vowels were full of sex, her consonants of money.

"Not at all, Mrs. Fullerton. Am I correct in assuming that you are the mother of the groom?"

"Precisely." She laughed into the receiver. I had read in pulp novels about women who laughed deep, throaty laughs — that is, before they were discovered to have shot their husbands. But Lois Fullerton did laugh a deep, throaty laugh, a kind of come-hither chuckle. "Now, I have not yet met your sister Mildred, but we have spoken on the telephone. As she has only recently lost her husband, like me I regret to say, I understand you are to give the bride away."

I decided against mouthing a sympathetic platitude. "That

is correct. Secondary billing. My name below the titles."

Lois Fullerton laughed again. This time the sound was a touch more shrill, which suggested she laughed from amusement rather than to create an effect.

"Very good. But I know you're busy. Since we are both involved in the wedding, our names below the title, as you put it, I thought perhaps we should meet. Would you come for a drink some evening, perhaps a bite of potluck supper?"

"I'd be delighted." I uttered the social lie with the ease born of practice. Drinks and a potluck supper with a total stranger have never been my idea of a good time, particularly when the stranger is a widow and, to extrapolate a diagnosis from her voice, running a temperature from the waist down. But, as I had known from the start, I had allowed myself to become involved in a situation where the sum of the parts would turn out to be far greater than the whole. Reason and courtesy both demanded I meet the mother of the groom.

"How about Friday evening, if you're free. Say around six?"

I paused, as if consulting a calendar dense with social engagements. The dull truth is that now I no longer go out to the sound of jungle drums, I far prefer to stay at home, a drink, a book, my VCR, and a couple of packages of *cuisine minceur* in my freezer. However, instead of rhythmic throbbing in my ears I heard the clarion bugles, loud and strident, of duty.

"Friday evening will be just fine," I replied.

The rest of the conversation dealt with logistics. She offered to send her chauffeur to fetch me, but I declined, preferring the independence of my own car. She gave me her address and telephone number and suggested the most convenient route to her house. Work reclaimed my attention, and I put Lois Fullerton and her potluck supper out of my mind.

People who are given to stating they are not religious are really saying they do not believe in God. As most of us have our notions of God shaped by long-dead Italian painters, notably Michelangelo, we tend to imagine the deity as a man with the physique of a stevedore wearing the untrimmed beard and uncut hair of someone who has just won a major poetry award. Possibly we have outgrown this image, even though most of us have the urge to make some sort of numinous connection with the vast unknown.

I have sometimes wondered if God is really small, frail, bald, nearsighted, and quite bewildered by the universe he once created on a whim and which has since spun wildly out of control. He is still capable, however, of arranging small epiphanies: a snowy owl perched regally in the back yard, the loose change found by a small boy beside a parking meter, a size 42 tall morning suit in mint condition on a rack in the Turnabout Shop.

An errand run on my lunch hour brought me into the vicinity of that volunteer emporium, whose proceeds go to a hospital. It is not a place I frequent, but whether I acted on a hunch or by some sort of extraterrestrial prompting, I walked in only moments after a shipment of clothing from an estate had been put on the racks. The tailcoat, vest, and trousers had been made in London. Not only were they impeccably tailored but the pockets were still sewn shut, suggesting the garment had never been worn.

Needless to say, I left with the suit over my arm and only a few dollars poorer. Perhaps I am selectively squeamish, but I do not mind wearing clothing that has once belonged to someone else. I do mind wearing costumes that anyone coming in off the street can rent, democracy at its most dry cleaned.

The sun hung glowing in a rare clear sky. Cold air nipped at my ears, seeped through my gloves, but I didn't mind. Crisp air is energizing, and my casual stumbling across a morning coat seemed a favourable omen. At that precise moment I felt I could handle my niece's wedding.

After laying the suit flat on the back seat of my car, I sought out a nearby bookstore to see if it carried a how-to book on weddings. "If you can't lick 'em, join 'em," and it had been more than thirty years since I buttoned myself into a double-breasted blue blazer and walked into the chancel to marry my bride.

The salesperson – every inch a lady – was just as I would have wished: her hair in a bun, a canada goose fastened to her cardigan, her tweed skirt ending only inches above her sensible Wallabies. She did not ask if I needed help.

"Are you looking for a specific book, or just browsing?"

"What I'm really looking for is a book which will explain the ins and outs of a wedding, a formal wedding."

She smiled. "Your daughter, perhaps?"

"My niece."

She went to the rear of the shop and began to search, giving me a moment or two to look around. Whether the bookseller was making a sly statement or whether she was short of space, I couldn't be sure, but the top shelf of the section marked Fiction was filled with diet books.

The saleslady returned, carrying a volume. "There are a number of wedding books on the market, but I understand this one is as good as most. They all say more or less the same thing."

"A bird in the hand," I replied, perhaps prompted by her pin. The book she handed me was *Fifteen Steps to a Lovelier*

Wedding, by Amelia Gates. I could hardly wait for Mildred to make her first blunder in wedding protocol, which I, with long-suffering tact, would feel duty-bound to correct. Not that I gave a damn about the finer points of nuptial etiquette. But Mildred was forever bringing conversations to a grinding halt while she pulled out her dictionary or her *Bartlett's* or her *Oxford Companion* so she could hunt down a word, a quote, a fact. The rest of us would sit in a state of social suspended animation while she pointed out that "A rose by any other name would smell as sweet" was in reality, "That which we call a rose," etc. Mildred is the kind of woman who gives Shakespeare a bad name.

As I walked back to my car I found myself thinking of my daughter. Had she lived she would have been almost thirty years old, possibly married, with children of her own. I would have been a grandfather. The state of grandfatherhood begins to overtake other men in their mid-fifties, but although in my mid-fifties, I still did not feel old enough to be a grandfather. I could not help smiling as I thought of the games we all play to deny age, *old* being the one adjective that declines itself backwards.

To wit: As a small boy I took pride in being the oldest child, looking down on Mildred for being younger and dragging out months, even days, to prove I was the oldest at games. Oldest stops at thirty, to be replaced by older. I have now reached the stage of being older, in which condition I will continue for some time: the older brother, the older man. Finally I will one day have to admit that I have passed older to become old.

The fact remains that men old enough to be grandfathers still have to be on time for appointments. As I did not have time for lunch in a restaurant, I ducked into a nearby supermarket for a package of cheese and a couple of apples to eat in my car. The self-service was discreet, courteous, and efficient. Through my windshield I could read not one but two bumper stickers on the car parked ahead of me. The first said simply: I ❤ Montreal. Across the second flew a flock of Canada geese with the legend: Honk If You Love Jesus.

Friday afternoon before leaving my office I telephoned the garage to learn whether my car was ready to be picked up. New winter tires were to have been installed on the rear wheels, the oil was to have been changed, the motor tuned up. I was informed that the car would be ready tomorrow afternoon. Small matter; I would take a cab to Lois Fullerton's house.

I made my customary stop at the liquor commission. Even though I still had Scotch, I wanted another bottle, just in case. I won't die if I run out of Scotch, but life, liberty, and the pursuit of happiness will become just that much more difficult. I also needed a bottle of wine to take along to my hostess, something French and red. I toyed briefly with a bottle of champagne, the wedding wine after all. But it is such a foolish drink, the bubbles suggesting a gay occasion (before that word fell into disrepute). My generation of homosexuals looks on champagne as a sissy drink. Real numbers don't drink champagne. I chose instead a Châteauneuf-du-Pape, then took a second bottle for myself, thereby guaranteeing I would get a shopping bag without a struggle.

I managed to find a cab without being waylaid by Westmount matrons bearing tidings. Once home, I poured myself a drink, just in case the prelude to the potluck supper turned out

to be sherry or sangria, or one of those aperitifs more suitable
drunk on a sunny Italian afternoon than on a chilly Canadian
evening. I washed my face and changed my shirt. On the point
of telephoning for a taxi, I remembered that Lois had offered to
send the chauffeur to pick me up. Since this evening had been
her idea, not mine, I saw no reason not to take advantage of her
offer. I telephoned her, explained how my car was unavailable,
and asked whether her driver could come by and fetch me.

"But of course," she replied in a husky contralto. "I'll send
him right down."

My apartment never looked more inviting than during
those few minutes it took to finish my drink. But duty, that
stern daughter of the voice of God, drove me out the door and
into the stairwell, where I narrowly avoided bumping into the
nelly old auntie who lives at the far end of the hall. He runs a
graphics boutique called Copies Charmantes, which loosely
translates as Prints Charming. That aside, the only way to live
comfortably in an apartment building is to pretend you are the
sole tenant. You may not get many Christmas cards, but at least
you are spared from being the resident fourth at bridge.

I pushed my way into the lobby thinking I would be on the spot
when Lois Fullerton's car arrived. At that same moment the
chauffeur pulled open the door and crossed to the porter's desk.
He did not yet know who I was, of course, so I had a chance to
study him unobserved. My eyes might not actually have popped
out, nor did my jaw drop, but I looked very, very hard. Six-foot-
two at least, with broad shoulders and narrow waist, he had
that olive-skinned handsomeness nurtured in a warm climate,

the Mediterranean or the Caribbean. His face had a sharpness of plane and clarity of outline that a movie camera would have loved to caress. In his navy blue uniform and peaked cap, he was anybody's wet dream of how a chauffeur should look. Had he been working for me, I fear he would have been far too tired to drive the car.

"Good evening," I said. "I am Mr. Chadwick. Did Mrs. Fullerton send you?"

The man turned, looked at me appraisingly, and replied, "Yes, sir," in a tone of studied neutrality.

He held open the door for me. Carrying my bottle of wine by the neck, as if about to fend off an attacker, I allowed myself to be ushered into the back seat of the large black vehicle. I confess I do not ordinarily mingle with those who keep a chauffeur on the payroll. Most of my friends either own cars or else risk their lives in cabs piloted by new Canadians who drive as though Montreal were a city under siege. As a result I was not sure whether I should talk to the driver or treat him as just another part of the car. Had he not been so good-looking I would probably have ignored him.

"Have you heard if more snow is on the way?" I asked, falling back on the weather, *faute de mieux*.

"No, sir."

There followed a pause. But Rome wasn't chatted up in a day. "Have you been working long for Mrs. Fullerton?" I inquired, moving my focus from the weather outside to the man inside.

"No, sir."

Another pause, this one longer. The car continued to climb up towards the very top of the Westmount mountain.

"Did you learn to drive in Canada?" The chauffeur certainly did not look like one of us, but he handled the large vehicle with a skill that would have put most Montreal car owners, accustomed to driving in winter, to shame.

"No, sir."

The negative reply hung, naked and unadorned. Had the driver felt disposed to talk he could have told me where he did learn to drive, leading to a discussion about country of origin. But like a rookie little league player, I had struck out three times. I retreated to gaze out the window until the car reached the top of the last incline. We drove past the lookout on the summit of the mountain, where generations of Montrealers have come to park, take a quick glance at the view, and indulge in what used to be called heavy petting. A final turn brought us onto Mayfair Crescent, and we pulled to a stop in front of number 15, a large, handsome house whose post-French-château architecture seemed at variance with the other Scottish Baronial mansions spaced along the gently curving road.

To use a current buzzword, Mayfair Crescent was a power address. Listing your place of residence as the Salvation Army Hostel or the Old Brewery Mission suggests that perhaps you don't file an income tax return. Mayfair Crescent, on the other hand, hints at tax paid in quarterly instalments on that income which slides without fanfare through the letter slot. All traces of the recent blizzard had been cleared away. Judging from the political clout represented by the collective residents, I'd guess it was probably one of the first streets in the city to be regularly ploughed.

Wordlessly, the chauffeur came around to open my door. Just as wordlessly, I nodded my thanks and walked up the freshly shovelled walk.

A black maid in a black uniform opened the front door. After I had shed my overshoes in the tiled vestibule, she took both my overcoat and bottle of wine, then ushered me through a spacious front hall, complete with tear-drop chandelier, into an oak-panelled room where a fire flickered invitingly in a brick fireplace. From the hall I had glimpsed a formal drawing room, Louis XV furniture, and flocked wallpaper in rows of panels. I confess I preferred what was obviously the library, although one corner of the room was dominated by that icon of the second-rate decorator – a sectional couch. It followed the angle of the wall and was upholstered in navy blue with a bold pattern of acanthus leaves. Had the couch been intended for a sun porch or a den, the pattern would have been bamboo. I crossed to examine the rows of books only to discover they were sets: Gems of Western literature, Great Ideas of Western Man, The English Poets.

In examining the spines, I had inadvertently turned my back on the door, something no self-respecting secret agent (or man with secrets) would ever do. As a result I missed the entrance.

"Mr. Chadwick," said a woman's voice, and I turned to meet Lois Fullerton.

I was glad I had put on a clean shirt. Lois Fullerton was the kind of woman who brings every masculine insecurity churning to the surface. Striking rather than beautiful, she radiated a no-nonsense femininity, which on closer inspection turned out to be artifice raised to the level of art.

"Mrs. Fullerton, good evening." I stepped forward and extended my hand to shake. Her hand was square, white, strong, with a mint-condition manicure on nails that did not appear to be acrylic. I have met bodybuilders with a more flaccid grip than that of Lois Fullerton. Her rich, heavy perfume reached out to envelop me.

"Two things. First of all, I think we should move on to a first-name basis. Second, what will you drink – Geoffry?"

"Scotch, please – Lois."

She crossed to a bar trolley, which had been left just inside the door, presumably by the maid, and poured a hefty shot of Glenlivet into an old-fashioned glass, then added an equal amount of water. This gesture of hospitality offered me an opportunity to examine her without seeming to. As I am far more accustomed to sizing up men than women, I found myself falling back on the vocabulary of adolescence. Lois Fullerton was "built," her sumptuous curves a stunning rebuke to the female fashion that equates scrawny with sexy and prefers anorexia to avoirdupois. A black velvet housecoat outlined her full bust and clung to the generous contour of her hip. Ash blonde hair, of a colour women like Audrey Crawford would have killed for, was pulled back into a chignon, which made her shoulder-length baroque pearl earrings seem even more extravagant. On the hand holding the glass she wore both a wedding band and an emerald the size of a Chicklet flanked by M&M-sized diamonds. I would have guessed her age at around forty-five. She looked more like the doyenne of a ballet school than the mother of the groom. But what I admired most was the obvious decision to ignore fashion fads, ill-fitting clothes and frizzed hair, and to wear what she believed suited her best.

She poured herself a Dubonnet, handed me my Scotch, and the two of us gravitated towards small but inviting upholstered armchairs on either side of the fireplace. As she sat, the skirt of her housecoat fell open to the knee, revealing a pair of gun-metal legs, (a swell pair of gams). Her calf curved outward below the knee and tapered to a slender ankle ending in a high-heeled black sandal, whose message was less "fuck me" than "nibble the inside of my thigh." She crossed her legs with that soft, abrasive sound which is supposed to drive strong men mad, and raised her glass. "Cheers."

"Cheers."

We both drank, I eagerly, she with the care of one who has painted on her lipstick with a brush, a slightly darker shade on the lower lip to minimize its fullness. She had wisely avoided blue eyeshadow to compete with her blue eyes; warm tones on the lids made them appear larger.

"As I said on the telephone, I have been talking to your sister, whom I look forward to meeting." She smiled, one of those five-thousand-watt smiles intended to disarm. "As we are both widows – she paused for a sip of Dubonnet and to let the fact sink in – "we have to rely on your strong right arm for the ceremony."

The strong right arm in question was still sensitive from a recent bout of bursitis, but I smiled at the figure of speech.

"However," she continued, setting down her glass with the air of one for whom a drink is no more than a prop, "I understand from your sister that you too were married once and that you had a small daughter. What a shock the accident must have been for you. I guess in a way we are all in the same boat."

I smiled a vague, noncommittal smile and took a couple of swallows in an effort to conceal my sudden, irrational rage. Not at Lois Fullerton, who was knocking herself out trying to be agreeable, but with my sister and her socially conscious, upwardly mobile snobberies that sprang from a sensibility as common as sewage. Quite obviously Mildred and Lois had enjoyed a long, matey, let's-be-instant-best-friends conversation during which the subject of Geoffry Chadwick had come up. When Mildred is trying to impress, all her geese become swans. I could easily imagine the puffed-up press release she had given Lois on my behalf: lawyer, distinguished, widower, such a bitter blow, never remarried, and so forth. Small wonder Lois Fullerton probably tripped over her feet in her haste to get to the phone and invite me to dinner.

There was another reason for my anger. Everyone has memories that, if not perishable, are still too precious to be exposed to bright light. Whatever my wife, Susan, and I had shared all those years ago belonged to me, and me alone. That file had been stamped Private and Confidential. I bitterly resented Mildred's trotting out for inspection something which happened thirty years ago; moreover, for the sole reason of tarting up my CV. My daughter will be given away by "my brother the widower," not "my brother the fag."

"I'm sorry, did I say something out of line?" Lois Fullerton dropped her question into a silence beginning to congeal.

I snapped to. "Not at all. Just woolgathering. I was married a long time ago, and I guess your remark sent my thoughts off the rails onto a siding. Do I have time for another pop?"

"Of course."

"Why don't I just help myself?"

"No, let me."

I could se she was determined to be ingratiating. I like whenever possible to pour my own drinks. That way I can keep track of consumption. Like most nondrinkers, Lois Fullerton's idea of hospitality was a drink the colour of strong tea. More is more.

"I suppose it is a bit unusual," she continued as she resumed her seat, "holding the wedding in the groom's home town rather than the bride's. But, as Mildred explained, your mother is not up to going to Toronto, and as she is paying for the wedding, your sister is quite prepared to accommodate her."

The blip that flashed onto my radar screen nearly knocked me out of my chair. Mother was to pay for the wedding? The implications caused such an information overload that I could barely bring myself to reply.

"Mother has never liked to travel. And now that she is old . . ."

"I fully understand."

I seemed to be learning about this wedding through dispatches, like news of a war being fought on several fronts. Unlike Audrey Crawford, however, a woman I have known most of my life, Lois Fullerton was a total stranger. Call it pride, call it privacy, call it family solidarity, I was not about to admit ignorance of the proposed financial arrangements.

"She is quite understandably excited about the first wedding in the third generation. As you probably know, Jennifer is the youngest. But I don't think either Richard or Elizabeth will marry for a while. They are both career-oriented at the moment."

Unlike Mildred, I did not feel obliged to fill in the blanks. Not only was Richard aimed towards a performing career, he was also gay, a fact that made his marrying remote. Elizabeth had won a scholarship to the University of Indiana to study singing, especially opera. She had spent the last two years studying voice in Montreal, and, according to the grapevine, she was getting quite a name for herself, but not as a singer. If she does marry, her husband will be either a halfback or a hairdresser.

"Mind you," Lois said, cradling the glass, an attractive gesture that put her remarkable hands into relief, "I fully expect to assume some of the costs of the wedding. The time has long since passed when the bride's family paid the whole shot. Both Mildred and I want the occasion to be memorable. It may be the first wedding for her, but as Douglas is an only child it will be the only wedding for me. You've met Douglas?"

"Not yet. The last time I went to Toronto he and Jennifer were in Montreal, and I just missed them."

"I think he's very special, but then I'm prejudiced. I know he's a bit young to get married, but he's a serious boy. He's designing the wedding rings."

"He's what? I mean – I didn't know he was interested in jewellery."

"He's very artistic. It was a toss-up between art school and a graduate degree in English."

"I see." A hearty swallow helped me to digest the bit about the wedding rings. There is sensitive and then there is sensitive.

It was almost with relief that I saw the maid appear in the doorway to announce dinner in her lilting Caribbean voice.

"Bring your drink to the table."

I stood, determined to make some effort to be pleasant over dinner. Up to now I had been about as scintillating as open heart surgery. So far the evening had been mined with surprises. I could only hope they had all been sprung, leaving me free to concentrate on being at least a civil dinner guest. I paused in front of a painting, one of those three-hour palette-knife studies of the trackless Canadian north, the thicker the paint, the more serious the intent.

"That is very fresh and arresting."

"I think so." Standing beside me, Lois put her hand lightly on my arm. I knew she would touch me sooner or later, the first move in the courting ritual. With her other hand she traced an arc across the upper half of the picture. "I love the way he has handled the sky. There is so much colour in each stroke."

"You're absolutely right." I agreed as I followed her hips towards the dining room. I really don't much like gooey paint, or impasto as it should be called. Except for Van Gogh. But he used his heavy paint with passion. Everyone else is merely sincere.

To live on the income of megabucks enables people to play games, one of which is to pretend that nothing really takes any effort. The rich float through life on a sea of diminutives: little dressmakers who charge by the stitch, intimate gatherings for no more than a hundred people, ten-day jaunts to Tokyo and Hong Kong. The sin lies not in having but in noticing one has.

A glimpse of Lois Fullerton's massive mahogany dining table, set with Crown Derby Imari flanked by baroque silver and softly lit by two immense ormolu candelabra, suggested the cook had been preparing more than potluck supper, an impression the oysters Rockefeller did nothing to dispel. A Gewürztraminer glowed in Waterford goblets. Knowing the mythology surrounding oysters, I wondered about the casual care that had gone into planning this particular menu.

Like Little Tommy Tucker I was raised to sing for my supper. To be a dinner guest is not unlike going on stage; one is expected to perform. By now I was feeling the beneficial effects of the Scotch, that temporary suspension of a week's fatigue, which is a kind of mild euphoria. Lois was an accomplished hostess, adroit at asking the right questions but not so forward as to be importunate. I told about the case I was currently occupied with, in broad outline naturally, for much of the information was privileged. We talked about *Masterpiece Theatre*, guilt-free television, that grab-bag program whose credits unroll against what appears to be a high-class garage sale.

The pillaged oyster shells gave way to a crown roast of lamb, neatly dismembered in the kitchen and handed around by the maid. It had been a while since I was served in this fashion – most of my eating out is in restaurants – but I remembered how. For all its supposed gentility, handing around food is awkward. The dish is seldom in the right position, certainly not for an arm twitching from the aftermath of bursitis, and the fragrant steam carries with it a good deal of heat. But my excellent Châteauneuf-du-Pape, decanted and acknowledged, went straight to my shoulder.

Lois and I continued our conversational *pas de deux*. During the exchanges, I looked as much as I listened. I suppose I was looking for a hallmark, like the one clearly visible on each knife and fork. But try as I might, I could not place Lois Fullerton, which I suppose is another way of saying she did not strike me as native to the community. I could not picture her wearing a down-filled coat and rubber boots, pushing a cart through the supermarket. If she once carried a hallmark, it had become illegible. My instinct told me she was a woman who had created herself in her own image, a do-it-yourself Adam's-rib project. Everything was right, almost too right. I looked in vain for the rough edge, the blurred line, the dropped stitch.

A lemon mousse the consistency of cloud followed by a

piece of Stilton, which must have been delivered by Brink's, brought to a conclusion a meal that had been less potluck than potlatch. Over decaffeinated coffee, which we had crossed to the library to drink, we returned to the topic that quite obviously concerned the hostess far more than either my work or my taste in movies did, namely the wedding. It was her suggestion that Mildred take charge of the ceremony itself and Lois pick up the tab for the reception. Having scant experience of weddings myself, I found her offer both reasonable and generous, particularly as she wanted to engage the Oval Room at the Ritz. It might not be available at this late date, in which case she would try the Four Seasons. To engage the Oval Room, one of the most elegant reception rooms in the city and to feed the guests, which included an open bar, *and* to underwrite an orchestra – no records or tapes for this reception, thank you very much – would take a sizeable bite out of any budget. It was perfectly evident that I was expected to endorse the suggestion, and I did.

"And now," she began, setting down her cup and leaning forward, "let's talk about you." I couldn't be dead certain, but I'd be willing to bet she had used just a touch of eyeshadow to emphasize her cleavage. She reached up to adjust one of her earrings, and in so doing exposed the palm of her hand. I read a magazine article once, probably in the dentist's office, which explained that when a woman shows a man the palm of her hand it means the light is green.

Two can play at body language. I crossed my legs so the outside of my left thigh blocked a frontal attack, sat upright in my chair, and held onto the cup and saucer.

"There's really nothing to talk about. If I tried to tell you about the real, the inner, the quintessential me, you'd be fast asleep in four and one half minutes."

She laughed a well-rehearsed dismissive laugh and flashed her laser dimples. "I don't believe that for a second. Attractive single men are always in demand."

I was already bored with the conversation. One thing about the gay subculture I do admire is the absence of sexual shadow-boxing, which, I suppose, is another way of saying that by the time you get around to speaking to someone who has caught your eye, going to bed is a foregone conclusion. Sometimes it's not necessary to speak at all. Even when I was younger and still trying to make it with this or that girl, my idea of flirting was to put my hand inside her blouse. Sex is something I like to do, not talk about, read about, or watch.

"Attractive men, yes. But I assure you, to know me is not to love me. I have been told that bracing truth so many times I'm beginning to believe it is probably correct."

It is sometimes a disadvantage to be taken for what passes as straight in a heterosexual world, especially at a time when declaring one's sexual taste is almost considered a virtue. Today's young homosexuals flaunt their preferences with a candour that threatens to give them whiplash. But, for better or worse, I was raised to believe that serving up your sexuality on a platter was bad manners, an attitude I have been unable to discard. Discretion is its own protective colouring, and to have been married, even all those years ago, has caused more than one woman to set her cap, or her cups, in my direction.

Lois was a case in point. "If that is true, I'd enjoy having the chance to find out for myself."

She rose and reached for a log from a small, neat pile on the hearth. The logs looked as though they had been dusted before they were brought into the house. After placing one on the now glowing ashes, she appeared to stumble. By putting her hand firmly on my knee, she steadied herself and rose to her feet, but not until I had been offered a bird's eye view of her splendid breasts hang-gliding above the hearth. I studied them with the detached interest of a judge at a country fair examining a fine Ayreshire heifer. I also decided it was time this *tête-à-tête* came to a conclusion.

I rose to my feet. "May I use the washroom?" I could certainly have used a pee, but I was more interested in shifting the pieces on the board.

Lois paused just a second before answering. "I'm sorry to say the powder room on the ground floor is out of order. Why don't you use the one off the master bedroom, just at the head of the stairs to the right."

As I climbed the wide, carpeted staircase I could not help thinking that Lois Fullerton would not tolerate a plugged sink or a blocked toilet for even an afternoon. A plumber would arrive, by limousine if necessary, to put the recalcitrant plumbing instantly to rights. In other words, I was being sent upstairs for a reason. As I turned into the master bedroom I realized what that reason was. In fact, I was so astonished by the room itself I almost forgot my reason for climbing the stairs.

I felt as though I had somehow travelled backward through time to land in a photo spread from *Life* magazine. Who would have believed an all-white bedroom could still be found in the 1980s, outside the Smithsonian Institute. White rooms belonged to the thirties, a fad of the jet set when it still flew in planes powered by propellers. White bedrooms were the stuff of screen legend, when movie stars seemed larger than life, both on screen and off. To find such a room on Mayfair Crescent struck me as no less astonishing than stumbling across a perfectly preserved pre-Columbian city in the Central American jungle.

Furthermore, the furnishings were bandbox fresh, no mean achievement in a city where the air pollution index is read daily by a radio announcer in a worried voice. Dominating the room stood an immense bed from whose canopy, shaped like a crown, fell luxuriantly draped billows of white brocade flanking a white quilted satin headboard outlined in scalloped white carving highlighted in gold. A counterpane of heavy white satin fell to the floor in pleated folds only partially subdued by a second, fitted counterpane of ecru lace. From white and gold valances, trimmed with swags of ivory brocade, hung heavy curtains of the same fabric. A dressing table surmounted by a large mirror framed in bare bulbs, like that of a theatrical dressing room, matching bureaus and boudoir lamps, occasional tables, a pair of Hepplewhite chairs (copies, one hoped), all echoed the white-and-gold motif against white-flocked wallpaper, their feet in casters sinking into the deep pile broadloom. On that untrammelled surface my footprints looked like those of the Abominable Snowman.

I waded across the carpet to an immense white bathroom, whose basic white plumbing fixtures looked perfectly at home. It is not even necessary to point out that there was a sunken tub, with Jacuzzi alongside a shower stall, bidet, double sink, everything necessary to scrub, sluice, soak, and soothe after a hard day at the orifice. I have always had mixed feelings about double sinks. Marriages can survive a good deal – adultery, abuse, prolonged absence – but not the daily sight of the other half brushing teeth.

I do not ordinarily wash my hands after micturition because I do not pee on them, but I felt obliged, positively compelled, by this pristine and gleaming sanctuary of sanitation. I ran water over my hands and blotted them on a velours pile hand-towel, whose colour I need not mention, lifted from a free-standing towel rack that looked like a crucifix. I left the towel folded over the edge of the counter, a sign of my passage like white pebbles or bread crumbs.

I mushed across the broadloom to the bedroom door, where I turned for one last, disbelieving look at that expanse of pristine vulgarity. I remember reading a supremely silly article written by a woman on how to seduce a man on home turf. She suggested the bedroom should be painted blue and filled with plants to give him the illusion he is making love in the great outdoors under a cloudless sky. Small wonder the gay population is growing by leaps and bounds.

But even if I were interested in grappling with Lois Fullerton, I would have found this bedroom daunting. Allowances made for muted lighting, with a few drops of her perfume on each light bulb so the heat sends her fragrance into the air, discounting the satin sheets, which I knew lurked under that counterpane, the whole effect was so self-consciously shop-girl erotic that it failed to arouse. To make love on that theatrical bed would be like shooting a porno movie without the camera. And I had been manoeuvred upstairs to glimpse this bower of bliss as though it were a preview of coming attractions.

It was quite obviously time for me to go home. But one difficult situation not covered by the *Boy Scout Handbook* is how to get gracefully away from a hostess who has absolutely no intention of letting you go.

The lights in the library had dimmed considerably by the time I returned, no doubt the result of a carefully controlled rheostat, and the cocktail clutter had been replaced by a tray of liqueurs, those lethal concoctions of alcohol and sugar that guarantee insomnia. The hostess was at the ready.

"Liqueur, or brandy? Or would you prefer a highball?"

"To be candid, I would really like all three, in that sequence. But prudence dictates I pass. I have to work tomorrow." The more patent the lie, the more glibly it must be uttered. I could easily have delivered the next line verbatim.

"Oh, but you can't leave yet. The evening is still young."

"I warned you, Lois. When they pick the ten dullest men in Montreal I will be the first seven. It has been a long week."

"We don't have to converse. I just had a compact disc player installed. The sound is quite extraordinary."

"I'm sure it is. But music, like anything else, requires concentration. And I fear mine is beginning to flag. I really should be pushing along. It's been a delightful evening."

"How would you like to put your feet up and watch a movie?" Lois dropped her voice, the way she had when she first telephoned my office. Her eyes suggested an infinity of unimagined delights. She managed the remarkable feat of seeming to pulsate while standing absolutely still.

"Not at the moment, thanks. I'll weaken and have a nightcap or three and feel slower tomorrow." I stepped towards the door.

Anticipating my move, she positioned herself beside the drink trolley in such a way that she effectively blocked the door. "One small drink for the road can't hurt."

I was suddenly weary with the charade, the elaborate meal,

the calculated outfit she had worn, the obvious sexual signals, the iron determination to be captivating, and the absolute refusal to decode the messages I was sending out in reply.

"I'll call you and we'll have lunch, when wedding plans are more fully under way. May I have my coat, please?"

For just a second her eyes snapped wide open, flashing a look subliminal but clear: "I'll get you yet, you son of a bitch!" Then pulling on a pleasant expression, like someone dressing in haste, she manufactured a smile. "Of course."

She led the way to the vestibule. I tugged on my overshoes, pulled on my coat, shook hands, said goodnight, and left.

The limousine, engine idling, waited at the foot of the walk. The chauffeur got out to open my door, and I nodded without speaking. Preoccupied as I was with the information picked up in scraps during the course of the evening, I made no further attempt to engage the driver in conversation as he turned off the crescent and headed down the hill. My vibes told me Lois Fullerton was a woman determined to get her own way. For myself I had no worries. Who can thwart a princess better than a queen? But I knew my sister and her whims of iron, her social graces forged in the Gestapo Charm School, where she had led the class. I could easily imagine Mildred and Lois meeting head-on, like two eighteen-wheelers on a narrow country road. I mistrust instant best friends; they can turn into instant worst enemies at the drop of a zinger.

Mildred is not a dishonest woman. How many times over the years has she used her probity to beat me about the head and shoulders? But a wedding is at best an expensive undertaking. Anyone would be tempted to add on extras, invite a few more guests, make the whole enterprise more up-market, if someone else is picking up the tab. Mother can afford to marry off her granddaughter. But I still did not want to see her taken advantage of, nor to see Mildred swanning through the big day, playing mother of the bride at ten thousand volts, having spared no expense for her darling daughter, and lapping up accolades while Mother signed the cheques.

More precisely, it was I who would be signing the cheques. I had signing authority for Mother's bank account. Once a month I went for Sunday supper, which truly was potluck, and paid her bills. It had been at the back of my mind for some time now to have Mother grant me a full power of attorney. Then in case of a real emergency I could act without consulting Mildred. Were I to get the power of attorney right away, I would be in a position to prevent my sister from being too lavish with Mother's money.

The thought of being placed in a discretionary position regarding my sister, of being able to tell her I really didn't think a certain expense was justified, gave me a little electric jolt of pleasure. At that moment the limousine pulled to a stop in front of my apartment building. Again the chauffeur got out to open my door.

"Thank you," I said. "Goodnight."

"Goodnight, sir."

He climbed back into the driver's seat, and the long, black automobile pulled away.

I decided to take the elevator up to my floor. Fortunately it was empty. I let myself into my apartment, turned the dead-lock, and attached the safety chain. I used to have the customary fantasies about tall, dark, handsome, and wildly randy burglars. But when I see photographs of the unwashed, unshaven illiterates who get caught pulling off nickel and dime jobs, I realize that agreeable fantasy is yet another victim of age and time.

Hardly had I hung up my coat when the telephone rang. A glance at my watch told me it was after ten, the hour after which only drunks or people in real trouble would dare to call. I picked up the receiver, fully expecting to learn that Mother had taken another nosedive. "Hello?"

There was a pause. Then an unfamiliar male voice spoke. "Chadwick?"

"This is he speaking."

"If you know what's good for you, you'll stay away from Lois Fullerton." The tone was muffled, as if the speaker was trying to disguise his voice.

I always treat crank calls as if they were quite routine. "But of course. Now, would you be kind enough to leave your name and number."

Obviously taken aback the caller hesitated before replying. "You've been warned." The line went dead.

"Just terrific!" I thought to myself. No sooner do I get home after having kept Lois Fullerton at bay with whip and chair than a threatening caller warns me to back off. If only he knew how little he had to worry, whoever the bastard might be. I unknotted my tie. I had been involved with my niece's wedding for one calendar week, and already I had a strong suspicion that June 13 was not going to be the happiest day of my life.

III

Knowledge is power, or so I remember reading when I was a student. Judging by the apparent knowledge of many in prominent government positions, whose IQ seems to be their weight divided by two, I find that statement open to question. Nevertheless, I decided to learn something more about Lois Fullerton, mother of the groom and possibly lethal dinner companion.

The person who immediately sprang to mind was Audrey Crawford, from whom I had learned of the wedding in the first place. Audrey is a woman whose hobby, pursued with almost votive calling, is to know about the people in our community. Her mind is a vast reservoir of genealogical tables, like those in the back pages of high school history books listing the kings and queens of Great Britain, their wives, children, in-laws. If anyone could fill me in on Lois Fullerton, it had to be Audrey.

I telephoned to suggest lunch; it really had been so long.

"Oh, Geoffry, I'd love to, but I really ought to say no. I'm on a diet."

"Even people on diets have to eat, unless you are fasting. Lunch does not necessarily have to be a double portion of lasagna followed by Black Forest cake."

"You're right, you know. But you must promise faithfully not to let me backslide."

"Scout's honour. Salad and tea and Melba toast, followed

by a slab of cherry cheesecake."

She squealed as if she had just been goosed. "You're really awful. Now I have to decide what to wear."

"How about a hair shirt, cut on the bias naturally, and the cowrie-shell necklace you picked up in Antigua. Come by my office around noon."

I hung up. Audrey is a professional dieter, at least in conversation. Plump girls really should be taught at an early age that if they indulge themselves in the luxury of four children they will have to practice girth control.

I took Audrey to a restaurant where I had taken to eating lunch at least twice a week, mainly, I suspect, because it was not decorated in grey with grey tablecloths and pink napkins. Nor did it have a salad bar. Audrey was fresh from the hairdresser, each hair a filament of epoxy resin. Under the sheared beaver she wore the basic little black nothing wool dress with enough gold chains to set up shop. Audrey is a good-looking, middle-aged, slightly overweight matron of medium height who daydreams of being a six-foot-one Las Vegas showgirl.

She declined the iced tea, because it was made with a mix containing sugar, and settled instead for a sweet vermouth, while I played games with white wine and club soda.

"I had dinner with Lois Fullerton last Friday night," I began as Audrey tore open the breadsticks, but only after lifting the butter to my side of the table. "It seems odd I have never run into her before. She is certainly a woman one notices."

"She certainly is, the way one notices the arches in front of McDonald's, or a mobile home parked in the driveway."

The dark-eyed and very humpy waiter put down a plate of bite-sized pizzas, compliments of the house. As the principal ingredient appeared to be tomato paste, heartburn to go, I found them easy to refuse.

"I really shouldn't ..." began Audrey as her hand, pulled by an invisible force, moved towards the plate.

"One also notices the Sun Life building or a Bentley at the beach," I added, nudging my lunch guest towards the tale I could see she was not reluctant to begin. Urged on by a second vermouth, Audrey told me about Lois Fullerton. If there was a bias to her story, it was that of one middle-aged blond talking about another middle-aged blond, whose waist may be smaller and whose income larger.

I learned that my first impression of Lois had been correct; she was indeed a self-made woman, the finished product a result of considerable trial and frequent error. She had been born in Magog, a small town close to 150 kilometres southeast of Montreal, the only daughter of British immigrant parents who worked in the textile mill. "You'd need a bushel basket to pick up the dropped *h*'s," was Audrey's observation.

Lois Fullerton, née Dalton, knew there was more to life than Magog; as far as she was concerned the yellow brick road led to Montreal. She finished high school and left town, having somehow managed to scrape together enough money to get herself into the city, where she enrolled in O'Sullivan's Business College to train as a secretary. She lived at the YWCA because it was cheap and respectable, and worked part time as a waitress at Murray's.

She led her class and graduated summa cum shorthand, or whatever it was they awarded secretaries. (Audrey Crawford had graduated from McGill with a degree in art history. She can tell a poster from a painting by running her fingers over the surface.) With her excellent references, Lois Dalton went right into the stenographer's pool of a large insurance company, where James Fullerton happened to be senior vice-president.

"She managed to – catch the eye – one might say," added Audrey, her pauses bubbling with malice. As she paused in her story to pop two more tiny pizzas, I could not help thinking that the striking woman Lois Fullerton had become must have been been truly radiant twenty-five years ago. Small wonder she had caught the eye and the fancy of James Fullerton.

As if doing penance for the pizza, Audrey chose the salad entrée. Having polished off the breadsticks, she broke a crusty roll onto her side plate, then, with only a faint tremor of hesitation, reached for the butter, to which she helped herself liberally. Heartened, she continued her chronicle.

It was not long before Lois was living in a nice little apartment in a building that James Fullerton happened to own. There was a problem, however; James Fullerton already had a wife.

"I know for a fact they slept in separate rooms," said Audrey with a look that suggested her own conjugal life scorched the sheets. And the first Mrs. Fullerton was unlikely to be dislodged, for her father was president of the company where James Fullerton worked. Lois was at liberty to – accommodate her boss, but there stood little chance of her marrying him. That was, until the first wife died, of a ruptured something. Audrey wasn't certain what.

The real certainty was that James Fullerton, now a widower, vice-president of a large corporation, due to inherit pots of money from the first wife, had become eligible. Whether or not he was available did not matter. He had become a catch, and more than one post-deb entertained fantasies of being chatelaine of 15 Mayfair Crescent.

That was, until Lois played her trump card. After three years of being one of Montreal's best-known secrets, and having successfully taken the necessary precautions, Lois suddenly found herself pregnant.

Audrey Crawford paused while the waiter sprinkled grated cheese over the cannelloni she knew she shouldn't even consider but had ordered anyway. I had to admit it looked a lot more tempting than the *cuisses de grenouille*, breaded Q-Tips, that I had been served. Lois Dalton had James Fullerton over not one barrel but two. First of all, he had been raised "to do the right thing." It had also become common knowledge how badly he wanted children, more specifically a son. He was even prepared to adopt, but the first Mrs. Fullerton wouldn't hear of it. One seldom knew the father of an illegitimate child; he could be a thief or a murderer or worse. One simply could not take the chance. Consequently, when James Fullerton learned that his beloved Lo-lo – here Audrey rolled her eyes to the ceiling, while I indulged in an uncharitable chuckle – was carrying his child, well, the rest of the competition might just as well pick up their kits and go home.

"I have it on good authority," Audrey said, leaning towards me as if she were about to whisper a secret message, "that he used to tiptoe up behind her, clap his hands over her eyes, and say, 'Guess who?' "

"Please," I said, "not while I'm eating."

At a shotgun wedding it is usually the bride's family who have their finger on the trigger. Lois was hustled into marriage so quickly she barely had time to buy a dress, no more than a couturier flour sack, for the pregnancy had really begun to show. The result of this same pregnancy was a son, christened Douglas James, now twenty-two years old and engaged to marry my niece.

Here Audrey paused for a sip or two of white wine, which she drank with the guilty gusto of a reformed smoker sneaking a cigarette. Having nibbled her way through a second well-buttered roll, she made a show of refusing the *table d'hôte* house cake in favour of a self-denying fruit salad. From the way she leaned slightly forward I could tell there was more to come.

Douglas was still a baby when James Fullerton and his sailboat parted company during a summer storm on Lake Memphremagog. Friends dined out on the terrible tragedy until the following Christmas. The young and beautiful Lois was now a wealthy widow. I noticed Audrey's observation that Lois had been beautiful, but the compliment was soon undercut by what followed. Lois Fullerton became a merry widow, the merriest.

What really irked Audrey Crawford was not that Lois Fullerton had lovers, but the expediency with which she took them on. The first was a notary who helped wind up her late husband's estate. The second was a real estate agent who advised her against selling Mayfair Crescent. The third had been an investment counsellor who steered her portfolio into high-yield order. And so it went: a salesman for Ford Motors who got her a buy on a Lincoln, a roofing contractor when the hugely expensive copper sheeting on the roof needed replacing, an interior decorator (think of that!) when she did over Mayfair Crescent and got rid of the first Mrs. Fullerton's chintzes and cretonnes.

"Do you suppose the decorator advised her on the bedroom?" I inquired over the double espresso I had ordered to help jolt me through the afternoon.

"Oh, you saw it, did you? Don't tell me . . ."

"No, Audrey, I did not." (Audrey Crawford has a vested interest in believing me straight.) "I merely went upstairs for a numero uno, as we say in sunny Italy."

"She claims she did that room all by herself, and I believe her. Period whoredom, the white period."

"Charity, Audrey."

"Even you have to admit it is a manicurist's daydream of high glamour. And white is so unflattering to skin. At her age she should surround herself in pink, or pale beige."

The idea of Lois Fullerton's bedroom in pink was enough to unsettle my lunch. I signalled for the check.

"Do you happen to know – I don't see why you should – if she was ever mixed up with someone, shall we say, unsuitable, dangerous perhaps?"

"I couldn't be certain. But when you've had that amount of turnover you're bound to come up with a bad apple or two." Audrey glanced at her watch. "Have to dash. I'm meeting Muriel Walsh at the museum; we're going to do prints and drawings. And I'm sure you have to get back to the office."

In the street we paused to say our goodbyes.

"You appear to know a great deal about Lois Fullerton. You must have been good friends at some point."

"Indeed not! Never could stand the woman." Audrey aimed a moist kiss at my mouth; she tasted of freshly applied lipstick. "Thanks for lunch, pet. We must do it again soon. Next time on me."

I watched her retreating figure with amusement. She knew more about Lois Fullerton, a woman she obviously does not like,

than I knew about my own sister. Perhaps that was just as well.
Moreover, Audrey Crawford is not without clout in the city.
She is Miss Volunteer Committee, with her picture in the paper
at least once a month. Face it; most people are more interested
in other people's sex lives than in what they do or think, and
Audrey knows who is looking at what ceiling. Maybe it is time
to rewrite the old saw and admit that gossip is power.

That afternoon after work I decided to swing by Mother's apartment. Things having been busy at the office, I had not been to
see her for over a week. I made a treaty with my conscience and
bought her a pound of pricey chocolates, the kind that go
straight to the thighs. Candy is not an imaginative gift, but
buying things for someone who seldom goes out is tough.
Mother already has more soap and handkerchiefs than a department store. I suppose Mother shouldn't eat candy, but nor
should she begin drinking at noon and smoking the second she
opens her eyes in the morning. But I am not my mother's
keeper. I do not consider it my disagreeable duty to scold her
about the two principal pleasures left to her, namely vodka and
cigarettes.

     Mother lives in an apartment building that boasts a secu-
rity guard as an advertising blandishment. Old high school
drop-outs do not fade away; they become security guards. After
several years of seeing me come and go with some frequency,
the afternoon guard has come to realize that I do not rape and
pillage and set fire to. There is a tradeoff, however. Instead of
being formally introduced and given permission to proceed as
though I were attending a reception at Government House, I

now have to pause for a short conversation that limps along on crutches.

"Afternoon, Mr. Chadwick." Small eyes set close together in an egg-shaped head squeezed themselves into a smile.

"Afternoon, Sam."

"So what do you think of the boys up there in Ottawa?"

I avoid thinking of them whenever possible, but some sort of hearty male-bonding reply was required. "They seem to be aiming at the sky and shooting themselves in the feet."

He nodded his head in ponderous agreement. "I'm a fishin' man myself. Think they'll ever get around to clearin' up the acid rain?"

"I sure hope so. I don't catch fish, but I sure like to eat them."

"It's them Americans. It's time we started talkin' tough."

Whenever I get into one of these pseudo-serious conversations, I feel as if I were suffocating. "I suppose you're right. But we have to remember that we are an enormous small country."

He looked puzzled. "If it was up to me I'd sure tell 'em."

"I'll bet you would," I said, edging my way past the desk. "Is Mrs. Chadwick at home?" We both knew she was; my question was no more than a signal that the conversation had ended.

"Yes, sir. A box of candy for your mother?"

I nodded as I walked towards the elevator. "Sort of. Actually they're chocolate-covered detonator caps. I really want to surprise her."

His reply was a blank look followed by a hearty ho-ho-ho as I stepped onto the elevator. The idea of his being responsible for building security is the stuff of nightmares, but fortunately Mother has a live-in housekeeper who would intimidate even the boldest burglar.

I gave the bell beside the door of her apartment three short rings followed by two long, my signal to the housekeeper that I was not a crank who had sneaked past the guard. Her immense starched white unsmiling presence opened the door. "*Bonjour, Monsieur Chadwick.*"

"*Bonjour, Madame. Ma mère est endormie?*"

"*Non, elle est dans le salon.*"

"*Des chocolats, pour Madame Chadwick,*" I said, pointing to the box.

Madame's granite features rearranged themselves into a smile. We both knew Mother would eat one, maybe two chocolates, then suggest they be put into the refrigerator to keep fresh. Once they were out of sight, she would forget about the candy, giving Madame the opportunity to finish off the box. I am more concerned with keeping Madame happy than Mother. Without a reliable housekeeper Mother would have to give up her apartment and move into a nursing home. That time will no doubt come, but not a moment sooner than necessary.

I hung up my overcoat and carried my propitiatory chocolates into the large living room, where Mother sat in her customary wing chair, wearing a wrapper and trying to bring the newspaper into focus through the new bifocals she hates.

"Surprise, Mrs. Chadwick, you have won third prize in the beauty contest. First prize was a trip to Afghanistan, second prize a weekend in Beirut, third prize a date with me." I kissed Mother on her wrinkled, fragrant cheek. She considers herself undressed without perfume, or scent, as she prefers to call it. Mother has always been a Guerlain girl, beginning with Eau de Cologne Impériale and moving through Shalimar and L'Heure Bleue to Chamade, which loosely translates as drum roll. Mother is more like an oboe played off key.

"Well, well, dear, I wasn't expecting you. Otherwise I would have changed. But Madame is cooking a little roast of beef. There will be plenty if you wish to stay for dinner."

"A few little chockies, Mater. They will make you big and fat and sexy." Like most old ladies who drink, Mother is so thin I am always afraid she will slide down the drain along with the bathwater.

Mother gave a wheezy giggle. "Oh, Geoffry, you are a caution. Are there any with cherry centres, or nougat?"

"Try that one there."

"Will you have one, dear?"

"Not at the moment, thanks. I'll have a biscuit instead." I reached for a wheat thin from a bowl of crackers Mother keeps in the living room to absorb excess humidity.

She put the top onto the box. "Mmmm, just delicious. But one will be enough for the moment. Be a dear and ask Madame to put them into the refrigerator. That way they'll stay nice and fresh."

"As long as I'm going into the pantry, I think I'll make myself a drink. Shall I give you a splash at the same time?"

Mother looked at her empty glass as though it had just materialized on the side table. "A little one, perhaps, just to be sociable."

In short order I was seated on a small couch facing Mother across a Scotch and soda. For someone who seems permanently out of focus, Mother has furnished her apartment with impeccable taste. The room is alive with muted colour, subtle texture, the gleam of dark wood, the glow of polished brass, the sheen of silken fabric. In her Viyella robe and the bunny-rabbit slippers my sister gave her for Christmas, Mother looks like a runaway hospital patient.

"Mother, we have to have a little talk."

"Indeed we do. Mildred wants Jennifer to be married in white taffeta with illusion yoke, Elizabethan sleeves, fitted waist-line, and cathedral train. Jennifer is pretty, but I fear she will be quite overwhelmed by the gown."

"So will you when the dressmaker's bill comes in. And that is what I want to discuss. I understand you have volunteered to underwrite the wedding."

"I was married in a white lace tabard over ivory crepe, very simple lines. And I carried gardenias. They were so fragrant. Jennifer should not wear a fussy gown. I suggested the Regency look – she has a small bust and ample hips – but your sister wouldn't hear of it."

"I read somewhere that hip interest is fashion forward this year. But if Mildred has her way Jennifer will come down the aisle looking like Chiquita Banana."

"Like who, dear?"

"An old movie star. Now, Mother, please listen carefully to what I am going to say. What I would like you to do is to grant me your power of attorney. That will allow you to forget about all the pesky financial details and save your energies for helping Mildred choose the wedding gown, plan the flowers, organize the ceremony. It will mean a great deal of extra work for me, of course, but we all want the wedding to be a huge success, now, don't we?"

I knew sooner or later God would get me for my guile, but my defence was that I did not want to see Mother unduly exploited.

"We most certainly do. And if you think my granting you a power of attorney is a good idea . . ." The rest of the sentence disappeared into Mother's glass. "So go ahead and do whatever is necessary. I have always had confidence in your judgement. You are so like your father. If only Craig could see his grand-daughter married. How I wish he were here."

"Me too. Then he could give the bride away. You realize I will have to drop by sometime this week with a notary. He will ask you to sign the document."

"Yes, dear, whatever you say. Now, if you are planning to stay on for dinner perhaps you had better tell Madame. She may want to prepare extra vegetables."

"Good idea. Why don't I save myself a trip and top us both up."

"Well, if you insist."

I carried the tumblers out to the pantry and spoke to Madame. Using the kitchen telephone, I called a friend from law school, a workaholic notary who stays late at the office almost every night. I asked him to draft a power of attorney granting me complete control over Mother's assets.

I had not expected Mother to be so readily compliant. After all, turning over full control of your property to someone else, even a son, is a tacit admission that the Grim Reaper is drawing nearer. But Mother was obviously far more concerned over Jennifer's gown than about any legal niceties.

"What do you suppose," she began before I had even sat down, "about my giving Jennifer four place settings of silver as a wedding present?"

"You're giving her the wedding. That's already beyond generosity."

"True enough, but I would like her to have something lasting. A bride should have flat silver."

"Why not give her yours? You hardly ever use it these days. Mildred was given silver when she married and so was I. You could buy yourself some handsome stainless steel flatware, and Madame wouldn't have to keep it polished. You will also be certain your silver stays in the family."

Mother took several sips of her vodka, a sure sign she was thinking. "You know something? You could well be right. Let me think about it."

Having brought Mother around to one major and one minor concession, I decided to change the subject. "Have you seen anything good on television lately?"

"Yes, indeed. Just the other night I watched a marvellous film, all about the American Civil War. I missed the credits, so I don't know the title. But it was about a girl named Scarlett. Do you know, at one point she wants to visit a dashing young man in prison but she doesn't have a thing to wear, so she makes herself a gown out of *portières*. Can you imagine, Geoffry? She just took them down from the parlour windows and sewed them into a gown. And very smart she looked too, I have to admit, even though I doubt she made French seams."

"I think I may have read the book."

I stayed on for dinner, carving the little roast and pretending not to notice that Mother's demitasse was filled with dark rum. Afterwards we went into the den to watch junk-food television, where actors who cannot really act find themselves in situations that are not comical and shout at one another so they can be heard above the laugh track, the whole interrupted at frequent intervals by commercials featuring tumescent teenagers drinking a variety of soft drinks in the pouring rain. But I knew it pleased Mother to have me there, a warm body in the chair beside hers. Soon, however, I noticed her head beginning to nod. After a couple of feeble tries to stay awake, she began to list heavily to starboard. I rescued her glasses, putting them on top of the television set, before fetching Madame to put her to bed.

As I rode down the elevator I realized how excited Mother must be over the wedding, as evidence of which she managed to stay awake right through dinner. Fortunately for me, the security guard was talking to another tenant, so I was able to sidle past without being quizzed on dirty dealings in the foreign arms market. A little learning is a boring thing.

IV

Truth is not necessarily stranger than fiction, but coincidence can sometimes be. Just happening to bump into Lois Fullerton in the lobby of my office building as I was leaving for the day bore the stamp of an artfully staged accident.

"Geoffry Chadwick! I didn't realize your office was in this building. I was just visiting my accountant. What a pleasant surprise!"

Startled, I took a second to take in the shimmering mink, such a deep brown as to appear black, and the face, framed by a black scarf tied like a wimple.

"Lois! Sorry to be asleep at the switch. I don't ordinarily take business problems home."

We stood in that strained, smiling silence of people whose immediate plans are quite different. The hall was alive with the sound of Musak. My present goal was to get home, with perhaps a pit stop at my carriage trade grocery store where the thirty percent markup is well worth the luxury of being able to charge. Not so for Lois Fullerton. She unleashed the full force of her great blue orbs, lowered her voice about half an octave, and suggested I buy her a drink, unless I had something better to do.

I was beginning to realize Lois Fullerton was locked into a time warp. That aberrant white bedroom aside, women today do not use their femininity as a blunt instrument. For a moment I felt a flicker of irritation. I had about seventeen better things to do than buy Lois Fullerton a drink. But last Friday night I had offered to buy her lunch; maybe a vermouth and some pretzel sticks was a reasonable tradeoff.

"There's a new hotel just down the street. The bar is pleasant."

"Sounds ideal. I'd better go and tell my chauffeur not to wait."

The bar was crowded; only a small table in the centre of the room stood vacant. Noise bounced off the hard, shiny hi-tech surfaces of marble, glass, steel, making conversation difficult. In this particular instance it was just as well. Surrounded by people and sound, Lois seemed ill at ease, a talk-show hostess without a microphone, although the definitely designer black sweater she wore under the fur drew glances, admiring and curious. A tribute to the current craze for glitter, its art deco patterns of blue and silver beads and sequins flowed diagonally from shoulder to waist, outlining her bust like contour lines on a weather map. It was a striking example of just how awful an ill-advised foray into fashion can be.

I watched with some amusement as she tried to deal with her mink coat, as much a uniform among matrons of a certain age and income bracket as the pleated tunics and Peter Pan collars imposed by the private schools to which they send their daughters. First, Lois draped the coat over the back of her chair, to be brushed against by every waitress or patron negotiating the narrow space between tables. After the waitress had taken our order, Lois draped the coat over her shoulders, making her look not unlike Bride of Nanook. A fur coat in an overheated room is suffocating, as evidence of which she tried with her hands to keep the garment from touching her shoulders. My better nature finally surfaced, and I borrowed a vacant chair from an adjoining table on which, after three tries, Lois managed to roll the coat in such a way that it did not slide softly from the seat onto the floor. I thought of my Prince Albert hanging comfortably on a hanger in the check room, where Lois had declined to consign her fur, and realized that personal vanity is a full-time occupation.

"I had a long talk with your sister on Sunday," began Lois, after a stern glance at the mink coat as though it were an ill-behaved child. "She has decided to increase the number of brides-maids from two to five. I expect that will mean more ushers."

"Likewise more frocks and flowers and limousines and places at the head table. Wouldn't it be ideal if they just got married at the courthouse, with a party afterward?" Already Mildred was being afflicted by grandeur. Five maids of honour could easily turn into ten, with escalations in all other trappings.

"That would be a bit bleak, don't you think?"

"Marriage is a bleak institution. And no amount of dressing up the bride and groom like Barbie and Ken, with Debbie and Cindy and Darlene dolls as bridesmaids and a couple of Cabbage Patch Kids as flower girls, is going to disguise the fact that Jennifer and your son are very young to be making such an important decision."

I could tell I had struck a nerve. Lois sat bolt upright and almost upset her vermouth. "That's not a very positive way to approach a situation which – where – we will all be working to-gether to make it a success."

"Perhaps not. but you must remember I have scant ex-perience. I was married only once, a long time ago, and the ceremony did not include a cast of thousands."

Lois laughed the laugh I had by now come to recognize as her way of clearing the air of tension. "You men! You're all alike. You all hate formal occasions and dress clothes and standing on ceremony, just like little boys. Now you just leave the planning to Mildred and me. All you have to do is turn up at the rehearsal."

She paused for a gracious sip of vermouth. If she had told me not to worry my pretty little head about the wedding she could not have managed to be more condescending, with that reverse female chauvinism which reduces any man to lovable lunk-head, unless he has an erection. What Lois did not realize is that I learned my lessons at a tender age from H. Ryder Haggard. I am She-Who-Must-Be-Obeyed. At some point Lois Fullerton and I were going to lock horns, but not in a crowded bar.

"What kind of gown do you think Jennifer should wear?" I asked. "Mildred wants something hugely elaborate, Elizabethan sleeves, cathedral train. Jennifer will look like a tea cozy. My mother, on the other hand, supports the Regency style."

"It's hard to say. She had better decide soon, or the dress won't be ready in time. A lot of brides are wearing gowns with appliqué: lace, pearls, beads, sequins, that sort of thing."

"Not everyone looks well in glitter. I seriously doubt Jennifer would." Having delivered that little zinger (call me a little boy at your peril), I caught the waitress's attention and held up two fingers, neatly avoiding Lois's eye. "I understand the bal-lerina-length gown is making a comeback. Jennifer is no Giselle, but at least she wouldn't trip."

"What did your wife wear at her wedding?" asked Lois with slightly strained sweetness. "You've never told me anything about her."

And I wasn't about to. "She wore white."

In the ensuing silence, a result of my refusing to rise to the bait, the sound of overlapping conversations from adjoining tables flowed between us. Murmuring something about how central heating dried out her skin, Lois opened her alligator bag, took out a small, coffin-shaped box with a mirror in the lid, and proceeded to repair her lip gloss. I watched, bemused. Heavy lipstick seems to have come back into style, bringing, to me at least, untidy memories of the forties and fifties. It was a time when all actresses in black-and-white movies had large black lips. It was also a time of heavy-handed chauvinism lurking under a veneer of shallow sophistication. "Candy is dandy, but liquor is quicker." "No woman needs an M.A. but a MRS." "When she was good she was very good, but when she was bad she was better."

During this time I had a brief fling with an older woman, by at least five years. She had been divorced, which pushed her by definition into the fast track. She once performed an act of love, which at the time made me uneasy, but, upon reflection, seemed pretty damned good. (Candy is dandy but a lick is quick.) I can still remember a moment of horrified consternation in the bathroom, when I thought I had contracted one of those dreadful diseases they used to warn servicemen about during World War II. It turned out to be nothing more than lipstick on my dork, but the experience left a scar. At least eyeshadow doesn't come off on your dainty private parts.

Watching Lois put on her mouth, I indulged in some random speculation best left unrecorded. Then I glanced at my watch.

"You'll have to excuse me, Lois, but I must go and collect my car. I'm meeting someone for dinner."

"Oh, but . . . In that case I'd better finish my drink."

I pulled out a credit card and paid the check, gulping the second drink I had ordered. Then I reached for the soft, slippery mass of fur on the chair and managed to shake it into the semblance of a coat.

As I helped her into the mink she smiled her disarming smile. "If it wouldn't be too much out of your way, could you give me a lift home? I dismissed the chauffeur."

When I drive from Montreal to Toronto I do not ordinarily go via Mexico City. To drive Lois up to Mayfair Crescent added a good twenty-five minutes onto my trip home. But it was another tradeoff. As punishment for lying my way out of dinner with Lois Fullerton, I had been manipulated into driving her up the mountain.

Although I can walk and chew gum at the same time, I cannot drive and talk, especially when traffic is heavy and roads slippery. I replied to Lois's inconsequential remarks with grunts; gradually she lapsed into silence. Outside her house we exchanged the standard remarks about being in touch soon, and I drove away.

As I turned down the hill I took comfort from knowing that once the wedding was over I would be clear of Lois Fullerton. However, I would not have wished Jennifer, or anyone else for that matter, to have Mrs. Fullerton as mother-in-law.

I don't as a rule take my car to work, but yesterday it had been snowing and my attaché case was locked in the trunk. I went down to the parking garage to pick it up. The envelope had been tucked under a windshield wiper. Across the front of the plain white business envelope had been typed "Mr. G. Chadwik." Inside, on a piece of standard bond paper, a message had been put together with words cut from an advertising supplement. "Stay away from L.F. You have been warned."

As I read this prop from a grade-B movie, I was struck by two conflicting impulses. The first was merriment. Did people in the real world actually cut out words and letters to paste into anonymous messages? The whole enterprise seemed like a game, something dreamed up by a frayed mother trying to keep a bored, sick child occupied. ("Come, dear, let's play ransom notes. Now you be the kidnapper . . .")

At the same time I found myself at a slow, angry burn. Far from being alarmed by the warnings, I was furious. How dare this unknown person threaten me, Geoffry Chadwick, lawyer, Westmount resident, respectable citizen (at least for the last few years).

The telephone warning I had been willing to overlook as a crank call. We get them on occasion, the childish questions, the tired obscenities. At least they are a change from the army of telephone salespeople who want to wash your walls at a discount, or the computerized voices who refuse to take offence when told to bugger off.

But here I stood, holding this juvenile letter, tangible evidence that I was being harassed, over a woman I would have gone to some lengths to avoid. I slipped the letter inside my attaché case. How best to deal with the situation posed a problem. The logical person to approach first was Lois Fullerton herself, but I found myself reluctant. My hesitation sprang not from fear at the crank caveats to avoid her. The fastest way to get any North American male to do something is to tell him he mustn't.

I did not want to approach Lois because I was leery of any involvement with her beyond that which was absolutely necessary. To admit that because of her I had been receiving threatening calls and letters would immediately make us allies. I did not want her springing to my defence. I wished to avoid her solicitude.

I did not even dislike Lois Fullerton. To feel negative about people burns up far more energy than it is worth. I saw her as a beautiful, rich, spoiled woman whose desire to captivate and conquer springs from motives of vanity and power. Well and good. But I did not wish to be charmed, conquered, and discarded as soon as the next challenge presented itself.

Most of all, I wanted to avoid the coyness of complicity. To share a secret with Lois Fullerton would punch a hole through my ozone layer, allowing her ultraviolet rays to come streaming through. I have sensitive skin.

Deal with the situation I would, however. I walked from the garage and headed downtown towards my office. The morning was bright, sunny, invigorating. The right solution would present itself. If only the mystery writer understood how willing I was to comply with his instructions, he would not have wasted time warning me off. But he was not going to fuck me over.

V

The following morning I collected the notary, Peter Boswell, and the two of us drove to Mother's apartment to get her signature on the power of attorney. By rights I should have taken Mother to the notary's office. But she hates to leave her apartment; moreover, I was anxious to get the power of attorney without fuss. I leaned on Peter Boswell a little, citing Mother's age, and he agreed to make a house call. Furthermore, I had just written a letter of recommendation to help his son enter an ivy league college. It is not difficult to recommend a young person who has been programmed to succeed since he was first plopped into his playpen with stimulating toys, and the favour had been done. To accommodate Mother, I traded on it.

I so seldom visit Mother in the morning that the daytime security guard glanced at me sternly, almost as if I were playing hookey. I resisted the impulse to say I had a note from my mother; I certainly hoped to have one when I left the building.

Although I have known Peter from college days, which makes him a kind of friend by attrition, I am never quite comfortable in his company. A small, tense, tight man, he even resents the time spent doing business because it could be spent doing other business. I fear one of these days he will simply implode, leaving his squeaky-clean wife and three overachieving children with life insurance, a tidy will, and airtight instructions about organ donations, cremation, and disposal of ashes. He is a man of whom I stand in awe but do not envy.

I had already alerted Madame that we would be coming by; she had laboured to make Mother presentable, a relative concept. At least Mother was not wearing bunny-rabbit slippers. She wore one of her "at homes," a garment inspired not by Balenciaga but by Omar the Tent-maker, in one of those mauve shades that looks wonderful on flowers, less so on human beings. The ballooning brocade folds collapsed around her emaciated body and made her look like a doll made of dowels draped in a table napkin. Unwilling to leave the apartment to have her hair done, Mother has taken to wearing wigs when receiving company. She owns several, severe toques of artificial hair whose uniform colour and aggressive sheen was never seen on human head. For Peter Boswell she had become a brunette.

I had deliberately organized a morning visit because Mother is passive and presentable before she begins to drink. She will not take so much as a sip before the stroke of noon, when the sun is over the yardarm, a notion she picked up from her own father and to which she clings.

"Mr. Boswell, so good of you to oblige an old lady and come to my house." Mother extended her hand to shake. "Geoffry dear. Now would you gentlemen like coffee?"

We declined. All I wanted was to get Mother's signature and scram.

"Perhaps we could waive the reading," I suggested.

Peter Boswell quelled me with a glance. I should have known he played by the rules. The document must be read, out loud and in full, to the person granting the power of attorney to make certain it was completely understood.

Mother was delighted. Any break in her daily routine is welcome, and the prospect of being read aloud to by the nice notary her son, Geoffry, had brought to call had her sitting up straight, hands folded in her lap, ready to listen. "Whenever you are ready, Mr. Boswell."

Peter Boswell slid on his shell-rimmed glasses, cleared his throat, and began: "On this thirty-first day of January, etcetera, etcetera, before: Mtre. Peter M. Boswell, the undersigned notary for the Province of Quebec, practising in the City of Montreal, appeared: Dame Constance Chadwick, retired, of the City of Westmount, Province of Quebec, therein residing at 25 West-mount Towers, unremarried widow of the late A. Craig Chad-wick, hereinafter called the 'constituent,' who does by these presents, nominate, constitute and appoint her son, Geoffry Chadwick, of the City of Westmount, etcetera, etcetera."

And on it went, and on. And on.

Peter Boswell was not a riveting reader. The Canada Coun-cil was never going to pay him a fee to read a power of attorney to a college audience. I sank into a trance of boredom. Mother, however, sat bolt upright, paying full attention, right to the bitter end.

"And after due reading thereof, signed by the Constituent with and in the presence of the undersigned Notary."

There was a pause.

"That was lovely, Mr. Boswell. So interesting, such wonder-ful language. My mother used to read out loud to me when I was a girl, especially Dickens. How we both loved Dickens. Every Christmas she used to read *A Christmas Carol* without fail. And *Bleak House*, and *Oliver Twist*. We read them all. It brings back such lovely memories. Would you be kind enough to reread the section which begins: 'To borrow money for such periods on such terms, rates of interest, and conditions as the said Attorney may deem advisable . . .' I did enjoy it so."

Peter Boswell looked frankly astonished. I am certain I did too. However, there is one quality for which I have to give Mother full credit. She is the real thing. Frail, comical in her brocade sack and acrylic wig, she remains a lady of the old school. People have always deferred to Mother, simply because she is what she is. And even though he was bursting to get back to his office, Peter complied and reread the section in question.

"Thank you. That was so interesting. Now I did enjoy the section beginning: 'To invest moneys in such investments as the said Attorney may deem proper . . .'"

"Mother, Mr. Boswell really has to get back to his office."

"Oh dear, I suppose he must. But it is such a pleasure to be read to. You never read out loud to me, Geoffry."

"Mother, this is the first inkling you have ever given me you enjoyed it. Next time I come for dinner I'll bring *War and Peace*. Now, would you be good enough to sign."

Like an obedient child Mother wrote her name on the appropriate line. Peter Boswell signed, and the deed was done.

Mother was all for our having tea if we didn't want coffee, but I was firm about appointments we both had to keep. We managed to disentangle ourselves and escape.

I drove Peter back to his office; he shot from the car before I could even offer to buy him lunch. Small matter; he will need another favour some day, and I will be ready to oblige. I felt a huge sense of relief at having the power of attorney signed, sealed, delivered. And the unchristian, shameful pleasure I was going to take in letting drop to my sister that I now had discretionary power over wedding expenses gave me such a blast of adrenaline that I ignored the elevator and took the stairs up to my office.

That evening, at one minute past six, when the reduced rates went into effect, I telephoned my sister in Toronto. Mildred answered.

"Yes?" she barked into the receiver, as though already certain the caller had dialled a wrong number.

"At the sound of the heavy breathing you will signal frantically for someone to run next door and telephone the police. Then you must try to keep me on the line so the officers of the law will have ample time to trace the call. Ready?"

"Geoffry, you are not in the least funny. I am peeling tomatoes."

"I used to, before I wised up. I would like to speak to Jennifer, if she's there."

"Oh, well, just a minute. I'll fetch her." Having informed me she was too busy to talk, Mildred was predictably miffed when it turned out I wanted to speak to someone else.

"Uncle Geoffry?"

"Jennifer, are you helping your mother peel tomatoes?"

"No, I'm chopping the onions."

"Are your eyes red-rimmed and unattractive?"

"Totally."

"Good. Just make sure your mother notices. I was wondering if you had any plans to visit Montreal in the near future."

"As a matter of fact, yes. Doug and I were thinking of coming down next weekend. We'll be staying with Mrs. Fullerton. I wanted to stay with Gran, but Mother says it will be too much trouble."

"Why don't you let your grandmother be the judge of that? I know she would love to have you stay. In any case, do you think you could pull yourself away for a private visit? Naturally I want to meet your young man, but there are a couple of things I would like to discuss, just with you."

"I already know the facts of life, Uncle Geoffry."

I found myself laughing out loud. "That's a relief. We can spend our time discussing the bathroom shower I do not intend to throw for you. I can take you to lunch if you can get away. Otherwise you could swing by my apartment."

"Sure thing. Why don't I give you a call as soon as I learn how the weekend is going to go?"

"Good idea. See you shortly."

"Hold on, Uncle Geoffry, Mother wants to say something to you."

I held on, knowing all along that Mildred would not let me get away without having a word.

"Geoffry?"

"I thought you were too busy with your tomatoes to talk."

"Geoffry, the last time we spoke I was so preoccupied with the wedding I never got around to asking about Mother, or your bursitis. How is your arm, by the way?"

"Better, thanks."

"Have you tried acupuncture?"

"No, nor do I intend to. I avoid all approaches to healing not covered by Blue Cross."

"You really should try it. I've been told it's very effective."

Mildred is the kind of woman for whom not to have an

opinion, regardless of subject, amounts to a confession of weakness.

"Now, tell me about Mother. Have you seen her recently? How is she?"

"I saw her this morning. She was a brunette. Actually I prefer the red wig. It makes her look more raffish."

"That is not what I mean. Is she eating properly? Is she taking any medication for her dizzy spells?"

"She is obviously eating enough to keep herself alive. And she only has dizzy spells when she is drunk. But then so do I, come to think of it."

"Geoffry, I simply do not understand you. Mother has this – this problem, and you refuse to do anything about it."

"Mother does not have a problem, Mildred, you do. She has made her peace with the world. She pays her rent and her taxes and goes through her days without giving any grief. I can't say that for many people of my acquaintance. Now, let's not play this tape yet another time."

A slight pause followed. "What were you doing at Mother's apartment this morning? Shouldn't you have been at the office?"

How Mildred has grown as old as she is without being punched in the mouth I'll never understand.

"Oh, just having her sign a power of attorney." I made my voice elaborately casual. "I already have signing authority for her bank account, but the power of attorney plugs the loopholes, gives me discretionary power, as it were. I can refuse to pay excessive or unjustified expenses." I studiously avoided any mention of the wedding. I knew Mildred would make her own connections in time.

"I see. This gives you full authority over her estate?"

"It does. Just a precaution. She is old and frail. And I am the one who sees her regularly. Trust me. I am not about to blow myself to a week at Disneyworld at Mother's expense. Nor do I intend siphoning her funds into a Swiss bank account. Now, hadn't you better get back to your tomatoes and onions? This is my dime. Jennifer will bring you a full report."

"She is so forgetful. She seldom tells me anything I really want to know."

"She is not forgetful. You simply have different priorities. I think I hear the doorbell, or the telephone, or is it the whistling kettle? We will communicate further." I hung up.

If Mildred had been a barnyard hen hatching eggs, she would have scolded the newly born chicks, not for breaking the shells but for not picking up the pieces.

The following day passed without a single reminder of the wedding. I had almost succeeded in putting the whole business out of my mind when Lois Fullerton telephoned that evening during my first drink to say she was giving a small dinner party on Saturday night for Jennifer and Douglas. In a husky, entreating voice, Lois hoped I would be able to come. (I trusted she meant only to the dinner.) She suggested it would give me an opportunity to meet Douglas, to whom I would be handing over my niece.

With the utmost reluctance I accepted. My idea of sinful luxury is to stay home on a Saturday night. To eat out means crowded restaurants and stressful service. Movie theatres are filled with patrons who chatter and cough, often simultaneously. People stand in line to get into clubs so they can stand in

line to get to the bar or stand in a different line and wait for a
table.

Private parties on a Saturday night turn into a life sentence; one is never permitted to go home. "Tomorrow is Sunday!" cry the hosts, meaning one can spend the following day
in bed, so do not even think of leaving. One can put in as many
hours at a Saturday night party as during a full working day.
Sunday mornings are precious to me. I tidy up my own life on Sunday mornings, paying bills, writing letters, sometimes working
through my attaché case and tidying up ends left loose during
the week. Last, but certainly not least, Saturday nights always
offer good old movies, black-and-white films whose dated
clothes and vintage dialogue cannot conceal the fact that they
were made with both craft and art.

Scarcely had I hung up the phone with Lois Fullerton than
Jennifer called. She had followed my suggestion and offered to
stay with her grandmother, who was predictably delighted. Jennifer's weekend sounded heavily booked, and we agreed she
should drop by my apartment late Saturday afternoon for a
visit. Then I could drive her up to Lois Fullerton's for dinner.
At least the evening would give me the opportunity for a visit
with my niece. That is, if we could prevent our hostess from
blocking the view.

VI

It was with some curiosity that I awaited my niece the following Saturday afternoon, I suppose the main reason being that I hardly knew her. I used to make occasional visits to Toronto for Christmas, when Mildred's children were a lot younger and, it goes without saying, so was I. The last Christmas visit had been a bit of a disaster, even moreso than the others. Mildred had asked a friend if he would volunteer to dress up as Santa Claus on Christmas Eve and hand out gifts to young and old alike. I had already met the friend, athletic, toothsome, and very possibly available. I wouldn't have minded in the least sitting on his knee, but he arrived stinko.

"I thing the anta-say is unk-dray," I stage-whispered to Mildred, reverting to the codes of our childhood.

"Don't be ridiculous," she hissed, at which point the Santa tugged "this goddamned pillow" from under his red jacket and demanded a dry martini, Santa Claus style.

"Call me when it's over," I said to no one in particular, and retreated to my room.

The party ended with Jennifer in tears, her belief in Santa Claus irretrievably shattered, the Santa himself led away in disgrace, and Mildred predictably furious. Most of her anger was directed at me, for no reason other than that I had removed myself from the arena before the kill.

After that I saw my nephews and nieces once in a while,

enough to be aware that they were growing up. And suddenly the small girl, who had stood saucer-eyed while jolly old Santa ranted and swore, was on the verge of being married. "*Où sont les neiges d'antan!*"

My intercom rang. "A Miss Carson to see you, Mr. Chadwick," said the porter.

"Thank you. Please send her up."

Unlike the security guard in Mother's building, horribly chatty and detestably affable, the porter in my building plays the Phantom. He blends into the furniture and doesn't miss a trick. I could easily imagine his wondering why a young woman was visiting Mr. Chadwick. Now, were the visitor a young man . . .

I walked to the elevator to meet Jennifer. As luck would have it the hall stood empty. I could hear the elevator clanking closer, then saw the shaft of light between the closed doors, which opened.

"Ta-da!" I sang by way of greeting.

Out stepped the old bag who runs Prints Charming. "The welcoming committee! Oh, Mary, you shouldn't have bothered!"

"To be candid, I thought you were my niece."

"I'm too old and too beautiful!" He swept down the hall and into his apartment. Loretta Young on television never went through a door with half the *éclat* of Prints Charming and his lynx coat.

By now the second elevator was en route. I waited until the doors opened to reveal a young woman who reminded me of my niece. But I had put all my spontaneity into that first ta-da.

"Jennifer," I said without fanfare.

"Uncle Geoffry!"

We embraced cautiously, two strangers who happen to be

related.

"This way." I led her down the hall to the door of my apartment, where Jennifer paused to remove her boots. To give credit to my sister, she has taught her children manners, the social graphite that eases friction between generations.

"Let me take your coat."

"Wow! I like your apartment, Uncle Geoffry. *Really cool!*" She put the last into the verbal equivalent of quotation marks.

"Thank you. I just had it redecorated, the second in fact I knew you were coming by."

"Very impressive! You sure know how to treat a girl."

"We try harder. Now, I know your Mother must have given you serious warnings about going to older men's apartments and drinking strong liquors, but under the circs I think you might take the chance."

"If she doesn't know about it she can't scold. Could I have white wine and soda, please?" She smiled a large, slow smile to reveal teeth tamed by a retainer into a perfect military row.

The same bottle of soda went into my Scotch and Jennifer's white wine. We moved to the conversation area, a couch and three chairs grouped around a coffee table.

"Jennifer, let us not beat about the bush. Mildred has asked me to give you away. I am happy to do so, although I did suggest your older brother was closer and possibly more suitable. Small matter. I would have been at the wedding anyway. Furthermore, your grandmother has agreed to underwrite the ceremony. As I am now her attorney, which means in effect that I will be paying the bills, I will be very much a part of the wedding, from the wings as it were. What I would like to know, without pre-amble or circumlocution, is what kind of wedding do you yourself really want?"

Jennifer put down her glass, but only after reaching for a coaster. She was interesting to watch, almost as if she were taking shape before my eyes. Already a young woman, she still had the round, fluid look of someone who, like moist clay, has not fully set. She would one day mature into beauty; what she had at the moment was that splendid glow of youth, the sheen of a fine pearl, which gave to her skin, hair, eyes a lustre that would have made cosmetics seem coarse and superfluous. Her heavy auburn hair fell in a French braid down her back. She wore a plain long-sleeved white silk blouse and a long black skirt, almost as if she were part of a group that specialized in unaccompanied choral singing.

After a moment's hesitation she spoke. "That is a serious question, Uncle Geoffry. If I don't have a ready answer it is because no one has asked me before. Once Douglas and I had decided to get married it seemed as if the whole thing was taken out of my hands. Mother was so excited at the prospect of my wedding that I couldn't bring myself to contradict her. And with Dad so recently dead it gave her something else to think about."

"You still haven't answered my question, Jennifer. What kind of wedding do you want? Remember, this is the one time in your life when you can legitimately be selfish. At the risk of sounding like a game-show host, this is your day. Obviously you want both your mother's cooperation and enjoyment. But whatever therapeutic value the occasion may have for Mildred remains secondary. The ceremony is to celebrate your marriage, not alleviate her widowhood."

The girl reached up to smooth her already sleek hair, the reassuring touch that convinces self really exists. She smiled a

nervous little smile. "To be honest, Uncle Geoffry, I would prefer no ceremony at all – a minister and two witnesses. But I
suppose there is no chance of that. Otherwise, I'd like a small
wedding. I want my sister, Elizabeth, to attend me, and Linda
Tyler; she and I have been friends since elementary school. I'd
like my brother, Richard, to be head usher, and I'd really like
you to give me away. For the rest, I don't much care, although
I'd prefer it small, smaller than it is. Mother wants me to have
five bridesmaids so the wedding will include cousins on Dad's
side of the family."

"It's your wedding, Jennifer. Do you want two attendants or
five?"

"Two. Perhaps I shouldn't even tell you this, but Mother and
I had a big row over the number of bridesmaids. I said I wanted
only two attendants. Mother gave me one of those looks, as
though I was three feet tall and retarded, and announced that
five bridesmaids are what Father would have wanted.

"I said how could she be so sure what Father would have
wanted. We only announced the engagement after the funeral.
Besides, Father was dead and I wasn't and it was my wedding.
Mother burst into tears. And you know as well as I do she never
cries. I was shocked. It was like watching Darth Vader cry. I decided that trying to cope with her attitude was too much effort.
Once I was married I would be moving away. And it just seems
easier to go with the flow than to have an argument over every
detail of the wedding."

I put down my tumbler. "Point taken re number of bridesmaids. Am I correct in assuming that you want the rest of the
ceremony and reception in proportion, which is to say small
and manageable?"

"Yes."

"Good. I'll see what I can do. Now, one more question. Do you have strong views on a wedding gown?"

"Not really. Mother has grandiose ideas for a dress. She wants me all bridey-widey. Not my style at all. I'd prefer something simple. I only hope we won't have another fight over the gown. But I don't want to look like a character on one of those costume movies on late-night TV."

"Your grandmother thinks you would look well in a Regency gown, rather like the heroine of a Jane Austen novel. I am not a designer myself, but I think the style would suit you very well. And as your grandmother is paying the bills, unless you have strong objections to the contrary, I think in this instance you could accommodate her."

"I love the Regency look. I don't have a waistline, and I never will. It's Mother who needs convincing, not me. Just so long as I don't have to wear one of those floral tiaras – a Walkman without sound. I'll be nervous enough as it is."

"Let me have a try at persuading your mother." I was about to add that Mother is the necessity of invention, but decided to curb my tongue. "And, truly, Jennifer, what is there to be nervous about? You have only to walk down the aisle on my arm, give your responses, and answer a few simple questions. Remember: a wedding is the only theatrical presentation I can think of where the prompter stands up facing the audience and feeds lines to the principal players. You couldn't go wrong if you tried."

"It's not just the wedding, Uncle Geoffry. It's what follows."

"You mean the future? That is a hurdle, I know. The problem with the future is that there's so much of it, for all of us."

Up to now the conversation had been a game of twenty

questions; moreover, I had learned what I wanted to know. "It's a big step you are about to undertake. And you appear to be going against the trend. People today seem to be delaying marriage, at least until they have one foot on the ladder of a career."

"You're right, Uncle Geoffry. To be honest, I wouldn't mind waiting for a while. There are lots of things I want to see and do before I begin to have children. I really enjoy teaching, and it would be interesting to teach in another country. But Douglas is very anxious to get married. And in spite of her claim of being totally liberated, Mother really does not like the idea of our living together. There is pressure on all sides. I decided it was easier just to have the wedding."

"I suppose it is," I added without conviction. Expediency does not strike me as an adequate reason for marriage. Maybe it was in the thirteenth century, when duchies, castles, vineyards, the very survival of the family depended on making the most useful alliance. But women are no longer chattels, to be traded and married off at the whim of an autocratic father or mother. Even parenthood, once a prime motive for marriage, has come up for reappraisal, what with single and surrogate mothers, artificial insemination, subsidized daycare. Fathers have become redundant. We will one day face an entire generation of fatherless children who will look quizzically at any man with warts or hair on his palm. "Daddy, is it really you?"

"But," I added brightly, "when what used to be called 'the tender emotion' strikes you down, you might just as well roll over and enjoy, smiling. Somebody once sent me a card which read: 'Love is the shortest distance between two hearts.' Is it still true? I've just about forgotten."

I was trying rather harder than I should have to inject a few carbon dioxide bubbles into the heavy water of our talk. I guess I hoped that Jennifer would giggle, laugh out loud, admit that she was happy, at least excited. Like an augur I was looking for a sign, a blush, a tear, a ripple of laughter that would indicate a heightened emotional state at the prospect of her wedding.

Jennifer did laugh, uncomfortably. "Come on, Uncle Geoffry, gimme a break."

"Okay, Jennifer. But remember: marriage is a big undertaking, even if you are one hundred and ten percent certain." I checked my watch. "We'd better think of getting along. I shouldn't imagine Lady Fullerton would like us to be late."

At once I was sorry I had been so flip. Me and my mouth. I glanced up to see Jennifer looking at me steadily. Our eyes joined in a glance brimming with eloquence. Young though she might be, Jennifer was no fool. How could she not realize her future mother-in-law was a bit much?

"I have a question, for myself," I began, trying to cover up my gaffe. "I would appreciate some direction on what you want for a wedding present. I am not about to lumber you with a silver-plated chafing dish, twelve twin-handled bouillon cups, or a wicker picnic basket with its own enamel plates and cups, which requires two hands to lift. How about a cheque? Then you can buy Tupperware in your favourite shade, or a set of presentation coins from the Franklin Mint."

"I'd like you to choose something, Uncle Geoffry. Whatever it is, I know it will be interesting."

"You lay on me a heavy burden. As the French would say: I will do my possible. Now we had better drink up and push off."

My first impression of Douglas Fullerton was that he was any mother's freewheeling fantasy of a prospective son-in-law. Tall and tailored, he moved with the assurance of a young man who, as a small boy, had been driven to day camp by the chauffeur. The dark suit showed off his athletic figure; I suspected the buttons on the cuffs actually buttoned. Tiny snaffle bits decorated his loafers, while across his tie marched a regular pattern of small objects, which on closer inspection turned out to be spurs.

"How do you do, Mr. Chadwick," he said, striding across the foyer after the maid had taken both my coat and bottle of excellent brandy, which I had chosen instead of flowers as a way of paying for my dinner. (The first rule in being a successful guest is to put your hostess on the defensive.)

"How do you do, Douglas," I replied, returning his smile and shaking his hand.

"Hi there." He acknowledged his bride-to-be with a quick kiss on the lips.

I watched without appearing to. I do not think engaged couples should dry-hump every time they meet, particularly when other people are present, but I couldn't help thinking this greeting was totally without chemistry. I felt as if I were watching a brother greet a sister who has been away for a while.

"Mother will be down shortly. My orders are to see that you are given a Scotch right away."

He led the way into the library, I was glad to see. There was something chilly and intimidating about that pale blue drawing room and its period furniture.

"May I pour my own? That way I won't slide in a drunken stupor under the dining-room table."

"Of course, sir. We got a wedding present today, Jenny. Come and have a look. Would you excuse us, please?"

"Reluctantly." I made myself a drink and stood in front of the fire. I wasn't the least bit cold, but there is something profoundly sensual in heat radiating from open combustion.

"You must be Jennifer's mysterious Uncle Geoffry," said a voice from the door. I turned to confront another young man. Short and stocky, he was buttoned into a grey flannel suit that threatened to burst seams and pop buttons, so snugly did it cling to the wearer's contours. A tangle of soft brown curls framed a face that made me think of a slightly debauched cherub. "You don't look nearly so terrifying as you were made to sound."

I gave a short laugh. "I assure you I am. The G really stands for Grinch. Mothers have only to mention my name and recalcitrant children are instantly reduced to whimpering obedience. You know my name, which is supposed to give you an advantage. Are you prepared to divulge yours?"

"At once, Charles Grant. Overjoyed, I'm sure." He extended a short, square hand. The grip was strong. "I'm to be the best man, in a manner of speaking. I'd far sooner be maid of honour, but my problem figure kills my chances every time."

"You know what they say. Always a bridesmaid, never a bride."

"True, but the rehearsals are such heaven, especially the one for the honeymoon. I thought Jennifer was coming with you."

"She did, but Douglas took her away to look at an early wedding present, and perhaps to greet her the way he couldn't in front of her uncle."

"I wouldn't bet on it. I suppose Auntie Lois is upstairs getting it all together. I wish I knew how she does it. Silicone? Polyfilla? Beauty secrets from Queen Hatshepsut? Now, shall I have a drink? Calories! Calories! I just checked out the kitchen, and there's a chocolate cheesecake for dessert that's to absolutely die."

With my mouth full of single malt whisky, the mere mention of chocolate cheesecake made my gold crowns jump. Charles moved to the drink trolley.

"Maybe I'll crack under pressure and have a gin and ginger ale, low-cal ginger ale."

"Sounds suitably innocuous," I replied. "Are you a friend of Douglas, from university, perhaps?"

"Right. We both did honours English. Who needs it? I mean, twelve books of *Paradise Lost* to learn Eve ate the apple? Doug went on to graduate school, and I went to work. I'm in the catering business. I'm going to have my own operation some day. A class act."

"You mean all those chicken livers wrapped in strips of bacon will actually be served hot?"

Charles Grant laughed, an intense, physical laugh involving every part of his body. His large, grey eyes wrinkled engagingly at the corners. I found myself laughing, more from sympathy than mirth.

"Correct. And those little mushroom patties are not going to crumble and fall, half into your cleavage and half onto the freshly shampooed wall-to-wall."

We continued to laugh. "Will you sit up until four A.M. ," I asked, "carving radishes into rosettes?"

"All night if necessary. But my real show stopper is a large cabbage with the centre hollowed out and filled with Russian dressing, fifty-fifty mayo and ketchup. Yuk! Then I cover the outside of the cabbage with toothpicks, and onto each toothpick I stick a shrimp. You take the toothpick, dip the shrimp into the sauce . . ."

"Which then drips down, half onto your Ralph Lauren tie and half onto the freshly shampooed wall-to-wall."

We were both laughing when Jennifer and Douglas came into the library. For just a fleeting second I had an intimation of absence, of absolutely no current flowing between them. Jennifer did not have the look of a girl who has just been kissed until her lips felt like grapes. Douglas did not stand with the base of his spine convex, his jacket carefully buttoned to conceal an erection.

I did not have time for further speculation for, with timing and panache that would have put any Las Vegas headliner to shame, Lois Fullerton made her entrance.

"Geoffry, how lovely you could come." She bore down upon me, a pre-Raphaelite vision in an artfully draped gown of sage, mauve, and teal. For all the yards of fabric gathered into the dress, it still contrived to leave a lot of Lois bare. She had that creamy, flawless skin that is its own presence. "And thank you for that sinful bottle of brandy."

(Was she going to say "You shouldn't have"?)

"You really shouldn't have. Jennifer!" Lois and Jennifer embraced in that curious way women can, without appearing to touch. "You've met Douglas?" She beamed at her son. "And Charles, our best man." The Douglas smile faded as she turned to him; her voice lost colour. "Now, I know the young people have plans for the evening, and there will be plenty of wine. Perhaps we might go right in to dinner?"

So that was the drill. We were to be hustled through the meal so the young people could hit the road, leaving me at the mercy of the hostess. And for this I was missing Garbo?

Wedding or no blasted wedding, I did not intend to spend the next four months being manipulated by Lois Fullerton every time we met. It was an easy pattern to fall into. I had been raised in that atmosphere of chivalry and condescension which saw men deferring to women the same way they deferred to children. One humours inferiors. But no more; my own consciousness had been raised.

"I would like another drink first, if I may." Without waiting for permission I moved to the trolley and poured myself a belt. Nor did I even glance at Lois.

"But of course . . . I only thought . . ."

"May I have a vermouth, please, Uncle Geoffry?" asked Jennifer, whose silence up to now had become apparent.

"Let me do it," suggested Douglas. "I'll have one myself."

"Why not!" announced Charles, more as a statement than a question, as he headed for the gin bottle.

Unable to quell the palace revolt, Lois made an exit, Andromache leaving the walls of Troy. "I'd better go and tell Cook to delay serving dinner."

Her departure created a vacuum in which we bobbed, clinging to our tumblers for security. From across the room Charles Grant winked to catch my attention and gave me a thumbs-up gesture of approval. I looked away, torn between complicity over the drinks and solidarity with my hostess, with whom I was aligned through age and station.

"What was the mystery wedding present?" I asked Jennifer in order to get the wheels turning.

I could see the corners of her mouth twitching ever so slightly. "A pair of silver napkin rings, engraved with our initials, *D* and *J*."

"As in John Doe or Disc Jockey. Pity they're engraved. That means you can't take them back."

"Not to worry," said Charles. "You can hang them from the rear-view mirror. Far classier than a pair of big fuzzy dice."

"Are your ears pierced, Jennifer?" I asked. "They could be very dramatic, with the peasant blouse and unbleached cotton skirt."

Jennifer, Charles, and I all started to laugh. Unwilling to be left out, Douglas joined in.

"I'm going to have a rebellious cook on my hands," announced Lois from the door. "Bring your drinks to the table."

VII

Were I to have concealed a small tape recorder on my person so as to capture the conversation at dinner, the tape would have made very dull listening. The table at which we sat, Lois and I at either end, Douglas beside Jennifer facing Charles across its width, was hedged around with constraint. All the baggage of gracious living – the silver, china, crystal, impeccable food, and a maid to hand it around – far from fostering ease only managed to inhibit.

On one level I did not really mind. There is very little people in their early twenties can tell me that I don't already know, except about computers. There is much we have to discover by and for ourselves alone. To be told with extreme seriousness that the sky is blue and the grass green fails to hold my interest.

I had hoped Charles might at least be amusing; I far prefer superficial to solemn, at least over dinner. But even he was cowed into obedience by the *mise en scène*: the coldly formal room, the table set as if for a photographer, and the hostess who, in spite of airs and graces, did not succeed at putting her guests at ease. Furthermore, it was evident that Lois Fullerton did not like Charles Grant, and he obviously had enough smarts to avoid the line of fire, as he sat in total isolation on the far side of the long table.

Jennifer played it safe, speaking when spoken to and keeping her answers short. She offered no conversational cadenzas or verbal arabesques, but took refuge in the simple declarative sentence. It fell to Douglas, himself on home ground, to carry the ball, as it were. He and I did what we could with what we had, conversing past Jennifer without including her. Occasionally I bounced a remark off Charles, who sat well outside the charmed triangle; but he too gave the minimal answer and, perhaps wisely, did not elaborate.

We skated over the usual subjects: Douglas's graduate work over cream of carrot soup. During medallions of veal we discussed free trade, or the idea of free trade. (Anyone who has cruised Dominion Square after midnight soon learns no trade is free.) Television saw us through a salad in which chunks of avocado and shards of endive jostled for prominence. Douglas Fullerton had the comfortable, slightly-to-the-left attitudes of a graduate student with a good profile and ample income. I suspected that by the time he was forty his point of view would have moved even further right than his snaffle bit loafers and patterned tie.

Lois was playing the role of hostess as though she had won the part after a stiff audition. She conferred with the maid, saw that wineglasses were kept filled, signalled the advent of the next course. She did much with her long, full, medieval-romantic sleeves, brushing back their scalloped edges with long, graceful gestures. At the same time she deferred to the men, which meant she took no active part in the conversation. I would not have been in the least surprised if she and Jennifer, and quite possibly Charles, had quit the dining room at the end of the meal, leaving Douglas and me with our port and cigars.

One episode, small but telling, stuck in my mind in sharp contrast to the bland conversation that, like white noise, had hummed quietly throughout the meal. By the time salad arrived I could see that Charles was having trouble keeping the lid on. Like a tightly closed cooking pot, steam inside was building up pressure. As we got onto the subject of movies, Charles began to join in. He evidently held stronger opinions on certain actresses and their wardrobes than on free trade. Outrageous he undoubtedly was, yet at the same time carried a kind of innocence. He did not intend to shock but to state.

The name of a certain television personality came up, one of those women whose main talent is for self-promotion.

"Isn't she something else!" exclaimed Charles, clapping his hands together. "I waited on her at a party once. Believe me, if her knockers were any bigger she'd need her own postal code."

Obviously two gins and a fair amount of wine had just spoken. But *knockers* is a no-no, particularly over avocado and endive on Baccarat plates. Lois, herself a prime contender for her own private listing (H3Y T1T), gathered herself in, tamed her sleeves, and asked in a frost-coated voice if we had finished our salad.

The arrival of the chocolate cheesecake helped to smooth over the contretemps. I do not avoid sweet stuff for any reason of weight or health or hypoglycaemia, that which used to be called a sweet tooth. I actually dislike sugar. But I helped myself to a wedge, the way I was expected to. At some point I would cut off a piece, mash it around on the plate with my fork, and leave it alone.

Lois coyly admitted the ingredients were a secret she did not ordinarily divulge, but that she would make an exception and give Jennifer the recipe for her card file. Jennifer thanked her politely, even though I am reasonably certain my niece is a nuts-and-berries kind of cook. Charles was so blissed out he could hardly even speak.

Obviously pleased by the reception to her dessert, Lois inquired if anyone would like a second helping. "Geoffry?"

"No, thank you. I haven't finished what I have."

"Jennifer?" (Had my own mother been hostess, Jennifer, being a lady, would have been asked first.)

"No, thank you, Mrs. Fullerton."

"Douglas?"

"Top weight, thanks, Mother."

"Charles?" She did not look at him as she spoke.

"Oh, I really shouldn't," he replied in the languorous tone of one about to fall voluptuously into the arms of a second helping.

"Then don't!" she snapped.

I could see Jennifer react as though she had been slapped. So did I, although I was perhaps better at masking it. I have never been one to throw down the gauntlet if there is another way out, but I found myself ready and willing to challenge Lois, even though I was still a guest in her house.

"Here, Charles," I said quietly, "why don't you finish mine. I've barely touched it, and it's far too good to waste." Upon which I handed him my plate.

The gesture compelled him to reach for it, meaning he had to give me his plate in return. Bad manners, indeed, but we can't always play by the book. As he handed me his empty plate, he looked directly into my eyes; I knew I had just made a friend for life.

The younger members of the party had been invited to join a group of friends en route to a nightclub. As Douglas and Jennifer were to be the nominal guests of honour, they decided to skip coffee and leave right away. Had I been they, I would gladly have traded the congenial atmosphere of a club for dreary demitasses with our mixed media group.

With commendable foresight Lois suggested that as they would perhaps be drinking she would prefer them not to drive. The chauffeur was to ferry them to the club; they could take a taxi home.

We moved in a wedge to the front door where the chauffeur stood waiting in the front porch, just as drop-dead good-looking as I remembered. For a moment our eyes met, locked. Lois gave him an order I couldn't hear, and he looked away. I had the oddest sensation that he had just given me what used to be called a dirty look. Then again, he had already demonstrated his total reluctance to make any sort of contact. And, democratic niceties aside, he remained a servant, one whose job it was to display distance and deference to his employer's friends. He was out of reach, but distance definitely adds charm.

In a flurry of goodnights and injunctions to have a wonderful time, Jennifer, Douglas, and Charles departed. The night was still young, to coin a phrase, and I was marooned way up here on the hill with Lois and her sleeves. Haven't we all been taught that one should try to make the best of any situation? I followed her gown into the library, where I headed for my customary chair on the far side of the fireplace.

Lois poured coffee as if preoccupied. A question was obviously formulating itself, but she could not seem to find words to frame it. After a moment or two she abandoned her quest for paraphrase and gave it to me straight. "What do you think of Charles?"

I understood precisely what she meant, but pretended not to.

"He seems a likable young man, bright, personable. He has a sense of humour, which I always appreciate in a person. I suspect he will reach whatever goals he sets for himself."

I had not given the answer she wanted. I knew it, and enjoyed watching her flounder.

"What you say is true, but doesn't it bother you that he is, well, so obviously what he is?"

"And what precisely is that?"

She gave a short sigh of impatience. "Geoffry, you're a man of the world. Do I have to spell it out?"

"I'm a lawyer, Lois, not a graduate student. I am trained not to deal in abstractions. In fact, whenever I see an abstraction heading into the room I hide behind a chair."

I wasn't giving Lois the slightest bit of help. She was dying to lay into Charles because he was gay, but she also wanted me to fill in the spaces. Well, screw her, in a manner of speaking.

"I think the current word is *gay*."

At least I had obliged her to say it out loud, obviously a problem for her. We had not said a word about my niece, the bride, or about her son, the groom on whom, if I had correctly read the signals, the sun rose and set. Instead we were discussing the best man, and not his role in the wedding party but his sexual orientation. The message flashing onto the screen read Proceed With Caution.

"Well, what about it? His personal life is his own business. Times have changed since we were youngsters, Lois. Sexual preference is no longer something to be concealed as if it were shameful. Being gay is no longer a major misfortune but a minor inconvenience."

"Yes, I know!" She tried unsuccessfully to keep the impatience out of her voice. "It's just that – I've never dictated to Douglas who his friends ought to be. But for his wedding? I mean, the best man is usually the groom's best friend."

"And what will the neighbours say? No more coffee, thanks. I think I'll have a highball, if I may. Face it, Lois, marriage is a fairly sound indication of heterosexuality, if that's what's bothering you."

"Indeed it is not!" she flashed with a bit too much heat.

"Would you prefer the best man to be some lout who stands in the receiving line chewing on a toothpick and who calls the bridesmaids broads? At the last wedding I attended, the best man was a football-playing jock who, I am sure, could not even read the diploma he had recently been awarded. By the time we got into dinner he was too drunk to toast the bride. I would be very surprised if Charles were not both articulate and amusing."

If not mollified, Lois at least paused to consider what I had said.

"I suppose you're right. And once Douglas and Jennifer are married it won't matter who their friends are. He hadn't – gone out with many girls before he met Jennifer. But she is such a lovely girl. I am sure she will make him an excellent wife."

"Did Douglas have trouble persuading you to give your approval?"

Lois laughed a brittle little laugh. "Not at all. I only hoped when he finally got serious about a girl she would turn out to be as nice as Jennifer. It's all happening just as I would have wished."

Lois put her empty cup onto the tray, then crossed to pick up mine from the occasional table beside my chair. "If only Douglas hadn't asked that awful little fairy to be his best man."

The remark came out so matter-of-factly that it jarred me all the more. It had the same harsh crudeness of her telling Charles at dinner not to have a second helping. I had noticed before that Lois had failed to catch up with the eighties. She still inhabited a time warp where men were men, women were women, and homosexuals were beaten up. It had also become abundantly clear that she was hugely relieved Douglas was getting married. To whom did not matter, in spite of protestations to the contrary. Jennifer might be cast as the bride, but she was still going to do nothing more than a walk-on cameo. I was beginning to have an uneasy suspicion that Lois wanted this marriage more than anyone else, so that her "sensitive" son, who was designing the rings, would be stamped, labelled, and presented to the world as she would have him seen.

My sister, Mildred, would have fallen right into line. By even the most stringent standards Douglas was a catch. With his WASP good looks, pleasant manners, soon-to-be-awarded Ph.D., and, let us not forget, bags of Fullerton money, Douglas was pretty close to a ten. Jennifer should be so lucky.

It all looked good on the surface, so good, in fact, that I felt uneasy. However, further speculation on the wedding was pushed to one side as Lois moved to the drink trolley. After studied deliberation she poured about an eyedropperful of Grand Marnier into a tiny glass, but instead of returning to her chair she sat on the small couch facing the fireplace. She gave the seat beside her a couple of inviting pats and shifted her voice into the key of G-spot.

"Why don't you come and sit here? Then you can look at the fire."

"I'd like to, but sitting in front of an open fire gives me a headache."

"I'll put up the screen. That will block a good deal of the heat."

"Don't bother. I'm perfectly comfortable where I am, and at my age inertia is perhaps the most powerful drive of all."

"If the fire bothers you we could go upstairs to the den."

"It's not the fire. I like that. It's just the blast of direct heat."

I realized it was some indication of how determined Lois was to nail me that she did not throw me out of the house into the street. I can well remember during my own younger days how I overlooked any amount of loutish behaviour for which today I would quite certainly ask someone to leave. Crotch fog not only obscures the view; it scrambles the thought process as well.

And in terms of the present situation, my own behaviour had been considerably below par. To be sure, I had not put my feet onto the table or flicked cigarette ash onto the rug or broken wind. But I had thwarted Lois enough times that, had our situations been reversed, I would have pleaded an all-purpose headache and sent me on my way.

But below those dimples of iron lurked a will of steel. Lois leaned slightly forward, brushed back her right sleeve, and laid her arm along the back of the couch. The gesture threw her bust into relief and made a graceful line of her jaw, neck, and shoulder. If, as feminists claim, penetration is colonization, she was ready for me to plant my flag. Poor Lois, she was running a marathon on a treadmill.

She smiled. "I have to admit, Geoffry, you are a difficult man to get close to." Her tone invited confidence.

"Not difficult, Lois. Impossible."

"How so."

How easy it would have been to tell her the truth. This so-called truth may not set us free, but it can permit us to uncross our legs. Yet one feature I have always admired about Arab countries is the importance of saving face. One must never pull the rug, prayer or otherwise, from under somebody's feet. To admit to Lois that I was homosexual would make her seem a fool. Why had she not seen the truth for herself? All this scheming and effort and manipulation so she could flirt with a fairy and make a pass at a pansy? She would lose face, that same face she had probably spent the better part of an hour putting on.

Furthermore, campy candour is not my style. I was not about to erupt into shrill giggles and admit I was as gay as a fuschia feather fan. I had given Lois ample notice of my intentions, or lack of them. I had hung out the Do Not Disturb sign, only to have her ignore it and pound on the door.

Instead of playing my queen I played my ace. "When one is climbing out of one relationship, Lois, one is not overly anxious to embark upon another."

There it was: alibi number two. The blazing torch held high. It had worked in the past when women tried to get close. Why not now?

"Geoffry, there's someone in your life?"

"Was."

"It's over?"

"Yes and no. Yes, in that we are no longer seeing one another. No, in that the bruises are not fully healed."

"Do you want to talk about it?" (Why did I know she would say that?)

"Not really."

"Some people think that a new love affair, even make-believe, is the best cure."

"To steal a line from a musical comedy, Lois, 'Some people ain't me!'" Although I have never hyperventilated, I was beginning to experience similar symptoms. My heart was pounding uncomfortably and my breathing had grown shallow. If only I could keep myself from blowing my lid.

Lois leaned forward, hands together in her lap, arms pressed tight against her sides. The effect was to give primary importance to her secondary sexual characteristics. "Two can mend a broken heart faster than one."

My impulse was to reply, "Not on a full stomach," but God helped me hold my tongue. Still, I was not going to let her off unscathed.

"Next you'll be telling me that love is the shortest distance between two hearts." That seemed to be my tag line for the evening.

There was a curious and totally unfunny irony in my situation. I had reluctantly relinquished an evening of old movies only to find myself playing in one: the appalling dialogue, the house furnished not as a house but as a set, and the hackneyed situation of the blonde femme fatale trying to put the make on a nerdy man who carries on as though his dork were solely to pee through. Even the aggressive way Lois plied her bust reminded me of an earlier time, when screen sirens wore snug sweaters and two inches of cleavage brought cries from the censors.

Even though Lois was doing her best to get me into that ghastly white bed, she was still an extreme sexual conservative.

In this more than anything else she betrayed her lower-class origins. I'd be willing to bet her parents had practised the flannelette-pyjamas-and-long-sleeved-nightgown approach to sensuality. They probably spoke of homosexual men as queers and refused to admit that lesbians even existed. They would also have endorsed the "when in doubt, don't" attitude to dating. Lois had obviously thrown off some of these attitudes. But to be a ready lay is not the same as being sexually liberated. Lois Fullerton made me profoundly uncomfortable.

Yet it was this same conservatism that allowed me to escape. According to her code, she could flash all the necessary come-hither signals, turn the lights green, talk in innuendoes; but it was still up to me to make the first critical move. I did not budge from my chair.

Lois cleared the air with a laugh. "It looks as though I have to admit defeat."

"Only if you believe there is something at stake worth winning. I assure you there isn't."

I finished my drink. At the precise moment my empty tumbler touched the table, Lois stood. "I hate to seem rude, but it's been a long day. At this point having Douglas to visit is like entertaining a houseguest. And then there's Charles. I hope you won't think me rude if I excuse myself."

"Not in the least," I replied, at once delighted and amused. No one would ever call Lois opaque. Once she realized, beyond all reasonable doubt, that she would not get to throw a leg over me, I was of no further interest. Finito! For the third time she had struck out. Stand not upon the order of your going, but go at once.

It was a no-frills goodnight. I thanked her for dinner and

the opportunity to meet the groom. She told me I was quite welcome, in the same way she must have spoken to the boy delivering the newspaper. I said I would be in touch. She said she hoped to see me again soon. There was the sound of the door closing. I glanced at my watch. If I went straight home I might still be able to catch Garbo as Mata Hari doing her temple dance. Perhaps only Dietrich in a monkey suit beats it out for sheer wonderful silliness.

Since it was Saturday night after all, I poured myself a highball to celebrate a safe return to my apartment. Snug in my Eames chair, the black-and-white images flickering reassuringly across the screen, I still found a part of my mind replaying a video cassette of the dinner party. I use *party* in its conventional sense, for there had been little real festivity.

Had I followed my own guidelines, I would have put the whole tiresome wedding out of my mind, except for my modest role. I could impose a budget on my sister, purchase the haberdashery to go with my morning suit, attend the rehearsal and the ceremony, and otherwise maintain an attitude of strict neutrality. With each passing year I have found it takes a little extra effort just to get through a day. There remains scant energy for causes, philanthropies, and the kind of high-minded meddling which our society passes for good works.

People in general, and that includes me, have a marked tendency to believe their way of doing things, if not the only way, is still the best. Thirty years have passed since I was married, in the church of St. Luke the Apostle, a smack-in-the-middle-of-the-road Anglican institution that has always advocated safe sects and that has acquired more of a reputation for rummage sales than for sanctity. The Geoffry Chadwick who took Susan Bradley to be his wife was a different man from the one remembering him now. It was as if I were a character in a play, a variation of which we have all seen, where four separate actors portray the same person at different stages in his life. How would I find the twenty-five-year-old Geoffry Chadwick were I to meet him today? Brash? Smug, perhaps? A bit too self-possessed, with a showy, self-conscious cynicism whose source was about ninety percent literary?

Dredging memory is like panning for gold. In among all the bits of shale, handfuls of sand, buckets of cloudy water, there are nuggets, gleaming and tangible. Even thirty years later I can remember how much I loved Susan. I am sure at times we believed ourselves in heaven, but there was also much of earth. In fact, from the time I met her, at a débutante ball, until the accident that killed Susan and our daughter, we were seldom apart. Most of the time it would have been difficult to push a putty knife between us.

She died while we were still riding the crest of the wave. We were married; we had our own apartment; I had just embarked on my career; and we had the only baby that had ever been born, to anybody, in the whole world, throughout time. I suppose had things turned out otherwise we would eventually have come down. It is oxygen that sustains the body, not ether. We would have been obliged to come to grips with raising children, buying a house, fretting over schools and slipcovers, and watching the bright shiny surface of our marriage acquire the muted patina of familiarity and habit. Perhaps my sexual orientation would eventually have driven us apart. I could speculate endlessly on the what ifs and if onlys. But of one thing I am certain. No matter what the disappointment and disillusion, I would still have wanted Susan alive.

And I firmly believed my way, and Susan's, of undertaking marriage to be better than the cool, almost rational, relationship I saw shared by Jennifer and Douglas. Even making allowances for changing fashion, that yesterday's love affair is today's neurotic attachment, I can't imagine embarking on something as daunting as a supposedly lifelong partnership without personal electricity.

Were Jennifer close to my age, with grown children from a previous marriage, I could understand the absence of passion, turgid and trite and penny-dreadful as that word may sound. People who marry in middle age have different expectations, unless they are caught in the grip of a sexual Indian summer and besotted with someone else's youth in an attempt to recapture their own. But youth is the time to draw irregular lines on one's emotional chart, abysmal lows and exhilarating highs. It takes the energy of youth for those blast-furnace fights and melting reconciliations. To grow older is to realize the universe is Copernican, not Ptolemaic, and that self and the loved one do not form the epicentre of the solar system.

I am sure there are people who are not capable of a real love affair, and perhaps those who do not really want one. But to have missed out, through ignorance or apathy or timidity, or just plain lack of awareness, is a lingering sorrow. I was afraid that Jennifer, mired in a safe marriage, might one day realize she had arrived in autumn, only to have missed out on spring. Jennifer is not like her brother and sister. Richard will never allow anything as intangible as love to stand in the way of his career, while Elizabeth has been in love more times since last March than I have been in my entire life. It remains Jennifer's choice, not mine. She is a grown woman and fully capable of taking responsibility for her own decisions. At least I would like to believe she can.

There is a time in a person's life when he can love with freedom and generosity and, why not say it, innocence. I do not mean the presexual innocence of a child but that brief state of grace before one has learned guile and the ability to lie to oneself. I had that experience with Susan. All that remains is the memory, but that memory is as bright as the large gold nugget every prospector longs to find. I would like to think Jennifer would one day find what I had known. I would be disappointed if she failed.

VIII

Because I had persuaded Jennifer to stay with her grandmother for the weekend, I was spared the Sunday lunch party Mother would otherwise have felt obliged to give, and which I would have felt compelled to attend. As a result the day stretched before me, unblemished by engagements of any kind. When I ducked around the corner to pick up the Sunday papers, I found the air cold and raw, perfect weather for staying in, which I did. *The Times*, television, a companionable highball: there are worse ways to go.

As dusk was falling I stood at the window of my living room, watching lights flicker on across the city, and thinking of all those tired weekend skiers battling heavy traffic on roads leading into Montreal. They are the four-day people. Monday, Tuesday, Wednesday, Thursday they allot to the town and whatever it has to offer. Friday afternoon, as soon as they can sneak away from work, they head off to "the little place in the country," often far larger and more elaborate than their urban digs. Sunday afternoon is haunted by the spectre of driving back to the city and the choices of killing the afternoon by leaving early, thus avoiding heavy traffic, leaving after skiing and making most of the trip bumper to bumper, or waiting until traffic has thinned out and driving in the dark. Thank heaven I am forever freed from the tyranny of a country house and the nagging obligation to get out there and enjoy it.

Monday morning I discovered my good gloves were not in the pocket of my overcoat. I strongly hoped I had left them in the car and not up at Lois Fullerton's house.

I took the stairs down to the garage, where I approached my car from the driver's side. With a slight sinking feeling I could see nothing on the front seat. I go through gloves the way most people go through paper napkins, to the point that whenever I see gloves on sale I usually buy a few pairs. The ones I probably left at Lois's house were good ones, though, suede lined with fur. Did I want those gloves badly enough to call Lois and arrange to drop by and pick them up?

So occupied was I trying to decide whether reclaiming my gloves was worth another encounter with Mrs. Fullerton that it took me a moment to notice the car was listing slightly to the right, the cant due to a flat on one of the spanking new tires only recently bought and installed. This flat tire in turn was due to a puncture, not ordinarily unusual. But in this instance the puncture had been made by a switchblade knife. Impaled on the knife was an envelope.

I watch enough television to know about fingerprints. I wrapped the handle of the knife in the clean handkerchief I always carry, before pulling the blade out of my tire. After carefully wrapping the weapon in the square of fabric, I stowed it in my attaché case. Then I read the note. Again it had been composed of words clipped from an advertising supplement, its message succinct: "This is your last warning. Keep away from L. Fullerton."

Suddenly I was shaking with anger. Nevertheless, I hesitated about taking the first, apparently logical step of reporting the matter to the police. My reluctance did not spring from lack of respect for the law; my profession imposed that. The boys in blue do a good job, some an even better one when they are out of uniform. I can remember many pleasant hours when the force was with me.

The fact remains that a slashed tire is a minor misdemeanour in relation to the volume of major crimes the police have to investigate. I would file a report, offer the few scant facts I had at my disposal, hand over the knife and notes as evidence, and wait for another, possibly more radical, warning.

I also wanted to shun publicity, to avoid becoming a titillating little paragraph in the paper about a middle-aged bachelor being harassed by an unknown male. I would not be given the benefit of the doubt. (That will teach him not to pick up rough trade.) I wanted the matter dealt with discreetly and at once.

One problem at a time, however. I returned to my apartment for other gloves and to telephone my mechanic about changing the tire. On my way out of the building I intended to warn the porter that a mechanic was coming by. As I strode into the lobby, I could see him talking to another man, who, as I drew closer, turned out to be Lois Fullerton's delicious chauffeur.

"Mr. Chadwick, you are just in time. This man has a package for you."

"Thank goodness! My gloves!" I exclaimed, reaching for the manila envelope that contained them. "Thank you, and please thank Mrs. Fullerton." I looked directly into his oblique dark eyes.

The chauffeur nodded.

Some people, regardless of disposition, carry with them an air of menace, a whiff of danger, which can attract and repel at the same time. Lois Fullerton's chauffeur moved in such an aura of sulphurous sexuality that I found myself wondering what or whom he did on his day off.

I tore open the envelope. Sure enough, my gloves were inside. "I'm very pleased to have them back." I looked up as I spoke. What I encountered, or collided with, was a look of such intense malevolence as to make me drop the gloves. From the centre of his narrowed eyes the darker pupils bored into my skull like drills tipped with diamond. Had I not been a true northerner I would have held up two fingers to ward off the evil eye. As I stooped to retrieve my fallen gloves I almost collided with the porter in one of those Alphonse-Gaston situations that had us each straightening up holding a glove. The chauffeur had taken advantage of the momentary diversion to make good his escape.

I explained to the porter about the car, dropped the extra pair of gloves and the torn envelope into my attaché case, and began to walk briskly towards my office. I was running late, and I have learned that if Monday gets off to a bad start the rest of the week tends to follow suit.

Hurrying along Sherbrooke Street, I had a flash of intuition which brought me up short. I belong to that generation which denied men – real men – the power of intuition. Women were allowed intuition, that intellectual shortcut which permits you to move from A to C in one smooth glide. But no man could be intuitive, unless it had to do with the stock market.

My anonymous caller and correspondent was none other than Lois Fullerton's chauffeur. The mere fact that I was playing a hunch, without a shred of evidence to back it up, made me none the less certain. My case rested on a look, the look that had caused me to drop my gloves. If looks could kill, and so forth.

Fortunately they cannot, but the whammy that man gave me was so filled with concentrated ill will that it stopped me dead.

I resumed walking. Giving someone a dirty look is not a felony, not even, unlike a slashed tire, a misdemeanour. You don't send a man up the river for failing to flash a toothpaste-bright smile. Maybe the guy was constipated. But no. I trusted my hunch. The problem now was how to proceed without sounding like an hysterical nitwit.

At my office, I took the gloves from my briefcase and tucked them into a coat pocket so I would remember to take them home. I was about to drop the manila envelope into the waste-basket when, from force of habit I suppose, I slid my hand inside to make sure it was completely empty. How many times have I discovered a proxy form or a return mailing envelope at the bottom of a discarded envelope?

To my surprise, I came across a folded piece of paper, which on closer inspection turned out to be a page torn from an ad-vertising supplement. It hardly seemed worth saving, only some sales. I was about to throw it out when I happened to notice one of the advertisements: "Warning! Fabulous Sale at Fuller-ton's Fabrics Ends This Weekend!" The ad continued in smaller typeface to suggest only those with unbalanced reason would fail to take advantage of this golden opportunity.

There on the page, incorporated in this simple-minded layout, were three of the words that had figured prominently in the warning notes, notably the name of Fullerton. It was not an unfamiliar name, to me at least; but on a hunch I checked the telephone directory. The Fullerton listing added up to fewer than twenty entries, making it a somewhat uncommon name, especially to find typecast and printed. Finding this random page in the same envelope as my gloves, following hard upon my hunch, only further reinforced my impression that Lois Fullerton's chauffeur was indeed the man in question.

I crossed to the window and gazed at a view I already knew by heart. Did staring into space really help one to think? In the movies a troubled character often walks to a window, the better to see into the future. Were I a character in a movie, I would hire a private investigator. And that is precisely what I decided to do. Yet once having made the decision to engage a sleuth, I found myself temporarily stumped. Hiring a detective is not like buying a car or a computer. You can't simply ask anyone at all for advice or recommendations, casually, over lunch, or when conversation starts to flag. I could not picture myself sidling up to someone and in a voice pitched barely above a whisper asking for a hot tip on a private eye. The very fact that the investigation to be carried out was private must suggest a violation of the Ten Commandments, most likely the one against adultery.

Another problem in hiring an investigator was the temptation to think in stereotypes. I did not want a down-at-the-heels sleazeball with a permanent squint from peering over transoms, nor did I want a rugged individualist, spiritual descendant of your frontier gunslinger, who acts in defiance of the law and who would resolve any personal disagreements we might have by knocking me out.

But as I reflected I began to recollect. About two years ago one of my partners had been handling a small merger between two companies owned by members of the same family. They had stumbled across a considerable discrepancy in inventory. A private investigator had been engaged who discovered that the sales manager of the larger company had been selling inventory privately, pocketing the proceeds, and falsifying the records to cover up the missing stock. The case had not involved incriminating photographs taken from the fire escape, nor assault charges against the investigator for punching out the chief of police. The name of that investigator must be on file. I decided to check it out.

The office building on the edge of Old Montreal was dated but scrupulously maintained. Brown linoleum gleamed with swirls of highly buffed wax, and even as I entered the small lobby a uniformed maintenance man was removing debris from the standing cylindrical ashtrays. Before I had even stepped into the elevator my first preconception had been shot down, namely that private detectives have their offices in seedy buildings.

My next surprise came from the neat gold lettering on the frosted-glass door: Patrick Fitzgerald Associates: Private Investigators. Had I really expected a hand-lettered sign on a piece of shirt cardboard taped to the door?

Another *idée fixe* was severely shaken up when, in the reception area, I was greeted by the kind of neat, personable, businesslike secretary I would have wanted in my own office. She did not look like a spinster languishing with unrequited love for her boss, nor was she a bimbo. Instead, she was quietly pretty, and wore a well-tailored suit.

I introduced myself.

"Please have a seat, Mr. Chadwick. Mr. Fitzgerald will see you just as soon as he gets off the phone."

I hung up my coat in a closet concealed by louvred doors and sat gingerly in one of two Breuer chairs, chrome and leather constructions that looked more like orthopaedic devices than casual seating. I slid my buns down the raked leather seat until brought up short by a horizontal leather band. Directly across from the chairs a Vasarely silkscreen billowed queasily off the wall, adding the one spot of colour to otherwise desert tones. Where were the battered filing cabinet, the cigarette-scarred desk, the chair spilling its stuffing, the Varga girl calendar, and the dented metal wastebasket overflowing with Styrofoam coffee cups? There was no place in my private mythology for tough detectives and tasteful decor.

A red light flickered on the secretary's telephone. "Mr. Fitzgerald will see you now, Mr. Chadwick." She ushered me through a door, which she shut behind me.

From the far side of a medium-sized office, a man wearing a tweed jacket came around from behind a handsome teak desk. The black hair may have turned iron grey, but the cobalt-blue eyes were unmistakable.

"Pat!"

"Geoff!"

"You've turned grey."

"So have you."

Uncertain of what else to do, we shook hands.

"Look," I began, "this was not meant as a joke. Would you prefer me to go back through that door and pretend it all never happened?"

"No, I wouldn't. I'm far too curious to know why you're here."

"I come as suppliant, as a prospective client. I honestly did not know that Pat had become Patrick Fitzgerald Associates."

He smiled to reveal those large white teeth that even now I could hardly believe were real. "I did not make the connection between Lyall, Pierce, Chadwick, and Dawson, and Geoff. Here, sit down."

I sat, in a small upholstered armchair that suited me far more than the wheelchair without wheels I had just vacated.

The surprise of recognition made us temporarily mute. Many years ago, more than I care to remember, Pat and I used to trick, a pleasurable activity that disease and disapproval have sharply curtailed. To trick is to have sex purely for its own sake, totally unencumbered by emotional complications of any sort. Tricking is perhaps the most extreme manifestation of consumerism, where you use another human being purely for your own pleasure and are willingly used in return. Formerly an almost exclusively homosexual activity, tricking has now branched out. Most of the men and women in singles' bars claim to be seeking true love, but they are more than willing to settle for a good fuck.

Tricking is the last natural high. It is not necessary to sip or sniff or snort or inhale or puncture a vein. All you need are two people and the right chemistry. North American society has always frowned on tricking. No two people should enjoy so much pleasure without pain.

"Now, tell me," Pat began, "what brings you here?"

"Before I begin, would you prefer me to call you Pat, Patrick, or Mr. Fitzgerald?"

"What do you feel most comfortable with?"

"Patrick. Pat suggests a relationship that ended long ago. And all things considered, I don't think I could call you Mr. Fitzgerald with a straight face."

"I guess not. Tell me something – Geoffry, if you can remember all those years back, did you ever call me after I went back to my wife?"

"Yes, I did, two, maybe three times. We had a good thing going. I was reluctant to give it up. Why?"

"My wife once mentioned, casually, a man had called, more than once. She said he had a cultivated voice and excused himself for dialling the wrong number, when most people just hang up. Given that, I knew it must have been you."

Patrick's voice was even more sonorous than I remembered. He spoke like an announcer, or someone doing voice-over for a wildlife special on the frozen north.

"I must have called three times, the magic number. I figured by then you and your wife had worked things out, and it was time for me to bow out."

"We tried, but it didn't work. We got a divorce. She re-married, and I faced up to the truth."

"We all have to, sooner or later."

"But you obviously did not come here to talk about the past."

"You're right. However, the clock on your desk says it's almost six. Shall I tell you my story here or over a drink?"

He smiled. "My mouth feels like terrycloth. How did you guess?"

"Mine does too. And we are both old enough to drink, I mean as part of our daily routine."

"I have a short call to make, and then we can push off."

"I'll wait for you in the foyer."

Seated in a far corner of the bar, as far away from the piano spilling Jerome Kern as it was possible to get, I signalled to a waiter whose four-inch sideburns did not divert attention from his receding hairline. I ordered two scotches with soda. Remembering that most bar drinks are measured with a thimble, I asked for doubles. "No problem," replied the waiter, although why a straightforward request for two highballs should present a problem escaped me.

I told Patrick the story of my involvement in the wedding, my meetings with Lois Fullerton, and the three caveats. I derived a curious kind of comfort from the mere narrative, at once less than a confession and more than an anecdote. To tell of any experience imposes a shape on the events; furthermore, I was spared a great number of explanatory digressions because Patrick and I shared a point of view. He understood my difficulties with Lois; he did not think me guilty of macho boasting; he did not think it strange I wanted to keep her at arm's length.

I showed him the notes, the page from the envelope, and gave him the knife, still wrapped in my handkerchief. Patrick listened carefully, with only the occasional interruption to clarify a point. At the end of my story he asked the question I knew he must. "Do you have any idea whatsoever of who this might be?"

I took a swallow of my drink. "Would you think me a little soft in the head if I said I had a hunch, but only that?"

"Not in the least. Which is another way of saying I assume your judgement is sound."

"I think it could well be Lois Fullerton's chauffeur." As he had not yet figured in the narrative, I filled Patrick in about my brief but possibly telling contact with the driver.

"You suggest he could be foreign. Were you aware of any trace of accent when he, or the unknown caller, spoke on the phone?"

"I couldn't tell for sure. I was startled, needless to say, and I had the impression he was probably disguising his voice."

"The notes themselves don't give us much help. Those snip-and-paste messages are almost as old as the printing press. But the note left under the windshield wiper has the letter *c* missing from your name. Chadwick spells itself phonetically; most native English speakers would get it right. There could be a connection."

Patrick reached for his glass, raised it halfway to his mouth, then set it down. "Geoffry, would you mind if I took on this case myself? I mean instead of turning it over to one of my partners?"

"I'd be delighted. It's far easier talking to you than to a total stranger. Now, have we reached the point in the script where I take out a wad of bills and peel off five one-hundreds as your retainer?"

"You've been seeing too many old movies. We charge one hundred dollars an hour prorated. If we spend fifteen minutes on the phone you are charged twenty-five dollars. You will receive an itemized statement at the conclusion of the investigation." He smiled. "Can I presume you are a good credit risk?"

"To the point where you are at no risk at all. Another drink?"

"I'd like to, but I have to run. I want to take these things back to my office for safekeeping. And I have a dinner engagement, with my ex-wife and her husband. Very 'Design for Living,' I'm sure you'll agree."

"Perhaps, but civilized too. I find it difficult to understand how some people can cut themselves off from those who have formerly been close. We can avoid people who have once shared our life, but we can't ever be rid of them. You are fortunate. Now, if you are running late just push along, and I'll deal with the check."

"You're the client; by rights you should outfumble me."

"You can get the next one."

We stood and shook hands. "Thanks, Geoffry. I'll get back to you as soon as I have something to report."

I walked home along Sherbrooke Street, bathed in the relief that comes from finally shaking off inertia and making a positive move. The ball was now in Patrick's court. All too often I am afflicted by a sound idea, such as seeing the doctor for a checkup, having my eyes tested, submitting to the dentist, even having my apartment repainted, only to find a broad plain of procrastination stretching between the onset of the notion and its execution.

I had taken steps to deal with my obscene caller. Heretofore I had thought him little more than a nuisance – until this morning, that is. That knife jammed into my tire suggested violence, and is not violence the ultimate obscenity?

My sense of relief sprang from more than just having taken a positive step in dealing with the situation. In his professional capacity Patrick Fitzgerald gave off an air of competence. My gut reaction told me he knew his business, an impression reinforced by his surroundings. Even though I had been truly surprised at seeing Patrick again after all these years, I had still managed to absorb a few details from his office, the handsome teak desk, the Japanese scroll hanging above the leather couch, which served to dispel my TV-induced notion that private investigators waited for clients in a clutter of Salvation Army rejects.

Striding along the street, I almost laughed out loud at the

incongruity of walking in to hire a private eye only to discover
we used to trick years ago. It is not as though I don't bump into
people I once used to sleep with. Whenever I go to the ballet,
which believe me isn't very often, I invariably see a vaguely
familiar face across a crowded room, who, on closer inspection,
turns out to be a former trick. Sometimes we exchange a glance,
sometimes a nod, on occasion even a smile. Most of the time,
however, we behave as though we have never met, particularly
if he is with a woman who looks like his wife, or a younger man,
obviously the current dearie. The alternate lifestyle has its codes,
none the less binding for being unspoken. And even though
the man with whom you spent an action-packed afternoon in
a musty motel room may cut you dead in the Ritz lobby, there
is a reverse civility in the gesture. By refusing to compromise
himself, he is also guaranteeing that you will be spared any
embarrassment.

Patrick Fitzgerald spun in and out of my life during the sixties, that watershed decade of peace and promiscuity. "Make
love not war." Truth is, we were all so busy making love we
couldn't have found the time for war. Life was a giant toy store
where teddy bears were alive. We all played games, the game of
sex, the game of drugs, the game of peace. As North Americans
take games more seriously than anything else outside of money,
these games usurped our lives. Sex became compulsive; drugs
grew addictive; peace demonstrations all too often ended in
violence. If there was one thing that we all feared more than
the Bomb, it was the tiniest curtailment of our personal freedom.

In retrospect the sixties seem like a latter-day Garden of
Eden. We drifted through an endless summer. Fish were jumping
and the living was easy. Were we expelled, or did the Garden

just wither from lack of tending? Marijuana and hashish and heroin (whatever happened to heroin?) have been pushed aside by angel dust and cocaine and crack, bringing with them a demography of destroyed lives. Far from disappearing, the nuclear threat has swelled. Reactors run amok, evacuating cities and disrupting ecosystems. Smoking a little grass, strumming a guitar, singing a little protest song will not make the problems go away.

And now there is AIDS, the scourge of our freewheeling sexuality. The Black Death was caused by fleas; AIDS is caused by a rogue virus. Both have been blamed on God. But he has always been the ultimate scapegoat. First it was blame the homosexuals. Then blame the Haitians. Blame the drug addicts. Blame Africa, which is already blamed for every disease except the common cold. Blame blood banks, singles bars, visible minorities. Blame someone. And when all possibilities are exhausted, blame God.

The closing years of our century will be known as the decade of the condom, as evidence of which the flag of the United Nations will one day be replaced by a giant inflated condom, floating above the East River, looking not unlike the Hindenburg, a tribute to safe sex and sterility. The final grim irony of this coda to the sixties, the joke that goes far beyond black, is that the only known cure for AIDS, the one certain way to check its spread, is the Bomb.

By the time I reached my building, I decided to skip the stairs and treat myself to the elevator. I was just about to press the button for my floor when a voice cried "Hold it!" and Prints Charming swooped across the lobby like a flamingo, if you can imagine a flamingo wearing a black leather coat. He takes up more room than any one person should be entitled to. I felt terribly compressed when the doors slid shut.

"Did you hear the one about the woman who went to her gynaecologist?" he began. "The doctor asked her if she practiced safe sex. 'Yes, doctor,' she replied, 'I never smoke after intercourse.'"

I laughed politely. "Good for her. Not every woman bothers to look."

IX

Just as a wet grey day can drive out all memory of sunshine, so did the prospect of a visit from my sister tend to push other, more important considerations into unused corners of my mind. Mother telephoned the morning after my meeting with Patrick Fitzgerald to tell me Mildred was coming to Montreal for the weekend. This unsavoury bit of news gave Mother an excuse to call and invite me to dinner on Sunday, but only after she had brought me up to date with the comings and goings on "Coronation Street," which she loves to watch, even though she finds the accents very lower class. I promised to be there at half past twelve, then undertook the not inconsiderable task of getting Mother off the telephone.

My sister's mind works methodically, but it works. She would never get from A to U without pitstops at the intervening vowels, but connections would ultimately be made. By now she must have come to grips with what my having power of attorney might entail. The spectre of austerity hovered over her plans for the wedding, and no doubt she wanted to clarify her position with Mother. Mildred was coming to Montreal to lobby.

Patrick telephoned during the week to suggest I avoid seeing Lois Fullerton for a while. If he could find a reason or reasons to suspect the chauffeur, then I could arrange a meeting with Lois, which would be carefully monitored. I was only too happy to comply with the request. With any luck I wouldn't have to see Lois Fullerton again until the day of the wedding rehearsal.

The week passed, filled with concerns of getting and spending, and blissfully free of anything to do with the nuptials. I no longer feel starry-eyed about my profession, as I once felt during the days when I was married. Then I saw the law as a noble calling, justice as a universal right. I soon outgrew those attitudes as I came to learn that the practice of law embraces more than its share of scoundrels and shysters, and that most people tend to get as much justice as they can afford. On the plus side of the ledger, however, I came to realize that what I lost in ingenuousness I gained in competence. The more unblinking my realization of what the law really entailed, the more skilfully I served my clients. I could never be a great jurist; I lack the hieratic spirit. I do not serve at the altar of the law; I practise my profession. Such satisfaction as I can derive springs from the knowledge that I handle my clients honestly and to the best of my ability. It is a small satisfaction, granted; but at my age it will have to do.

Sunday morning, I stopped at the local greengrocer, a Third World small-time entrepreneur who stays open from dawn to dusk seven days a week. I wanted some cut flowers to take along to Mother, who enjoys the idea of a present far more than the gift itself. I'm just getting my own back, I suppose. When I was a small boy, the very first question I asked if either parent had been away, even overnight, was, "What did you bring me?"

The only flowers the greengrocer had left was a bucket of early daffodils in late middle age. We worked out a deal: three dozen for the price of two. I hoped perhaps the sheer volume of blooms might help conceal the fact that they would barely last through the afternoon.

Carrying an armload of flowers, like Tosca making her first-act entrance, I pushed my way into the lobby of Mother's building. The security guard stole time from his Sunday paper to check me out.

"Morning, Mr. Chadwick."

"Morning, Sam."

"Says here there's goin' to be a by-election, Conservative versus NDP. Who do you think'll win?"

"The Conservative, naturally. You know what they say: 'A fool and his money are soon elected.' Is Mrs. Chadwick at home?"

"Yes, and your sister just got back from church a few minutes ago." He began to laugh. "That was a good one."

I smiled and moved towards the elevator. Mildred doesn't believe in going to church any more than I do. I guess the idea of a legitimate sermon seemed a lesser evil than watching the sermonizing on television with Mother. Not in the least concerned with the niceties of dogma, Mother feels that so long as someone is talking about God it is *ipso facto* good for you, like calcium supplements.

I gave Mother's doorbell my secret ring.

"I'll get it," brayed a voice, and the door flew open to reveal Mildred in all her mourning glory. "Geoffry!"

"Sorelina!" If we had embraced any more stiffly we would have clanked.

"Flowers for Mother? How thoughtful. Here, I'll go and arrange them. You hang up your coat and say hello to Mother. Make yourself a drink," she threw over her shoulder as she disappeared through the swinging door.

Mildred has a way of taking over. On those infrequent occasions she comes to my apartment she manages to make me
feel like a guest in my own house. And I always have the over-
powering urge to do the reverse of what she says, like throwing
my overcoat onto the floor and stamping on it, cutting Mother
dead, and going on the wagon.

But, as I have occasion to remind myself, I am an adult.

Mother sat in her favourite wing chair wearing a blonde
wig, which looked as though it had just landed. From a central
part, two waves swooped low over her forehead before taking
flight in U-shaped curls over her ears. The shiny acrylic fibres
quite overpowered Mother's small features, from which time,
cigarettes, and vodka had erased all traces of former prettiness.

"Here he is, Mother, number six on your list of dream dates,
hot on the heels of Cary Grant, Gary Cooper, Douglas Fair-
banks, Ronald Coleman, and Harpo Marx. Do blondes have
more fun?" I gave her the customary kiss.

"Your sister brought it down. It makes me feel like a loose
woman, but I have to wear it while she is here. Fetch me a drink,
will you, dear? Mildred said I wasn't to start until you arrived."

"You should have asked me to breakfast, not dinner. On the
double, Ma."

I pushed my way into the pantry, where Mildred was cutting stems and sliding them into one of those devices made of
wire mesh which holds flowers at angles that defy gravity. She
had on her beautiful flower face, corners of her mouth slightly
raised in a kind of blissful smile, rapt, in awe of nature's bounty.

"You were badly taken on these daffodils, Geoffry. They're
just about gone by. You really should take them back, only
Mother would be so disappointed."

I paused a moment. Whenever I am with Mildred I find myself counting up to ten more often than a kid watching "Sesame Street." "They were all he had. Sunday and all. What's with this locking up the liquor?"

"I thought it wouldn't hurt for Mother to wait for you before she started drinking."

"Mother waits for nobody. She has her first drink on the stroke of noon. It is her house. It is her liquor." By way of emphasis I added an extra, generous shot of vodka to Mother's drink, then added a little soda to my own before pushing my way backwards through the swinging door.

"Thank you, dear," said Mother. "Cheers!" She took that long, first swallow, which is always the best. I followed suit.

"Have you had a pleasant weekend with your baby daughter – who is currently engaged in making something very lovely with the daffodils I brought you."

"That was thoughtful, dear. I do so enjoy daffodils."

Mother took another swallow and ignored my question. She has always endorsed the "least said, soonest mended" approach to family differences. We sat in silence, bracing ourselves for the onslaught of Mildred and my daffodils, for which her painstaking arrangement would entitle her to grab most of the credit. Mother and I can sit together without speaking for long periods without feeling the least bit uncomfortable. We drink and, in our own private way, are convivial. I respect people with whom I can share silence. I have even loved a few.

Mildred entered the room carrying the bowl of daffodils as though it were the head of John the Baptist on a platter. "See what Geoffry brought, Mother? They're beautiful, but a bit passé. I had to cull and cut the stems." She went to put the flowers on a cherrywood commode.

"Not there, dear," said Mother, just this side of sharply. "The bowl will draw moisture and mark the wood. Put them on the glass top."

Mildred complied and returned to the pantry for her drink, which by rights I ought to have poured and brought in. Not bloody likely.

"Geoffry," she began, even before she sat, "I'm glad you're here. There is much we have to discuss." She picked up Mother's ashtray and emptied it behind the fire screen masking a purely ornamental fireplace. Madame would have to vacuum up the butts on Monday morning.

"I'm listening," I said, consciously avoiding Mother's exasperated look.

"I had dinner with Lois Fullerton last night."

I grew instantly interested, but did not let it show. "That's good. It's high time you two met. Did you have a pleasant evening?"

A slight pause preceded Mildred's answer. "Yes, although she did give me a false impression. On the telephone she talked about a little potluck supper, and I dressed accordingly, high neck and a short skirt. She sent the chauffeur to pick me up and served a meal which would have put Escoffier to shame."

I could not quell a small chuckle. "Tell me, was her neckline at the 49th parallel, the Mason-Dixon line, or the equator?"

"She makes no attempt to conceal her thorax, if that's what you mean. I had no idea she was so – so flamboyant. And that house! The rooms are to be admired, not lived in. Five quid for the complete tour including the garden. Throw in an extra ten shillings and see the secret staircase."

"But she is underwriting the cost of the reception."

"True enough. That means we can spend more money on the ceremony itself."

"Within reason. Have you once sat down with Jennifer and discussed what she would like? It is her wedding, after all."

"If Jennifer had her way she would be married on the back porch with a reception in the high school gymnasium. She has already insisted that she does not want the ceremony video-taped."

"Good for her. Neither do I. I have no intention of joining ACTRA so I can give the bride away. And I repeat: it's her wedding, not yours."

"Your father was so handsome on the day we got married." Mother spoke from the depths of her chair, already adrift on vodka and memories. "Mind you, he was always handsome, but on our wedding day he was particularly handsome. Poor Craig." Her glass stood empty.

"I'll get you another drink, Mother."

Ignoring Mildred's censorious look, I reinforced both Mother's drink and my own.

"I had a talk with Jennifer last weekend," I began as I returned to the room. "She wants only two attendants, her sister and her best friend."

"Bruce's brother has three daughters. We must include them in the party."

"Why, if Jennifer doesn't want them? They'll be at the wedding. I'm sure Conchita, my cleaning woman, would love to be a bridesmaid, for a gringa. She could be your token ethnic."

"You're just being foolish."

I said nothing. I was not about to slug it out with Mildred

over wedding expenses with Mother in the room.

"I had hoped to have a word with the minister this morning after church, but he ducked right out after the service without even greeting the congregation."

"Maybe he had a heavy date." On those few occasions I have attended St. Luke the Apostle, I never listened to the sermon. Usually I study the Reverend Cameron and wonder: does he or doesn't he? Good looking, in an austere way, he has the kind of profile that compels devotion. I suspect he may even have a sense of humour. A small, hand-lettered sign beside his official parking lot reads: Park Not Lest Ye Be Towed. However, I must confess I have always shied away from men of the cloth. I prefer men who undress, not defrock.

"I understand his wife recently ran off with a doctor of theology," I continued. "Nobody would have paid much attention had the doctor of theology not been a woman."

Mother spoke. "I read *The Well of Loneliness* once, a long time ago. Extraordinary book. Who would have thought?"

Mildred said nothing. A rigidly conventional woman, she is nonplussed by sexual irregularity of any sort.

"As long as we're on the subject of the wedding," I continued, "isn't it about time for you to think of getting married again? Some nice guy, divorced or widowed, who hates living alone and wants companionship?"

"How can you say that, even as a joke?"

"I'm perfectly serious, Mildred. You are what passes in the community for a good-looking woman. Also you are a skilled household engineer. You still have your teeth, so get out there and bite the apple. But you've got to shed the mourning. Slide gracefully into matronly mauve, or menopausal mulberry. Better wear that wedding ring on a shoelace, around your neck. And I hereby volunteer to give you away. Mother, do we have time to top up before dinner?"

"If we are prompt."

I escaped to the pantry before Mildred had a chance to huff and to puff and to blow the house down. I suppose she really is a good-looking woman, if you happen to like the type. She takes after Father more than I do, and he was a fine-looking man. Mildred has all the necessary components – regular features, good skin, clear eyes, abundant hair – but she lacks the inner radiance without which no woman can be beautiful. My wife, Susan, was as plain as a split-rail fence if you examined her feature by feature; but she had vitality and a sense of luminosity that made her beautiful, to me at least.

Much as I enjoy pulling Mildred's leg, I was more than half serious about her getting married again. Mildred lacks the imagination to apprehend the future. With Jennifer married, she will suddenly find herself alone, rattling around the house where she has raised three children. At a time when Toronto real estate has never been more vigorous she might well be tempted to sell the property and return to Montreal, to take care of her elderly mother. It was a prospect I did not wish to contemplate, at least not until the wedding had been dealt with and my pen pal laid to rest, preferably in a block of concrete.

"Geoffry, there is something I would like you to do for me, for the wedding," began Mildred no sooner had I entered the room, "and that is to find a good photographer. It makes more sense to hire someone local than to bring a man down from Toronto."

"But, Mildred, I know absolutely nothing about photographers.

I avoid them even more willingly than I avoid a friend in need. The last time I had my picture taken without protest I was six months old. Why don't you ask Lois to engage one?"

"Because I don't want the wedding photographed through a lens smeared with Vaseline so that she will look younger."

"Vaseline! Oh, goodness me." Deep in her wing chair, Mother shook with silent laughter.

"Last night she showed me sketches of the dress – gown – outfit she is having made for the wedding. One might even think she intended to jump out of the bridal cake. And speaking of cake, she wants to have a groom's cake, one of those heavy, dark fruitcakes stuccoed with almond paste which is cut into little pieces and put into little white monogrammed boxes for the guests to take as souvenirs. What could be more old-fashioned, not to say banal? I suggested dragées, little baskets of sugar-coated almonds, but she insists on the groom's cake. She even wants to pay for it."

The ramifications of putting a piece of dark fruitcake into a white box had me stifling giggles. "I have always favoured comfits myself," I volunteered with a smile having nothing to do with my remark.

"Do you know she even has a software program, on a floppy disc, for her home computer? The Failsafe Wedding Planner, it's called. She showed me the menu: Wedding budget, Gifts received, Rehearsal guest list. What could be more trite? If there is a power failure we'll have to cancel the wedding. She even wants to know the colour of the bridesmaids' gowns so she can coordinate the tablecloths. Someone really ought to tell her the only thing the mother of the groom has to do is wear beige and keep her mouth shut." Mildred paused for a sip of her drink.

"Never mind; she is giving the children a house as a wedding present."

"I thought it was the bride who was supposed to bring the dowry. Are you sure they really want a house, or are even entitled to one? Starting married life in a house is like playing your first recital in Carnegie Hall. Where is there left to go? Do you know where they are going to live? Teaching jobs are scarce. Douglas will have to go where the work is."

"They'll settle in Toronto, or Montreal. Universities are always in need of funds. Lois is certain something can be arranged."

"You mean buy Douglas a job with an endowment?"

Mildred said nothing, but she sat there looking like the proverbial cat who has just swallowed the canary.

"Poor Douglas." I shook my head. "With a mother like that I'm surprised he doesn't still suck his thumb."

"They must have a microwave oven," said Mother, who tunes in and out on her own frequency. "I understand they are quite indispensable for young married couples who are working. Keep it away from the children, though. I heard of a little girl who put her bowl of goldfish into the microwave. Quite spoiled the appliance."

"I'll bet the fish were even less happy than the parents."

The housekeeper's massive starched presence filled the doorway. Ordinarily Madame's expression makes the Lincoln Memorial look jolly. Today, however, she looked particularly thunderous. No doubt Mildred had been dropping a few household hints. My sister would not hesitate to tell the Angel Gabriel he was playing flat.

I rescued Mother from her chair and steered her into the dining room, where an overdone roast of lamb waited to be carved. My sister is one of those women who cannot walk across the room without her handbag. She takes it to the telephone, she carries it to the bathroom, she probably tucks it under her pillow at night. Needless to say, she marched it into the dining room. After I had carved the lamb and served the vegetables from Mother's silver-plated vegetable dishes, which conduct heat away from whatever is inside, I sat and watched Mildred open her bag and spread a variety of coloured brochures on the table in front of her placemat.

"We were taught it was rude to read at the table. Lift your fork, Mother." I began to eat. Having had no breakfast, I was hungry, fortunately.

Mildred ignored me and spoke to Mother. "I still haven't made up my mind on Jennifer's china pattern. I have to inform the bridal registries before the invitations go out. Did I tell you the invitations are to be engraved, with individual names written in by a calligrapher? It will cost a bit more, granted, but so much more distinguished."

"After the wedding you can have the copper plate from the printer made into an ashtray," suggested Mother, still awake as a result of her curtailed vodka ration. "I still have mine. I use it for hairpins."

"Good idea," I chimed in. "But shouldn't you let Jennifer choose her own china pattern? She has to live with it."

"Jennifer wants pottery!" replied my sister. "When she gets to our age she will realize a sideboard filled with good china can be a comfort."

"Perhaps," I replied, unconvinced. In the basement storage area of my apartment building sits a small wooden crate marked simply "china." Inside, carefully wrapped, are the four place settings of Royal Doulton with which Susan and I set up house-keeping. I have not used the china since Susan died, but I cannot bring myself to give it away. I guess that crate is my own private archaeology, shards of a past life that once was mine. Whoever sorts through my possessions after my death can deal with the crate. By then I will no longer care.

Between bites of lamb, Mildred riffled through pages. "You certainly can't fault Aynsley. But not Pembroke. I couldn't stand facing that bird day after day. Even the exotic garden is a bit much; Jennifer won't be serving dinner at the Taj Mahal. Thank goodness there's more to Wedgwood than Jasperware. I've had more than my share as Christmas presents. And More-croft, all those puce flowers. I really don't think Jennifer wants that Greek key marching around the rim of the plate for the rest of her life. It looks like the kind of thing children draw around the pages of their exercise books, don't you think? And nobody, but nobody, could live with a pattern named California."

Mother put down her fork. "You must choose an open pattern in case you want to replace breakage. Lydia Parsons once threw the soup tureen at her husband, and when she went to replace it she discovered the pattern had been discontinued. So she decided on a plain white one. It did look clinical."

"Well, Ma," I said with a chuckle, "I don't think Jennifer will be leading a soup tureen sort of life, unless she fills it with dried apricots."

"Royal Doulton has some lovely patterns," continued Mildred, oblivious to everything but her booklets. "But most of them are too opulent, for Jennifer anyway. And pattern all over the dinner plates does compete with the food. The Majestic

Collection is a possibility, but those flowers are a bit twee. It's one thing to be feminine, another thing to be simple-minded. I have always loved Coalport, but the designs tend towards Fu Manchu. It's not as though Jennifer were going to marry Charlie Chan's number one son. Maybe we should choose Royal Worcester, one of the simpler patterns, in gold and white perhaps. One never tires of gold."

"I do hope Jennifer will carry gardenias," Mother spoke from Cloud 9, where she had taken refuge from Mildred and her brochures. "I carried them at my wedding. They are so fragrant. But you have to be careful not to bruise the petals, or they will turn brown. Jennifer will look like that poor girl in the opera who dies of consumption. *Il Trovatore?*"

That was pretty close for Mother, who has spent a lifetime resisting information, but Mildred could not let the slip pass without correction.

"Don't you mean *La Traviata*, Mother?"

"No, she means *Die Walkyre*. With you and Lois to deal with, Jennifer would be well advised to carry a spear and shield."

Silence settled over the table. By pretending to scratch the back of my hand I stole a glance at my watch. In a moment of filial foolishness I told Mother I would take Mildred to her train. We still had coffee to get through, and one of Madame's stolid desserts. Then goodbyes before Mother went to crash. I could have sworn the hands on my watch were standing still.

How long, O Lord, how long?

When the time finally neared to take Mildred to the station, I was suffering from a terrible energy leak, a condition caused by drinking in the middle of the day followed by a stodgy meal taking its own good time to digest. My disposition teetered on that fine line between the smile and the snarl. I suggested to Mildred that were she to get to the train early she would have her choice of seats.

"Mildred, I have something to say which I did not want Mother to hear. As you already know, I have her power of attorney. This gives me discretionary authority over which expenses she will or will not pay. I have no wish to stint on Jennifer's wedding, nor do I intend to let Mother underwrite a Cecil B. De Mille spectacle."

"I think Mother is the best judge of that."

"You know as well as I do that she is not. I will not stand to see her browbeaten or manipulated. Also, I will happily contradict her, if I consider it necessary for her own best interest. It is quite evident you want a far more grandiose wedding than does Jennifer, the bride. What I propose, therefore, is that you submit a budget, for a wedding that includes three attendants for the bride. The cousins can draw straws for the honour, or the chore."

I could see Mildred drawing a deep breath, but I held up my hand. "If I consider your budget reasonable, I will approve it. If not, I will submit your proposed expenses to a bridal consultant. I may anyway. Mother will pay for a reasonable wedding. Should you wish to add bridesmaids, flower girls, ring bearers, should you decide to turn the chancel into a tropical paradise of exotic blooms, should you want to provide ten stretch limos, horse-drawn floats, T-shirts, and a big brass band, you are at perfect liberty to do so. Only you will pay for them yourself."

I put down my cup. "Finally, do not fall into the trap of trying to compete with Lois Fullerton. If she chooses to throw an elaborate reception, it is her right. But we do not have to live up to her party. I have the distinct impression that Jennifer would prefer a simple ceremony and a low-keyed reception afterwards, but she is going along with Operation Wedding to accommodate you. That you must work out for yourselves. I am not siding with Jennifer against you. My concern is that Mother pay no more than is reasonably necessary to finance this tribal rite. Is there anything more dreary than a wedding? Now, I think it's time we left for the train."

Mildred looked at me as though I had just drowned a sackful of angora kittens, then went to get her coat. On the way to the station she was uncharacteristically quiet. Like many people who tend to bully, she backs down in the face of real authority. Furthermore, I had the law on my side.

I handed my sister and her suitcase over to a redcap, tipped him, gave her a perfunctory kiss, wished her a good trip, and promised to be in touch. Then I climbed into my car and headed home. I wanted a nap so badly I could taste it.

X

Because I had postponed my nap I did not doze lightly but slept heavily. I awoke feeling sodden and disoriented, and lay without moving until my bladder prodded me out of bed. My mouth felt like North Africa, and I wondered briefly whether I should be wise and make tea, which took minutes, or foolish and pour myself a Scotch, which took seconds.

The telephone rang. "Hello," I said in a medium-grey voice.

"Geoffry, it's Patrick. I have some information for you. Can I come by your office tomorrow sometime? Or could I drop by now, if you're not busy?"

"You don't rest on the Lord's Day?"

"Sunday is just like any other day in my business."

"I was just about to pour myself a drink. Come on over and I'll pour one for you too."

"Ten minutes."

I washed my face in cold water, combed my hair, and pulled on some clothes. In ten minutes to the second, my buzzer rang, and I instructed the porter to let Patrick proceed.

In short order we were facing one another across a matching pair of highballs. In sports jacket and jeans, Patrick looked as trim and preppy as when I first knew him. Only the grey hair and deep lines like parentheses bracketing his mouth revealed the passage of time. It was easy to see why I had once found him attractive.

"I've dug out some information about our chauffeur: Manuel Alvarez, a.k.a. Marcello Adorno, a.k.a. Melvin Abrams. There could be more. Originally comes from the Dominican Republic. His mother was American, which suggests he must be handy in English. He got mixed up with the wife of someone pretty high up in the government, who found out. For reasons of health, Manuel Alvarez skipped to Cuba."

"May I ask how you discovered all this, in what seems like a short time? In novels the detective usually tells the story himself, so we always know."

Patrick smiled. "Would you discuss your clients' affairs with me?"

"Point made. Question withdrawn."

"Let us just say it is my business to find out. That is why you hired me. Verdad?"

"Si."

"Our man arrived in Havana just about the time the island was being opened up for North American tourism. You must remember."

"See the picturesque peons cutting cane down among the sheltering palms."

"Precisely. Anyhow, Alvarez managed to get himself on the wrong side of the law. There was an attempt on his life; very possibly the outraged official in the Dominican Republic put out a contract. The upshot was that he became *persona* very *non grata* and shipped out on one of those boatloads of refugees and riffraff that Cuba unloaded on the U.S. in 1980."

" 'Give me your tired, your poor, your huddled masses.' "

"From Key West he went to Miami, where, we suspect, he

got involved in the drug trade."

"Are you sure you haven't watched too many episodes of 'Miami Vice'?"

"Quite sure. He had occasion to leave Miami in rather a suspicious hurry, without even packing a bag. We lose track of him for a while until he ended up in Canada claiming refugee status before it became such a popular thing to do."

"I have to hand it to you, Patrick. You have not been idle."

"There's more. But all this talking is thirsty work."

"So is listening." I poured two more highballs, and Patrick continued. "I made another interesting discovery while I was tailing him, which I'd like to run by you. As you probably know, Lois Fullerton owns two cars, a grey Buick sedan and a Cadillac limousine. She obviously has brand loyalty. Ordinarily the chauffeur tarts her around in the limo. Supposing, however, the two of them set out one day in the sedan and drive to one of those apartment buildings on the edge of downtown, which has recently gone condo. The chauffeur lets her out at the door, and she goes inside. There is no doorman, so she uses her key. The chauffeur parks the car and returns to the building. He too has a key and goes inside. I check the names beside the bells and discover one L. Dalton, her maiden name, right? After an hour or so he comes out and goes to collect the car. By the time he drives up to the front door she has come outside. The two of them drive off. Has anything occurred to you?"

"Yes. Their fuck is costing me one hundred dollars."

Patrick laughed. "Don't worry. I give discounts for stake-outs, particularly if I'm in no danger."

"When you sell the rights to this story for daytime TV, I insist on a percentage."

"Sure thing." He smiled as he drank. "Okay, Geoffry, this is where I begin to speculate. We have a still beautiful woman who enjoys male companionship. And, speaking off the record, that chauffeur is a bit of all-right, even if he does look like the heavy in a TV miniseries. However, this woman is beginning to realize time marches on; she wants a permanent relationship, marriage even. But since she did not originally come from the top drawer, she has had to work hard for the social position she now enjoys. She is not about to marry the chauffeur, even if he is a winner in the feathers. At this point a new character is introduced: a widowed lawyer, middle-aged, distinguished, not even bad-looking." Patrick turned down the corners of his mouth as if in contradiction to his words while he paused to drink. "In other words, the kind of man she would like to marry. Furthermore, she is too shrewd to sleep with her chauffeur in her own house, under the knowing eyes of maids and cooks. At 15 Mayfair Crescent it's strictly mistress and chauffeur. At the condo it's mistress and mattress. In the meantime – I'm still winging it, mind you – the chauffeur understands that so long as he keeps the boss lady satisfied in the sack he will continue to drive her car. Should she become interested in someone else, however, he will be let go. One does not ordinarily keep old lovers on the payroll."

I was tempted to suggest that I had just put Patrick on mine, but decided it would be better to keep the interview strictly professional.

"Now, let me put something to you, Geoffrey. I'm certain there were more household servants in your background than in mine. Doesn't it strike you as odd that a servant, someone who puts on livery and drives a car, would dare to threaten one of his employer's friends? Servants have been known to lie and steal, but to make warning calls and send threatening letters?"

"You're quite right," I replied. "Unless for some reason it was critically important for him to keep his job."

"My reasoning exactly. And considering his past record, he does not strike me as the kind of man who is going to settle down comfortably and spend the rest of his life driving a car for a wealthy widow. Not unless he really needs the job as a cover for something else."

"Ah-so. And along comes this importunate lawyer who somehow manages to capture his employer's fancy, and the driver feels threatened."

"My idea exactly. I still maintain that servants, even jealous ones, do not threaten their superiors."

"But wouldn't he run the risk of the lawyer – me – going to the police?

"You're not certain of his identity. And whoever sent those notes left no fingerprints. He is probably counting on both your inertia and your reluctance to call in the law. Professionals like you tend to shun the spotlight. But the one possibility he probably did not take into consideration is that you would go to a private investigator. What we must rule out now are the other possibilities. Can you think of anyone, anyone at all in your past or present, who might have sent those notes?"

"No. Face it, Patrick; old male lovers, even cast off ones, do not ordinarily want you to stay away from women. Under different circumstances I could easily suspect my sister. But considering that she has strongarmed me into being a member of the wedding party, I can't see why she would object to my meeting the mother of the groom. Seriously, though, I can't think of anyone. The kind of law I practise does not send people up the river for twenty years, where they brood darkly on what they will do to me when they get out."

"If you'll pardon my observation" – Patrick tried, unsuccessfully, not to smile – "you strike me as a man some people might go out of their way to avoid, but not to threaten."

I too tried not to smile. "That's the nicest thing anyone has said to me in years. In the meantime, what's the plan of action?"

"For the moment, business as usual. Avoid Mrs. Fullerton if possible. I do not believe you are in any real danger. If Alvarez is working on a caper – drugs, I strongly suspect – he won't want to risk drawing too much attention to himself."

Patrick's scenario had a certain wild logic, only I could scarcely bring myself to believe I might figure in so unlikely a story.

"Now what about Lois? Is she in any danger? She may not be my favourite person – and I shall never forgive her for having made that toothsome sonofabitch – but I wouldn't want to see her come to any real harm."

"She's his cover. And she's no fool. If she knew or suspected anything, she wouldn't keep him around."

"Hey-ho." I drummed my fingers on the arm of the chair. "You want me to sit tight and do nothing?"

"For the moment, yes. We may be on the verge of something big, Geoffry. A case of simple harassment . . ."

"Watching and besetting, as the Criminal Code would have it."

"Watching and besetting, then. This routine case might turn out to be important. Trust me. If there's the slightest hint of danger I'll have you put under surveillance."

"I really do not believe all this is happening to me."

I sat for a moment feeling almost stunned. The sensation did not arise from fear; I was not concerned about my personal safety. To date the threats had been too clumsy and amateurish to be truly alarming, but now something out of the ordinary was definitely going on. My modest role in the wedding of my niece, a quiet, uncomplicated girl, had turned me into a quarry, on one hand pursued by a lusty widow intent on adding my initials to her monogram or, at the very least, my name to her hit list. On the other hand I was being tracked by her surly chauffeur, who feared I had wandered into his drug-smuggling operation and was trying to intimidate me into backing off. There was no chapter covering these contingencies in *Fifteen Steps to a Lovelier Wedding.*

Somewhat unsettled, I cast about for reassurance. I was already working on my second highball. Another might be fool-hardy, at least without food on the way.

"Patrick, to change the subject for a moment, have you eaten?"

"Not yet."

"I'm going to send out for barbecued chicken, one of my Sunday night rituals. You must join me."

"Only if you'll let me pay."

"It's a deal. I'll go and telephone the order. Give me your glass and I'll top you up."

"Done!" I announced as I returned carrying a small tray on which sat our tumblers and a ceramic bowl filled with dry-roasted, salt-free peanuts. "Help yourself to the lavish *hors d'oeuvres.* Do not stint. I have ashtrays if you want to smoke."

"No, thanks. I gave it up years ago."

"Cheers!" I drank. "Now can we drop the investigator mode and talk like people? What have you been doing with yourself since you left me to return to your wife – in twenty-five words or less?"

Patrick shifted uncomfortably. "I thought it was the right thing to do at the time, but – we all make mistakes."

"Speak for yourself." I smiled. "Obviously it didn't work out."

"No, it didn't. I stopped lying to myself. I guess you could say I came out. There were three or four action-packed years."

I laughed into my drink. "Only three or four? And then you met someone you liked? None of my business, really, but I am as curious as the next person."

It was Patrick's turn to smile. "You're absolutely right. I did meet someone. We lived together for almost twelve years, until he died."

I was fearful of saying the wrong thing. Silence thickened between us. "Sorry to hear that, Patrick," I offered lamely.

"I know what you're thinking, but he didn't die of AIDS."

"Was I thinking that?"

"Who doesn't? People today hear of a gay man's death and they jump to one conclusion, especially if he's under sixty. He survived the first heart attack but not the second."

"Dead is dead, Patrick. It still leaves you out in left field."

"Does it not. Twelve years is a long time. We were very – I suppose *compatible* is the word. What I really missed were the shared habits, having someone with whom to talk over the day, to argue with over whose turn it was to stay in for the plumber. The trivia of daily life. I grieved. Then I realized I had to get on with my life. But by then the scene had changed. When I went out, the men were so much younger I felt like a chaperone. AIDS had changed the rules. And I really wondered if I could go right back to the beginning and start all over again with someone many years my junior. I tried a couple of times, with pleasant, decent men, but we kept running into blind alleys. Which is another way of saying we had little in common but a mutual desire to get off the streets. All the people my own age had settled into stable relationships, or resigned themselves to solitude. At the moment I seem to have opted for the latter."

"There are worse things than living alone," I suggested. "And I should know. I cleaned up my act long before I had to. The running around one did at twenty becomes exhausting at fifty. Twenty years of the morning after begins to pall. I suppose we all hope one day to meet that certain someone, one more time. It gets easier to fool other people as you get older, but a lot harder to fool yourself." I paused for a sip of my drink. "God only knows, I've certainly had my share of love affairs – and doesn't that very term date me. Who has love affairs today? Relationships are the thing. What is a love affair but a kind of neurotic confrontation. When you're not in the sack you're squaring off over slights, which are mostly imagined. A love affair gives you good head. It also gives you good headache. I'd willingly give up sex in the shower, or under the kitchen table, for someone compatible to share a weekend in Vermont."

"Amen to that." Patrick nodded approvingly.

The arrival of our food helped to dissipate the soul-searching. Appetite has a way of banishing abstraction. Patrick and I ate chicken with our fingers and washed it down with beer from the can.

"Well," said Patrick comfortably after he had rinsed his fingers under the kitchen faucet, "burp and scratch. That really hit the spot. And now I must move along."

The day was winding down. I walked Patrick to the elevator, where we said goodnight and shook hands before he stepped into the conveyance. We seemed to make rather an issue of shaking hands, reconfirming with each salutation and separation that our relationship was purely professional. Whatever had passed between us had ended a long time ago.

Patrick and I met in men's underwear. I had gone to one of the department stores to replenish my supply of jockey shorts, the ones advertising "comfo-crotch" without whose support I could not get through the day. I had not been living alone all that long and had yet to master several of the domestic arts: laundry, for instance. I speak now of that innocent age before ring-around-the-collar turned into a national issue. The fact remained that my underwear was decidedly tattle-tale grey, and one day I bleached it. Did I bleach it: fifty-fifty liquid bleach and boiling water. My jockey shorts came out looking and feeling like whipped cream, with just about as much tensile strength.

The garments disintegrated as I pulled them on. For a week I went to the office wearing underwear looking as though it had been stitched from fish net. Finally I made time late one afternoon to go shopping, an activity I thoroughly dislike unless I am looking for something frivolous.

As I searched through the department store shelves for my waist size, I noticed a man looking at boxer shorts. I looked again. Tilt! That truly devastating combination of blue eyes and black hair. I guessed he was probably Irish, the type of black Irish that always make me think of toora-loora-lay. As I checked him out I could tell he was sneaking furtive glances at me. Much more adroit at making pickups than doing laundry, I knew that anyone buying boxer shorts was not going to make the first move.

I edged closer, under the guise of looking at undershirts, which I have never worn.

"Does that brand have deodorant freshness in every stitch?" I asked. "One can't be too careful."

His startled look gave way to an uncertain smile as he realized my intentions were friendly. "My wife usually buys these for me, but she's out of town."

God bless her for that! I thought to myself before I spoke. "Unattached husbands can easily get into trouble. Let's have a drink so I can keep an eye on you." I was young then, and youth is unsubtle.

For a moment Patrick stood irresolute, like a figure in a comic strip with a tiny angel hovering over one shoulder saying, "No! No!" while above the other shoulder a diminutive devil whispers, "Yes! Yes!" The devil won.

On the way back to my apartment I learned his name was Pat and that he worked for a living. That was all. I figured along with the out-of-town wife he probably had a closet full of hangups.

We all start out with inhibitions of one sort or another; some of us shed them earlier than others. Patrick undressed with his back to me and slid furtively under the sheet. Even that brief glimpse was enough to show me he had a body most men would have been proud to flaunt.

Sex was at once passionate and perfunctory. It took him about seven minutes to shower, dry, dress, and disappear. The only traces he left were a damp towel and a scrap of paper on which he had written "Pat" and a phone number.

We met maybe half a dozen times after that. Once he realized I was not going to crack the code and invade his privacy he began to relax, but such conversation as we had remained cryptic. He was a truly masculine man, free of aggression and able to be active or passive, or both in tandem. What I remembered most clearly, far more than the couplings or the clichés of sex – "Oh, God! It's so good. Don't stop. Please don't stop!" and "I'm coming!" gargled as though it had about thirty-seven syllables – what I truly remembered were his eyes. They were the most extraordinary blue I had ever seen, deep, clear, the blue of fine china, lapis lazuli, an October sky. They were eyes into which one could easily tumble and drown, but in those days I was a strong swimmer.

As I opened another beer I found myself idly wondering whether Patrick still wore boxer shorts, surely the most asexual garment ever designed. To be sure, he never had them on for very long, but I remember the wide cotton legs billowing from the crimped elastic waistband like failed culottes. Take a man, any man, put him into a pair of boxer shorts, an undershirt – the white cotton kind before they went chic and became tank tops – add a pair of mid-calf socks held up by elastic garters, and you have a safe sex object that would turn off the devil himself. Maybe we should add boxer shorts to the growing list of safe sex devices, although the underwear lobby might balk at the suggestion.

Anyhow, the wife returned from the mother she had gone home to. There had obviously been an attempted reconciliation, which did not take. But, to give Patrick due credit, he did give it the old college try. We did not see each other again.

I settled into my Eames chair, and for a while wandered the

grounds of Mansfield Park and listened to Fanny Price's rather mean-spirited disapproval of what seemed to me like perfectly harmless amateur theatricals. Imagine disapproving of play-acting in the drawing room.

The old order changeth.

XI

An opportunity arose for me to go to Toronto to clear up some business for the office, and I jumped at the chance. Ordinarily my reluctance to visit that metropolis springs not from negative feelings for Toronto itself, for it is a city I enjoy, but from the obligation I am under to see certain people who live there – my sister, for instance. Should she get wind that I am planning a visit, she will telephone long distance to inquire what night I am coming to dinner. I know perfectly well she doesn't want to see me, a feeling reciprocated with compound interest; but her code demands we meet whenever geography permits, like heads of state whose military alignment cannot totally conceal their economic rivalry.

Toronto also harbours a friend from childhood, one of those sentimental barnacles that attach themselves to our lives and cannot be scraped loose. Larry, or Lawrence Townsend II, has never outgrown the idea that he was put on this earth to have a good time, all very well. Now in his late fifties, he still thinks of good times as those he enjoyed at twenty-five, as evidence of which he wants to turn my Toronto visits into three-day drunks. The result is that I find myself sneaking in and out of the city, coat collar turned up, hat brim pulled down, like one of the ten most wanted men. I walk the streets in fear, lest I bump into someone at Bay and Bloor who will betray my unheralded presence and earn me a dressing down on the long-distance phone.

On this weekend, however, I would be able to stride along University Avenue with head held high. Having so recently endured my sister over Sunday dinner at Mother's, I was under no obligation to see her, telephone her, or even be obliged to offer an excuse as to why I did not. Furthermore, Larry Townsend was spending two weeks in Nassau, ostensibly soaking up sunshine and rum, and, I strongly suspect, getting the lay of the land. I do not know whether it is better in the Bahamas, as the ads suggest; but if anyone can find out for certain, it is Larry. I only hope he is being careful.

The result was that I could enjoy the luxury of a weekend in Toronto, first-class hotel with reduced rates, and no obligations beyond those of a little business I could easily mop up on Friday afternoon.

Perhaps the reason I have always enjoyed Toronto is that I do not waste time comparing it with Montreal. The two cities are as different as chalk and cheese, to borrow a threadbare analogy; although having once tasted chalk as a child, to the teacher's predictable and boring dismay, I am not certain I don't prefer it to that goat's milk cheese with which Greek restaurants encumber salads. For comparisons with Toronto one should look to major American cities, Chicago, or Houston. Montreal is less a city than a cluster of neighbourhoods. The old loyalties of English, French, Protestant, Catholic, and Jewish are giving way to alliances based on whether you approve of the Olympic Stadium, where you go to buy *pâté campagne* and Boursault, and in what part of Florida you own real estate.

I flew to Toronto and, perhaps unwisely, asked for a seat in the no-smoking section. In future I will risk death from secondary fumes and request the smokers' part of the aircraft. Smokers keep to themselves. Along with cigarettes, those who smoke carry briefcases and portfolios, books and magazines. They puff and drink and read and do not strike up conversations.

Unfortunately, the same could not be said for the woman by whom I was trapped against the window. She was one of those meek who shall inherit the earth because they trample all civilized defenses, refuse to read body language, take no for an incentive. By radiating a kind of determined helplessness, she coerced one of the other passengers into folding her coat trimmed with Hudson seal and stowing it in the overhead compartment. Then she squeezed her adipose hips into the centre seat, under which she made several unsuccessful attempts to wedge her plastic shopping bag. Next, she unzipped her galoshes and managed to dig me in the ribs three times as she fished around for the ends of her seat belt. From a large, ugly chintz knitting bag she took an unfinished baby sweater, in one of those unpleasant pinks which has too much blue, and began, ostentatiously, to knit.

I could see her trying to catch my eye as I turned the pages of my national news magazine. I was just as determined not to be caught.

"They say that's a good magazine," she said out loud to no one in particular. "I don't read it myself. Don't have time to read magazines."

She gave her strand of pink wool a tug, causing the ball to pop out of the knitting bag and land in my lap. I handed the ball of wool across the arm of the seat without looking at her, but that small gesture provided all the opening she needed.

"Thank you. That was clumsy of me. But I have to finish this sweater and make another one too. My daughter's just gone into labour, ten days early, and they say it will be twins. We were that surprised. There's no twins in my family, or my late husband's. But they can tell nowadays if it's going to be a boy or a girl – or twins. The X-ray, you know. Anyhow, there I was, halfway through a batch of chocolate chip bran muffins, when they telephoned to say she had been taken to hospital and could I get on the plane and come right up. And me without even a bag packed."

And she was off. Nor could I turn her off. Once started, she needed no further encouragement than the sound of her own voice, nasal, petulant, incantatory. By the time the coffee trolly had rattled to a halt beside our seats, she had moved beyond the unfolding birth to the trials that lay in store. "And I always have the same argument with my daughter, but she will put powder in the washing machine. I use the liquid myself. Spot soak the stain before I put it in; always do. But she claims the powder is more economical. Maybe it is if you buy them big boxes nobody can even lift. And she will use a dryer, even in summer. I always say you can't have fresher clothes than those as is hung on the line, in the good fresh air."

I sat there, stoically trying to read about surrogate mother-hood, but my mind kept returning to that scene in a James Bond movie where the villain is sucked through the broken window of a plane. However, I suppose it would be difficult to pull off a similar stunt on a crowded aircraft without attracting attention.

Then, just as suddenly as she had started, the woman stopped, as if someone had pressed a switch. The adrenaline-fuelled excitement of flying towards grandmotherhood dissipated itself. In moments she had fallen asleep, the knitting lying in her lap.

I had to prod her awake so I could get off the plane.

An excellent lunch at Fenton's went a long way towards restoring my good humour. An hour or so in a handsome office overlooking the University of Toronto campus took care of the business I had come to transact, and I stepped into a mild afternoon, a suggestion of spring softness already in the air.

With no schedule and time on my hands, I walked down to Dundas and along to the art gallery. I did not go into the special exhibit, or even the permanent collection, but headed, as I always do, straight to the large hall housing the Henry Moore collection. I love this room, hushed, tranquil, with the huge, spectral, yet benign figures who seem to communicate with one another in a language I can sense but not hear. To stroll among these monolithic, gentle presences is to enter a dimension of time suspended. Much as I love the large reclining Henry Moore at the northwest corner of Dominion Square in my own city (drive past it and watch how fluidly it moves), it stands alone, stripped of the resonances that here echo from one figure to another, each in itself a whole and at the same time part of a greater whole. Although I have never meditated, I should imagine that the ease and tranquillity of spirit attained are not dissimilar to what I experience in this extraordinary room.

The small group who had been visiting the Henry Moore hall when I entered now left, and for a few precious moments I had the place to myself. From a corner of the room I turned for a new perspective just in time to see a man walk through the door. Even distant he seemed familiar; a moment passed before I made the connection and recognized him as Charles Grant, the young man slated to be best man at my niece's wedding.

I confess I felt a small pang of regret. Unless I were to crouch behind the nearest pedestal and duck from exhibit to exhibit, like someone in a counter-espionage movie, I would have to make my presence known and step back into time as motion. The greeting would break the spell.

Often against my better judgement, I remain a social creature. I walked across the room until I was close enough to Charles to speak in my normal volume. To call out in this room would be unthinkable, bad manners at their most uncouth. These giant figures were my hosts; as mere intruder and guest I must tread softly, speak low, tender courtesy.

"Charles."

He turned, registered who I was, and dissolved into a grin. "Uncle Geoffry! I mean, Mr. Chadwick. The last person I expected to meet."

I could not resist his grin and smiled as we shook hands. "This is where people of taste always meet. Now, as I am neither your uncle nor your employer, why don't you call me Geoffry."

"I'd like that. You're into Moore too, eh?"

"Love it. A trip to Toronto always includes a visit."

"I wanted to be a sculptor," said Charles, "but I didn't have the money. And I didn't want to become a Canada Council bum, existing from grant to grant. It takes money to be an artist. There's nothing ennobling about being poor. Maybe I should find myself a rich patron." He laughed. "But it would help if I looked like Rupert Brooke, not Dylan Thomas."

I too laughed at the analogy. Charles Grant was attractive, moreso than he realized. He had the glow of youth and such an abundance of vitality one could feel him without touching.

"From what I've heard about Dylan Thomas, I wonder when he found time to write poems. Do you come here often?"

"Whenever I'm in the area. I'm a gallery member, so I can duck in and out. You're in Toronto on business?"

"That's the excuse. Business, and a bit of goofing off." I glanced at my watch. "It's perhaps earlier than I usually start drinking, but one ought to break training once in a while. Are you at liberty to join me?"

"Love it."

"Tell you what. You just arrived and would like to look around. Let's meet at the front desk in, say, half an hour. That will give me a chance to roller-skate through the permanent collection and whatever else has been laid on. By then we will both have earned our drinks."

"The Protestant ethic speaks?"

"Correct. Thirty minutes. Let's synchronize our watches."

After half to three-quarters of an hour in any picture gallery anywhere in the world, I find my rapt contemplation interrupted by lower back pain and a pressing need to find the men's room. Charles was already in the foyer when I got there, clutching his down-filled parka as though it might at any moment take flight. A short taxi ride brought us to my hotel, and soon we were seated in a corner of the bar off the main lobby, amidst wicker chairs and silk ferns, where a cocktail waitress with crimped hair and purple eyelids brought us drinks I am convinced she measured with a teaspoon, not a jigger.

I poured soda water into my glass, which I raised. "To the wedding!"

Charles made a wry face as he lifted his glass. "I suppose."

"You sound a bit glum for someone who's going to see a good

friend get married, to a radiant bride, in white, on the happiest day of her life. To judge from your expression, she ought to be wearing black bombazine."

"Maybe she should. I don't think Doug should get married."

"May I ask why not?"

"That's one question I didn't think you'd have to ask."

"I'm not sure I follow you," I fibbed glibly.

"I think you do. I think you have gone through your life with your eyes open. You are old enough, and smart enough, to know which end is up."

"You mean, only the young die good?"

In reply he smiled. I always drink my first highball quickly, and took a moment to snag our waitress's attention before I continued. "Could you be referring to that same sensitive side of Douglas's nature that compelled him to design the wedding rings?"

"I think we understand one another."

"Well, Charles, as long as we seem to be laying our brass tacks on the table, let me ask another question. Are you and Douglas lovers, or have you been?" I am not generally so perfunctory, not to say tactless, but I had not brought the subject up. Charles did not seem in the least surprised by a question that, had it been directed at me, would probably have earned the response, "None of your damned business!"

"No, nothing like that," he replied, leaning forward. "Douglas is still locked in the closet – and that cloned mother of his has the key on a string around her neck. Doug is going to be a late bloomer. But it's only a matter of time before he unties the apron strings and puts on an apron himself. Up to now, whenever Doug catches cold Lois blows her nose. You must have seen how much she dislikes me. She hates the idea of her son having a gay friend. Guilt by association. I don't know to what extent she realizes Doug is gay, or will be one day. But she is absolutely determined he will marry, Jennifer or someone else. Marriage will make him legitimate."

"Charles, that kind of thinking went out with corsets." I felt uneasy at having my suspicions so roundly confirmed.

"Which she probably still wears. And her dear late husband probably wore red ties, in a Windsor knot. Oi! As you can tell, Geoffry, I'm not too happy about Doug and Jennifer as mister and missus, even less so as I introduced them. Doug is one of my best friends, and I think Jennifer's a terrific girl. But I don't think they should get married."

"Have you and Douglas ever had what people of my generation used to call a little talk?"

"We couldn't. Doug's pretty defensive about that side of his life. It's strictly Keep Off the Grass, even when he's smoking a joint. I don't know how much he knows or suspects about himself, but if I went charging in it would only create bad feeling. I know they've been sleeping together. But they're both pretty naive."

"You mean they are mistaking the novelty of sex for love?"

"Exactly." By now Charles had finished his gin and diet ginger ale, and I signalled the waitress to bring us both another. I remembered the night of the dinner party at Lois Fullerton's house, and how I had been struck by the absence of real chemistry between Douglas and my niece.

"Charles, I am genuinely curious. You are just about the same age as Douglas, twenty-five perhaps, yet you are years older in point of view."

He made a grimace, not quite a smile. "One of the advantages of being a disadvantaged child is having to grow up faster. I was not insulated by money from some of life's more abrasive realities. These days being naive is a perishable commodity, like soft cheese. You need a controlled environment to keep it fresh."

"I guess. But even you will have to admit that many successful marriages have been built on friendship," I suggested, temporizing. "Douglas and Jennifer may well forge a partnership that works for them."

Charles rubbed his short curly hair the wrong way; it sprang back into place of its own volition. "For a while, yes. But once they've put up the valance boxes and found throw cushions that match the wallpaper, once they've grown used to walk-in closets and quality paperbacks on the night table – happiness is two in a rowboat; this is your McLife – they'll have to take a second look at one another."

"Don't you think a baby or two might keep them off the streets?" I am convinced that nothing widens cracks in a marriage more quickly than children, but I wanted to hear what Charles had to say.

"They both claim they want to postpone having a family. That's a plus. It will make the divorce easier if there are no children involved."

I was beginning to feel the comforting effect of my albeit tiny scotches. Laughter welled up at the slick cynicism of this young man, no older than the prospective bridegroom. "Have you thought of talking to Jennifer?" I asked.

"I don't think I could do that. I don't know her well enough. And what could I say? I don't think you should marry Douglas because one day he will go gay? She would be sure to repeat the conversation to Doug. And he would get sore. Now, if you were to talk to Jennifer. You're her uncle."

"By a sheer accident of nature. I am a far cry from the kindly avuncular figure you used to find in a Normal Rockwell *Saturday Evening Post* cover. I scarcely know the girl. A girl to me, a young woman to the rest of the world. And that's the crux of the matter. She is an adult, in charge of her own life. One of the things I have come to learn, the hard way, is that to interfere in somebody else's life is a serious matter. Jennifer would listen to me because I am older and she is well brought up. Our very lack of closeness would make me just that much more plausible. Think of how potentially devastating it could be for her, for anyone, to have a remote, respected figure warn ominously against the marriage for which invitations are being addressed as we speak." I paused to add a little soda to my drink.

"Charles, I know what you are trying to do. From the best and kindest of motives you would like to prevent their making what you consider a mistake. But maybe it's not a mistake. Maybe this marriage is a necessary step on their – you must pardon the metaphor – journey to self-discovery. We have all done foolish things, made right choices that led to dreadfully wrong results. How else can we move towards – I falter – wisdom, maybe? Enlightenment? Salvation, perhaps? Jennifer and Douglas have a right to their mistakes, lapses in judgement, whatever. And the best thing you and I can do is to suck in our guts, fasten those striped trousers, tug on the tailcoat, and see them through, with a smile on our lips and a song in our hearts. And, not to overlook the bottom line, they will be practising safe sex." I spread my hands open, palms upward. "You have equal time."

Charles opened his eyes wide in mock astonishment. "Mr. Chadwick, you are totally awesome."

"Totally tiresome is more like it. However, on a lighter note, I am beginning to think seriously about dinner. Are you free to join me, on my plastic?"

"And how. But I'll have to make a call."

"Good. You make your call and I'll take my briefcase up to the room. I'll meet you in the lobby in seven and one-half minutes."

Charles fished around in his trouser pocket. "Could I scrounge a quarter for the phone?"

"I can see you're not a cheap date."

He laughed. "On the contrary, I'm as cheap as they come."

In my room I took the opportunity to change from the suit I had worn all day into a jacket and slacks. Without turning myself into Joe College, I wanted to appear less at variance with Charles in his crew-necked sweater and chinos under the down-filled parka: out of L.L. Bean by Eddie Bauer.

"Yo, Geoffry," he called as I stepped off the elevator. "You changed."

"My clothes, not my point of view. These are my older-man-not-wanting-to-look-like-sugar-daddy duds."

A doorman costumed as though he were the Grand Duke of Ruritania flagged down a taxi, a two-dollar bill discreetly changed hands, and we were off, into the magic and mystery of an Ontario night.

At Charles's suggestion we ended up in a crowded, fun restaurant with natural brick walls, tiled floors, menus written in chalk on large blackboards. The overall decorating motif was noise, fluid, enveloping, self-renewing, so pervasive as to be a presence, a third, uninvited guest at our table. With the heed-less energy of youth, Charles happily shouted over the din. I knew if I tried to compete with the uproar, my larynx wouldn't last past the Melba toast; instead I pitched my voice low, pro-jecting the tone like a stage whisper. Judging from the amount of waving back and forth and table hopping, the restaurant had to be a popular hangout of the under-forty set. I felt a bit like a chaperone.

Across a few more drinks and immense portions of whole-some food, we managed to communicate. We did not converse; that gentle art does not flourish in decibels like those of a rock concert. Charles seemed quite ready to chatter away in a quiet scream, and I was more than content to listen, an activity that included reading his lips from time to time in order to double check the message.

Still, a picture began to emerge of a young man, com-fortably self-centered, as young men of his age generally are, but not without a set of what my mother would have called principles. Orphaned young and raised by an aunt and uncle, who sounded like the worst kind of Bible-thumping Christers, he had still absorbed a value system that, if mostly rejected, remained a measure of conduct to be followed or ignored. He had intelligence more than intellect, and did not allow a formal education to short-circuit his common sense. I also came to realize, with relief I have to confess, that his slightly camp flippancy was more in his mouth than in his conduct. And, astonishing as it might seem, we managed to negotiate the entire meal without mentioning AIDS.

In a curious kind of way I was enjoying myself. At this point in my life I do not meet many people Charles's age, at least not for extended periods. I got rather turned off youth by those foolish, unkempt, self-indulgent flower children of the sixties, while the so-called yuppies are just like me, only younger. Listening to Charles in this den of din, I felt almost like a sociologist, or an anthropologist, studying behaviour patterns different from my own. Perhaps the only difference between an anthropologist and a private investigator, both of whom report on the sex lives of others, is that the anthropologist gets paid by the government.

To leave the restaurant and step into quiet brought a rush of exhausted relief, not unlike that I felt as a child when I could finally go home from a birthday party: musical chairs, and pin-the-tail-on-the-donkey, and blind man's bluff, and cross adults, and kids throwing up, and fighting over favours in the birthday cake. The best favour of all was being able to leave.

The evening had reached the point when, had I been Charles's age, I would probably have gone out on the town, in a search for the adult version of the child's party with sex as the favour in the cake. I told Charles that I was old enough to find my way home alone, if he had plans for the shank of the evening. Announcing that he was totally at liberty, he insisted on buying me a brandy or a nightcap. The offer seemed genuine, and since I was on a kind of mini-vacation, I accepted.

By mutual consent we walked for a while, both to allow that home-style cooking to settle itself and to clear our heads of sound. Talk was inconsequential, of restaurants, movies, clothing, in which Charles had an interest far exceeding his budget. We skirted problems: acid rain, fluorocarbons, nuclear reactors, whale hunts, free trade, and taxes. Earnest conversation about the lamentable condition of the Niagara River does not clean it up. After a particularly bleak and windswept stretch of avenue we found ourselves approaching a large hotel whose porte-cochère beckoned invitingly.

The bar stood almost empty, a welcome change from the *son et lumières* through which I had eaten my calves' liver and home-fried onions.

"Geoffry," began Charles, leaning forward, both feet flat on the floor, hands squarely on the arms of the chair, "may I ask you a personal question?"

"You may. I don't promise to answer, but ask away."

"Do you live alone, I mean really alone?"

"You mean, do I have a lover? No, I don't."

He made a gesture with his entire body that made me think of a dog shaking itself after a swim. "Would you be willing to accept an offer for the job? Say, a young man who can cook, clean, and perform a variety of services, public and private?"

The combination of alcohol, fresh air, and digestion had lulled me into a comfortable stupor. "Some Filipino pal of yours wants to hire himself out as a houseboy, with maybe a little modelling on the side?"

"No way. I am not applying by proxy. I want the job myself."

My comfortable lethargy fell away like a wet raincoat.

"Hold on a minute. Are you suggesting what I think you are suggesting?"

He grinned his enormously appealing grin. "That's right."

"You mean, you are asking for my hand in – dalliance, not to mention et ceteras?"

"And how. For you I'd even do windows."

I laughed, albeit uncomfortably. "Wait a minute, Charles, aren't you running the movie backwards? Shouldn't it be the older man who buys the dinner and puts on the make?"

I was playing it light as I played for time. Usually I know how to swim with my head above water. I am too old to lie to myself, but not even subconsciously had I harboured designs on Charles. Aside from liking him, I confess I found him attractive, in a brash and bouncy way. With all that verve and energy, I am sure he would be wonderful value in bed. But at my age sex begins in the brain, not the crotch; and my brain had not been programmed to put the make on a man at least thirty years my junior and who was to be best man at my niece's wedding.

And yet, goddammit! I am not dead. How could my vanity fail to respond to being courted by a man half my age? More than one middle-aged man or woman has fantasized about finding himself in just such a situation, against all probable odds. Poor Eve, that much maligned woman, drawn irresistibly towards an action that her better judgement told her to avoid. What is temptation but the pull of passion over reason?

All this flashed onto my mindscreen in seconds, far less linear than I make it sound.

"Geoffry, since you have retreated into the eighteenth century with your talk of dalliance, let me say I don't care a fig for your script. I am making you an honestly disreputable offer. Do you want references?"

I smiled, at once amused and dismayed. "But you're located in Toronto."

"Not permanently. I have been thinking seriously about moving to Montreal, even before I met you. For anyone in the food business it's a much more interesting city than Toronto."

"But, Charles, have you really thought of the implications? I am more than twice your age." I could see him about to interrupt so I made a stronger, more forceful gesture and continued. "You are still living in an endless present. So did I at your age. It goes with the territory. Supposing, just supposing, we took up together. In ten years you will be thirty-five, just hitting your stride, the best years still ahead. I will be sixty-five and thinking of retirement. At forty, when you will be in your prime, like Miss Jean Brodie, I will be seventy and about to embark on old age."

This time he would not be quelled. "But you're throwing up barriers we might face at some point in the future. What about now?"

"Now is the easy part. How very easy and agreeable it would be to fall into bed and turn on. But you are not someone I met casually in a bar, someone whose knee brushed mine in a movie theatre. We did not strike up a conversation in a record store, or meet at a laid-back party. Grim though that dinner party at Lois's may have been, there was decorum. I met you with protocol, as fellow member of the wedding party, as a friend of my niece. Age aside, we can't just jump into bed and hope things will work out. Which is to say we could, but it wouldn't be wise."

"You know something, Geoffry? I never suspected you were so stuffy."

"How long have you known me, and how well? We would have to start from scratch. How could you possibly fit in with my patterns, at your age?" Believe me, Charles, it is not through lack of good will. I like you, very much, very much indeed. I listened to you over dinner, and I listened between the lines. To begin with, I'm fully prepared to believe you don't want to play games with handcuffs and enemas. I believe you put cucumbers in salad. I also believe you are going to be one hell of a forty-year-old. I only wish you were that age now. You began by asking if I live alone. I do, with all that entails. I have habits, patterns, priorities, and I know they would not suit you. Take a recent example: you were right at home in that restaurant tonight. I watched you, a fish in water. I felt as though I were being brainwashed by noise. I was the oldest person there. That is not meant as a reproach, but an observation. One thing I do know: the man I used to be at twenty-five could not possibly live with the man I am now."

Charles put down his glass with determination. "Now you just listen to me. You have been making a great many speeches this evening, and it's my turn. You keep harping on age. Can't you see that is one of the main reasons I think you're, well, great? Ever since that night at Mother Lois's, when you had another drink and stopped her dead in her tracks, you became my hero. And the cheesecake! That was cool. You have to be at least fifty to pull off a stunt like that. You have so much more experience than I have. You could teach me so much."

I smiled inside myself. The charming egotism of youth. I was almost tempted to suggest I was not a one-man cram school, or charm school for that matter, but I decided to hear him out.

"You know and I know it's a jungle out there. Everyone my age with a three-figure IQ – who's gay, that is – dreams of meeting someone who's prepared to play it straight, who won't be tricking around on those nights you have to work late. Imagine being able to have sex, the old-fashioned unsafe kind, without condoms and rubber gloves and pieces of latex and water soluble lubricants and spermicides and the rest of that shit."

He paused, overheated. "Don't get me wrong. I'm not just looking for a safe partner; they can be had. I'm looking for" – in spite of himself he laughed – "what the Classified Ads call a serious relationship. And I've found the person I want to have it with. I'd like to say more, but you know what I mean."

We sat, not looking at one another, as silence grew dense.

"Look, Geoffry, I know I've been coming on pretty strong. I don't want to move in and take over your life. I couldn't even if I wanted to. All I want is for us to give it a try. If it doesn't work out, no hard feelings."

"If it didn't sound so vulgar I'd be tempted to suggest you wanted to try me on for size."

Charles gave a reluctant laugh. "I don't understand what you mean. I'm just laughing to be a good sport."

I smiled, then grew serious again. "Charles, forgive me if I appear to pull rank, but I know things you don't. When you are fifty you will know them too. But you don't know them now. You are right in what you want, or rather whom. But I am not he. Jesus Christ! We shall both die of pronoun poisoning."

I managed to raise a faint smile. "You will have to take me on faith, but I am not the person you are seeking, at least not in that capacity. I am reminded of a song Libby Holman used to sing; she was before my time, let alone yours. 'This is how the story ends. He's going to turn me down and say can't we be friends.' That is what I would like us to be, Charles: friends."

He looked directly at me for the first time since I broke the silence. "You mean that, don't you, just friends."

"Yes."

"And there's no way I can change your mind about – very good friends?"

"No. There is much I could add, but some things are better left unspoken. And now, even friends must let one another get some sleep."

Charles paid the bill, a welcome distraction. Wordlessly, we pulled on our overcoats and left the now empty bar.

"I'm only a few blocks away from my hotel," I said. "I think I'll walk."

"I go the other way."

"Goodnight, then. Lunch or dinner when you next come to Montreal?"

"Sure thing." Suddenly, as if giving me a present, he flashed his winning smile. "Well, Geoffry, you have to admit I have excellent taste."

"Never doubted it for a second. And remember: there's no fool like an old fool."

We shook hands and went our separate ways.

Perhaps I had been an old fool, but not in the sense of the saw. Had I reached an age when I could so easily turn my back on life, on something as affirmative as a love affair with a young man prepared to follow me to Montreal? Perplexed and uneasy, I went straight up to my room, where television failed to exert its usual soporific effect. After I switched it off and lay in the dark, in that overheated room, I was chilled. My skin felt dank, pallid in the semi-dark, stretched uneasily over my bones. Reluctant to admit the truth, even to myself, I felt very much alone. After fitful sleep invaded by dreams, I awoke to a heavy, overcast morning. Light snow had fallen and melted, making the streets look slick and unwelcoming. I might have said the day matched my mood, but I resisted, pushing the pathetic fallacy into a drawer and closing it firmly. I rang for coffee and a newspaper and sat down to plan my day. I thought of doing the galleries and checking out state-of-the-art art. I considered browsing through the shops on Bloor, fingering the overpriced merchandise and snootily refusing offers of help from supercilious salespeople. I might pick up something for Mother at Creed's; she would enjoy the box as much as the contents. A leisurely visit to Toronto is incomplete without a visit to the Royal Ontario Museum and its collections, which might loosely be called eclectic. I love the ROM, Canada's own white elephant sale without price tags.

I also thought of telephoning Charles and suggesting lunch. We would drink gin, he with ginger ale, I with vermouth in a stem glass. After lunch we would return to my room and go to bed, possibly for the rest of the weekend, with time off for room service. You don't need sunny skies for sex. A simple phone call.

I made a call, but not to Charles. Instead I telephoned Air Canada and booked a seat on the mid-morning flight. In less than an hour I had checked out of the hotel and was on my way to the airport in a cab.

I knew perfectly well I was running away, not from the lunch and subsequent lovemaking, but from the expectations such an encounter would create. I can remember being twenty-five, when skin was the gateway to the soul and a good fuck was forever. Still, to turn somebody on, fully realizing that you will soon have to turn him off, is not the act of a responsible man.

I had an odd feeling in my gut, a hollow sensation in the pit of my stomach as the plane taxied down the runway. And I am not afraid of flying.

XII

"Geoffry?" My sister can turn a question into an imperative with the flick of a phoneme.

"Right first time. What's up?"

"I have several things I'd like to discuss. Are you by any chance coming to Toronto during the next few days?"

"No," I replied without elaboration. To say nothing about Friday's recent visit was not the same as telling a lie. "But if it's to be a long call, even at Sunday rates, would you like to hang up and I'll call you back? Consider it my modest contribution to the festivities."

"That won't be necessary."

My offer had been genuine. A phone call, of any length, was a small price to pay for avoiding an evening with Mildred in Toronto. Also, I had managed to put her on the defensive. "What's on your mind?"

"I would like to hold an engagement party, but I don't know whether it should be here or in Montreal. Either way, some of our friends will be unable to attend."

"Why not hold two parties, one in each city? One for Jennifer in Toronto, another for Douglas in Montreal. That way you can invite everyone you like and soften them up so they'll all be sure to cough up a wedding present."

"That's not a bad idea," said Mildred, who managed to

suggest, even as she agreed with me, a slight astonishment that I could come up with anything so constructive. "I'll speak to Lois. She may well decide to have the Montreal party at Mayfair Crescent. Heaven only knows, she has the space. Her drawing room is only slightly smaller than the lobby of Union Station, and about as welcoming. I might be able to get the Faculty Club, as Bruce's widow, or through a colleague." A long long-distance pause followed. "Would the engagement party be considered a legitimate wedding expense?"

"I don't see why not, provided you don't invite the entire city."

"Believe me, Geoffry, I don't know the entire city. I must say this Montreal-Toronto arrangement is a bit of a nuisance." There was a slight rustle, as if Mildred were consulting lists. "I am seeing about the announcements in the *Globe and Mail* and the *Star*. Lois will look after the *Gazette*. I sent her a photograph, a good one too. Douglas looks very distinguished for so young a man."

"What do you think of Douglas?" I asked casually, as if the thought had just occurred. Heretofore the groom had been conspicuous in his total absence from our conversations.

"What do I think of him! What do you mean, what do I think of him? He's going to marry my daughter, isn't he?

"Up to now that is the impression I've been given. But you still haven't told me what you think of him. I know he's rich, handsome, well mannered, and about to graduate with a prestigious degree. But there must be something about him you like."

Obviously flushed with her success over the engagement party, Mildred so far forgot herself as to laugh, gravel pouring off a dump truck. "I think he's a perfect dear. And you're right about his manners. Just last week he came to dinner with old Mrs. Tyson. You must remember her; you met her here one Christmas."

"That old bore! She spent the entire evening telling me how to grow African violets under fluorescent light. Don't tell me you invited her to dinner with Douglas. Are you trying to sabotage this marriage? Whatever will we do with those cast-by-the-lost-wax-process-and-set-with-the-birthstone wedding rings?" Much of Mildred's reputation for being a brick stems from her opening the door to a string of retired dropouts, rich bag ladies, and darling eccentrics the rest of us would cross the street to avoid.

"She's a remarkable woman for her years, make no mistake. I only hope I'm half as alert at her age. She and Douglas hit it off at once; he was perfectly charming to her. I was most impressed."

"Good for him." I am always uneasy around young men who hit it off with old ladies. Birds of a feather, and so forth. Quite obviously I was going to get no more than the pleased mother-in-law party line from my sister, so I let the matter drop.

"Well, Mildred, I only hope Jennifer is making the right choice. Marriage closes so many doors. As Czar Nicholas was heard to remark as he was led away to be shot, 'Don't put all your Fabergé eggs in one basket.'"

"What has Czar Nicholas to do with Jennifer's wedding?"

"Nothing. Is there anything else you wanted to discuss? My secretary is tracking down a reliable photographer."

"Yes, could you suggest a good hotel, not too expensive? Most of the ushers will be from Toronto, and we are trying to hold down costs."

"If I am not mistaken, the groom pays for the ushers' accommodations."

"No, you're quite wrong. I'm certain that is an expense of the bride's family."

"Let's check," I said, reaching for my copy of *Fifteen Steps to a Lovelier Wedding* on the night table. The book can send me to sleep in minutes. "Here we are, page forty-two: Expenses of the groom and his family. Hmmm. Here it is! 'Hotel accommodation for attendants and ushers when necessary.' Amelia Gates never lies."

"I see." Admitting error has never come easily to my sister. "Now, I suppose we will be dealing with a Montreal florist?"

"No doubt. But flowers are for girls. You can work that one out with Lois. Oh, and make sure Jennifer has a portable iron tucked into her hope chest. That way she will be assured of a wrinkle-free honeymoon. I read it in a magazine. Anything else?"

"Not at the moment. That's a good idea about the iron. I'll lend her mine."

After the usual wind-down we hung up. Mildred is so depressingly literal. I had meant the quip about the iron as a joke, but she took it as wisdom. The real joke will be trying to get the iron through airport security.

I really had read about the portable iron in a magazine. At the Toronto airport yesterday I ducked into a newsstand for something to read during the flight. I felt low, and the usual array of informing and improving magazines failed to catch my interest. Then I spotted it, a special issue of a national magazine featuring "101 Wedding Ideas for Today's Bride."

Paying for it was another matter. Had it been soft-core, even hard-core pornography, I would have felt considerably less self-conscious about approaching the cash register. Were the cover to have featured Vampira and her kiss of death – hip-length, high-heeled boots, cache-sexe, bullwhip, domino mask only partially concealing a cruel sneer – I would have looked the cashier straight in the eye. Instead, the cover featired a bride and groom of such surpassing vapidity that I spent those long moments during which the cashier counted change studying the sugar-free gum. I guess it proves I would rather be thought depraved than foolish.

The contents turned out to be as vapid as the cover. "Bride's Beauty Countdown," with radical suggestions like losing weight, getting plenty of sleep, having your teeth checked, and, as the big day drew near, deep-conditioning your hair, cultivating beautiful nails, taking care of troubled skin. From what I had seen of Jennifer, she would prepare on the big day by taking a shower and brushing her teeth.

There followed pages of coloured photos, gowns for a size eight bride with a pair of size ten bridesmaids. Romantic honeymoon hotels, all featuring a garden restaurant on the roof, boardwalk on the beach, Jacuzzi in the tub.

About to give up on the magazine and write it off on my income tax as a business loss, I came across an article entitled "25 Ways to Keep the Romance Alive," which turned out to be pure pay dirt. Twenty-five struck me as an arbitrary number. Why not nineteen, or twenty-seven? It was also worth noting that the responsibility for keeping this romance alive rested squarely on the shoulders of the bride. Many of the suggestions had to do with keeping the house or apartment spotlessly clean and well stocked with fresh flowers and candles, almost as if the newlyweds planned to live in an area where power failures were the norm. Other tips had to do with the element of surprise, springing the unexpected on the unsuspecting husband: dinner out on a weekday (Who pays?), or tickets for a concert bought on impulse. Any concert would do, Pachelbel's Canon or Beethoven's Ninth; the element of stunned astonishment was what mattered. At all times the wife must look her absolute best, impeccably made up, not a hair out of place, wrinkle-free. She must also have in her trousseau some sleazy underwear and a tarty nightgown, so that once she has washed the supper dishes she can turn into a call girl.

Not a few of the suggestions were enough to cause heartburn. Tuck a note into his briefcase so he will learn at the office how much you love him, possibly in the middle of a sales conference. Hold hands as you watch Saturday morning cartoons on television, happily wasting the most important morning of the week. Go to an amusement park and ride the roller coaster. Scream a lot. He will put his arms around you and feel protective. Picnics at romantic spots, like those in cigarette ads, are a surefire way to spark romance, even if the suggested foodstuffs take three days to prepare, not to mention the entire week's food budget.

The beginning of our descent into Montreal was announced just as I was trying to picture Jennifer and Douglas splashing happily in a bubble bath, but my imagination simply could not make the leap.

There remained the problem of what to do with the magazine, still hidden in my briefcase. (Thank goodness one did not have to go through Customs between Ontario and Quebec.) As the publication had set me back a few dollars, I was unwilling to toss it out. Nor did I want it seen in my possession. Perhaps I would give it to Conchita, my cleaning woman who could look at the pictures. But I wondered if my Spanish was up to explaining that my niece had left the magazine behind, accidentally, by mistake. *Que lastima!*

Mighty oaks from tiny acorns have been known to grow. My casual suggestion to Mildred that there be two engagement parties, one in each city, produced immediate results. On Monday morning at half past nine Lois Fullerton telephoned my office. As I was not with a client, I took the call. The subject on her mind was the engagement party she planned to throw for Douglas and Jennifer the weekend after next. She had received a call from Mildred, who relayed my excellent suggestion of holding two parties. By way of response I inquired whether it wasn't the prerogative of the bride's family to make the announcement and give the party, the first one anyway. Yes, I was quite right, she assured me, but since Mildred did not yet know where to hold the party and since Lois herself had such a large house, they agreed to make an exception and let Lois kick it off, as it were. As there seemed to be no hard and fast rules governing the engagement party, she had more or less decided on drinks first, with plenty of hot hors d'oeuvres handed around, followed by a buffet. Did I not agree that might be the best way of dealing with what might turn out to be a very mixed crowd?

When a woman like Lois says she has "more or less decided," her decision is about as mutable as the Magna Carta. I was expected to agree with her and I did. Of course, she went on to explain, she had thought of giving a tea, but cups, for that many people?

I agreed, a totally unrealistic number of cups.

Were the ground not covered in snow, she continued, she could have put up a marquee in the garden and held a barbecue.

But that puts the hostess at the mercy of the weather, I suggested. And the menu is so limited, hamburger or chicken, franks or ribs, a vat of baked beans, a mountain of garlic bread. And a dessert built around vanilla ice cream. Anybody in her right mind would opt for a buffet over a barbecue.

I had said what she obviously wanted to hear; furthermore, I added the usual empty assurances, that I was certain Jennifer would be delighted, so would Douglas, and that we were all going to have a wonderful time. By this time the conversation had run out of steam, and I was able to hang up.

For a moment I couldn't help wondering why she had even bothered to telephone. She had obviously made up her mind about what kind of party she intended to give. I had contributed nothing outside of a few vague affirmations. Was I being kept track of, against the time when my quote-unquote broken heart had mended sufficiently to contemplate another romance? Whatever the reason, I soon found my attention claimed by work, which precludes thought. Perhaps that is why work has always been popular in North America.

Lois wasted no time. Two days after her call to my office an invitation arrived, special delivery. There is something vaguely intimidating about that red special delivery sticker. It compels obedience. Aside from a casual disregard for cost, the invitation suggested, albeit politely, that you had bloody well better show up at the party in ten days' time, or else produce an iron-clad alibi.

I telephoned Patrick and told him about the invitation, which, as stand-in for father of the bride, I was obliged to accept. However, I would be no more than a face in the crowd, one of many. Patrick agreed – the anonymity of a mob scene. Then he suggested I arrange to get him invited to the party. That would give him a chance to check out the situation under cover of numbers.

I confess that for a moment I hesitated. Did I really want to pay Patrick Fitzgerald one hundred dollars an hour so he could crash my niece's engagement party and freeload to his heart's content? Laughter came down the wire. "Don't worry, Geoffry. I don't expect you to pay me for having a good time. From what you have told me, Mrs. Fullerton will throw quite a bash. I haven't been to an engagement party in years. All you have to do is get me in."

Put out at being caught out, I still had to laugh. "A hundred dollars saved is a hundred dollars earned. Have you any more info on the chauffeur?"

"No, he's keeping a low profile at the moment. But the word is out through the grapevine that there may be something big afoot."

"I see. Now what happens if the party's a dud, a real bore? Will you charge me time and a half?"

"No, I'll just have to postpone buying the trenchcoat."

"Come again?"

"You know as well as I do, Geoffry, that all private detect-ives wear trenchcoats. But have you tried to buy one recently? They've all gone designer and cost a mini-fortune. It's cheaper to wear mink during a stakeout."

"And far less conspicuous, especially with a snap-brim fedora. I'll call you about the party."

I telephoned my RSVP to Lois and, in one of those off-the-cuff by-the-ways, mentioned that an old friend, divorced, was coming to Montreal for the weekend of the party. He had tele-phoned asking me to have dinner Saturday night. Naturally, I had to refuse, but would it be possible –

Why, of course, Lois had replied before I even had a chance to complete my sentence. By all means bring him along. An extra man is always welcome.

That bit of lore harkens back to another era. Women of my mother's generation always tried to flesh out a dinner table with an extra man and the unspoken but wicked hint of sex up for grabs. The fact that most "extra" men were as gay as a carousel did not ease the unfortunate truth that extra women were considered a liability. My experience with extra men at parties has not been all that great. They eat more, and certainly drink more, than the other guests. They make passes at the help and sneak off to the furnace room for a quick bit of in and out. They are seldom amusing and frequently bad news. But most people take parties very seriously. They are occasions to network and make contacts, business, social, sexual. The idea that one would go to a party merely to have a good time seems frivolous in the extreme.

The one ironclad rule laid down by *Fifteen Steps to a Lovelier Wedding* was that the prospective bride and groom both be present at the engagement party. As for the other members of the family, they should attend if possible. I fully intended going to Lois's party; I even had an escort. Whether I would go up to Toronto for the party Mildred planned to throw in three weeks' time seemed very doubtful. When it comes to engagement parties, once is more than enough, even though one can be reasonably certain there will be nothing to wave, wear, or blow.

Nothing could have kept my sister away. She was coming down from Toronto, on foot if necessary, to play her part as the not-too-quietly-understated mother of the bride.

That left Richard and Elizabeth, Jennifer's brother and sister, head usher and maid of honour respectively. Both were in the middle of academic terms at universities. It seemed un-realistic, to me at least, that they should interrupt their studies twice in one month to fly first to Montreal, then to Toronto, for these parties. Nor did I consider ferrying them back and forth a legitimate wedding expense, as I told Mildred during a terse telephone conversation.

She called while I was performing the irritating task of trying to fold a fitted sheet into a neat square so it could be stored in an inadequate linen closet. My cleaning woman had been laid low with flu, and I was playing house, not my favou-rite game. Housework is just that, all work and no pay. Not surprisingly, Mildred wanted Richard and Elizabeth to attend both parties, at Mother's expense, a suggestion I vetoed at once. We were not running a travel agency.

Before Mildred had a chance to embrace martyrdom, I made a counter-proposal. Why not have each sibling attend the nearest party? Richard could fly up from New York for Lois's party, Elizabeth from Indiana for the one in Toronto. The compromise was nonnegotiable, and Mildred accepted with all the charm of a slammed door. She was already sorry she had allowed herself to become involved in these beastly engagement parties. Lois Fullerton had made such an issue of holding the first party, by rights the prerogative of the bride's family, that Mildred was forced to agree. Either that or tell the silly female off. As I had anticipated, there was trouble in paradise.

Pouring oil on troubled waters has never been my long suit, to mince the metaphor, but I suggested to Mildred that Lois was less overbearing than enthusiastic. Nobody could fault her for that. Furthermore, anyone who mattered already knew about the wedding, so the party was to be no more than just that, a party and not an official function. Lois was obviously going to a lot of trouble and expense, so why don't we all just plan to have a good time.

Not in the least mollified, Mildred muttered something about women with dollar signs where their brains should be, and hung up. I returned to folding my contour sheet, a trick that made Rubik's cube look easy.

Possibly one of the surest signs of encroaching age is that one grows more willing to spend money on services than on goods. Far more important than the designer label on the shirt is the nearby laundry who will wash the garment, press out the wrinkles, fold it, and slide it into a polyethylene bag. I have always considered the hotel, where one can rent a room with adjoining bath scrubbed daily by a maid, to be one of mankind's highest achievements.

Not so my sister, who considers hotels an invention of the devil. I know I will not have to protect Mother from unjustified hotel bills, for Mildred would almost prefer to sit up all night in the concourse of Central Station than to incinerate money by paying for lodgings.

Lois Fullerton's impending party was to cause an exodus from Toronto: Jennifer, Douglas, Mildred, and Charles. My nephew Richard, the head usher, would be flying in from New York. I knew the idea of anyone staying in a hotel would be anathema to my sister, but I made no attempt to offer a solution.

I have protected myself by having no facilities whatsoever for putting up guests. My couch does not unfold into a bed, nor is it long enough for anyone to sleep on comfortably, one of the features that occasioned its purchase. When I retired from the arena of one-night stands and meaningful relationships that lasted seventy-two hours, I exchanged my king-sized bed for a regular double and made my bedroom seem twice as large. People who want to crash in a sleeping bag on my living-room floor are unwelcome. I far prefer to put such out-of-town visitors as I have into a hotel and pay the bill, a small price compared to tripping over them in the early hours of the A.M.

Not surprisingly, Lois came to the rescue, insisting she had heaps of room for the young people. Furthermore, Douglas and Richard, who had yet to meet, could get to know one another. Mildred would stay with Mother. All these bedding-down arrangements took an unnecessary number of phone calls, but at least I would not have a body sleeping in my bathtub.

All that I have ever wanted from my sister is that she leave me alone. In her case, absence may not make the heart grow fonder, but it does keep the disposition sweeter. Were I the kind of person who allows himself to feel guilt, a vain, self-indulgent emotion that permits one to feel a bathetic responsibility for events over which one has no control, were I to get off on guilt, I might have felt differently about Mildred's missing her daughter's engagement party. As anyone who lives in Canada well knows, in the midst of winter we are in flu. Poor dear Mildred was flat on her back.

She had all the classic symptoms: fluctuating temperature, aches, chills, fever, and a head that did not feel attached to the rest of her body. Only the ministrations of a kindly neighbour enabled Jennifer to leave the patient and get down to Montreal. Sick though she might have been, Mildred was not too sick to telephone and tell me just how sick she really was. I felt she would ultimately recover.

It was only when I had hung up the phone, after suitable expressions of solicitude, that I realized Mildred's illness landed me with a major problem, namely, that of getting Mother to the engagement party. Up to now I had considered Mother as Mildred's responsibility for the evening. But my sister was now *hors de combat*, and I certainly wasn't going to saddle Jennifer with her unpredictable grandmother. Although Mother leaves her apartment only when it is absolutely necessary – the doctor, the dentist, the ophthalmologist – she had expressed a determination to attend her granddaughter's engagement party. My heart plummeted at the thought of Mother turned loose at 15 Mayfair Crescent. Steering myself through that evening would take all my concentration, not to mention having Patrick in tow.

Under ordinary circumstances I would have put myself out to accommodate Mother, to pick her up, transport her safely to Lois Fullerton's house, to keep her under constant surveillance while she made her token appearance, and to whisk her away the second she started to fall apart.

I also understood that Mother was more intrigued with the idea of the party than with the gathering itself. It was time for me to carry out the intellectual equivalent of a mugging, and it was with deliberation and premeditation that I reached for the phone.

"Mother?"

"Geoffry. How very nice." I could tell by Mother's voice that she had just about started on her third vodka of the day.

"You've heard the news about Mildred?"

"Isn't it awful. Poor girl. And with Jennifer's party this weekend. I guess I will just have to attend in Mildred's place."

"That's what I wanted to talk to you about, Mother. Can you put your hand on your overshoes?"

There was a pause and a tinkle. "I don't really know. I suppose so. But why would I need overshoes?"

"We may have to walk down the hill after the party to find a taxi, or else take the bus. There's a long-range forecast for a big storm, and getting around will be a problem. If the night is stormy I won't be driving my car. And be sure to tie a scarf over your wig."

"Couldn't we hire a limousine?"

"We could, at exorbitant cost. Probably a good idea, though. We can put your wheelchair in the trunk."

"Wheelchair, Geoffry? Why would I want a wheelchair at an engagement party?"

"There will be a great many people and not much place to hunker down. With your own wheelchair you will be guaranteed a place to sit."

"I see." Pause. Tinkle.

"You know what these cocktail parties are like, Mother. A bunch of drunks standing around talking at the tops of their voices. But that won't matter to you, as there won't be anyone there you know, outside of Jennifer and Richard and me. And we'll all be pretty tied up with the other guests."

"True." A long pause but no tinkle. I pressed on, ruthlessly.

"But I wouldn't worry about being entertained. If I know Lois, she'll probably have musicians, or at least a pianist. I can wheel you over to the piano and you can listen to the cocktail music."

"Cocktail music?" I could hear Mother take a long swallow before she continued. "Do you suppose – I know it's dreadful of me even to suggest it – but do you suppose it would be really awful of me not to attend?"

"No, I don't. You're all grown up, Mother. In fact, you're old enough to be my mother. Why should you even remotely consider doing something you don't want to do? Tell you what. Should you decide you really don't want to go, I'll do my best to square it away with Jennifer."

"That's very good of you, dear. Perhaps you should. I don't really think I would have a very good time."

"Whatever you say, Mother. Now, if you hang up right away I just may be able to catch her at home."

"Well, if you think it best . . ."

I rang off, pitilessly, and called my niece. I blandly suggested that if she wanted her unwilling grandmother at the engagement party, she would have to dress her, groom her, transport her, and make sure she stayed off the sauce prior to departure. I was fighting dirty, and I won. Jennifer didn't stand a chance.

"What you might do," I temporized, "is stay with your grandmother. Now that Mildred can't come to Montreal, the guest room will be free. I know Mother would enjoy having you there."

"Good idea, Uncle Geoffry. I would prefer to stay with Gran. That way I won't have to spend the weekend avoiding Mrs. Fullerton's aura."

The plan was for Jennifer, Douglas, and Charles to drive up to Montreal along Highway 401, boring in summer, an endurance test in winter. Hell must surely consist of driving for eternity along the 401, in a car that never needs refilling, with kidneys that never need draining. Richard, who was careful with money, his or anyone else's, was coming up from New York City by bus, a wise choice, for nothing can shut down an airport faster than a snowstorm. Although I am not frequently given to gestures of male solidarity, I volunteered to take Douglas, Charles, and Richard to lunch on Saturday, a kind of bachelor party for the groom. Unlike the bachelor parties of my youth, however, the groom would not be doused with beer and pushed into the shower fully dressed, all in the name of good clean fun. The lunch party would also serve to get the three young men out from under Lois's feet on that big and busy day.

Perhaps the most extraordinary thing about the week preceding the party was that I managed to get some work done. On a couple of evenings I stayed late at the office, quietly clearing my desk with the slightly smug feeling that the telephone in my apartment was probably melting down.

Lois Fullerton's obvious gratitude that I was taking the houseguests off her hands on the day of the party convinced me that lunch had been one of my better ideas. I would have a chance to see my nephew, whom I liked; I could get to know Douglas away from his mother; and I would be seeing Charles in a situation that would not be charged with what if. Yes, indeed, a pleasant occasion.

It was only after I had made the reservation that the full implications hit me: a lunch party of three gay men and one on whom the jury was still out. (Aside from what Charles had told me about Douglas, those wedding rings made me very nervous.) But I was both the oldest man and the host. It would be my responsibility to make sure civility did not degenerate into camp and that comedy did not descend into farce.

We certainly had an impressive cast. If not a true queen, I can certainly be a grand duchess when the occasion demands. Richard was our visiting princess. (You don't have to be either Jewish or female to be a princess.) Charles would play the lady's maid, the wenchy kind whose breasts are always billowing over her *fichu*. And Douglas was the naive young man from the provinces who falls into the clutches of these three harpies. For parallels one would have to turn to French comedy more than English, Marivaux perhaps, Beaumarchais, even Alfred de Musset. Then again, we were just four men meeting for a pleasant lunch. I would unobtrusively make certain that all the hairpins remained in place.

Late that afternoon, after waking from my nap and before showering, I made tea, a little jolt of caffeine to get the motor turning over. I had about an hour before Patrick came to pick me up and drive me to the party in his car. I had followed his suggestion and moved my own car from its customary parking spot downstairs, just in case my unknown admirer decided to play more tricks on my hapless Cadillac. I drove over to Mother's apartment building and left the automobile in the parking space she rents for guests.

To my mild astonishment, lunch had turned out to be pleasant and civilized. I took my guests to a Swiss restaurant whose food is outstanding. Granted, the cowbells and alpenhorns take a bit of getting used to, as do the Franz Lehar waitresses in dirndls. I could see Charles giving the restaurant the once-over, his gaze resting on the bar, which reproduced the façade of a Swiss chalet. He happened to catch my eye, then made such a dumb show of trying not to smile that I burst out laughing, to the puzzlement of Douglas and Richard.

I had not seen my nephew in over a year. Preparing an advanced degree at the Julliard School of Music is no easy undertaking, and he worked hard. Initially, like most young musicians, he had wanted a career in performing; music is written to be heard, after all. I had suggested that rock concerts can easily sell out hockey arenas, but harpsichord recitals seldom play to a full house. With an advanced degree from a respected institution he would have more options. He could teach, full time if recitals dried up.

I would also like to think that at a critical point in his life I gave him some sound advice. The burden of my message was that he accept his sexual orientation without turning it into an issue. This conference had taken place during that simpler age before AIDS began to grab headlines from acid rain. Sexual politics had turned shrill and strident. Nelly little numbers in skin-tight jeans and T-shirts with the sleeves rolled up to the shoulder confronted men in three-piece suits and hair parted on the side. The gay libbers screamed in uncivil fashion for civil liberties, as they stamped their sneakers and tossed their blow-dried curls in an orgy of Them and Us. The slightest hint that they simply shut up and accommodate themselves to a heterosexual society in which they were a minority group met with outraged cries. They lusted for confrontation; they de-manded obedience. But haven't we always known that when you scratch a fairy a fascist bleeds through?

I had not wanted my nephew to fall into this unattractive pattern. And, I was pleased to see, he had not. He was a serious young man, but that quality was due in part to the harpsichord. Musical instruments whose strings are plucked – the harpsi-chord, guitar, harp – tend to be solemn, as opposed to those whose strings are bowed. What is jollier than a cello? Richard had inherited the best genes from both parents and, perhaps un-fairly, was by far the best looking of Mildred's three children. Tall, well built, broad of forehead and straight of nose, he had the intensity that springs from serving in the temple of music. There was a time when I found that kind of intensity in a man quite sexy. Now it wears me out.

Douglas Fullerton was, as I had initially expected, an air-head, or, to use an expression borrowed from my father, a bit of a lightweight. I also suspected his lack of weight sprang not from a limited intelligence but from a lack of direction. My own prejudices leak through, but I have always thought that going to graduate school to study English is not unlike attending a world-renowned cooking school in order to learn how to eat. At grade school one learns to read and write, add and subtract. At college one applies these skills to learning about the history of our civilization. At university one learns a profession. Only those who have the true vocation of scholarship should pursue doctoral degrees in literature, history, philosophy. A Ph.D. is not a degree for amateurs. I suppose what bothered me about Douglas was his lack of vocation; he had read a lot of books, but he was not a scholar.

Of the young men around the table I felt most comfortable with Charles, the man of intelligence with no pretensions to intellect. I'd wager that as a child he learned to tell the time and tie his shoelaces without the help of adults. He knew enough to take shelter when it rained. I felt certain he was deft with tools and understood electrical wiring. In comparison with the other two tall, conventionally handsome young men, whose prototypes looked at you from the pages of glossy fashion magazines, Charles seemed solid and square. His centre of gravity was low; his feet rested firmly on the floor.

I was also interested to observe that whereas at Lois Fullerton's dinner party he had chafed under the heavy decorum imposed by house and hostess, as my dinner guest he was just another young man at the table, a listener as well as a participant.

As a matter of fact, Charles and I found ourselves spectators to a conversation between Richard and Douglas that grew increasingly animated with each glass of wine. It was one of those discussions graduate students are given to having, about whether music or literature best expressed the spirit of the eighteenth century. I interrupted to suggest perhaps they were not mutually exclusive, but I could tell they listened out of politeness, not conviction. The second I had made my point they were off and running. Charles tipped me the wink as I turned to summon the waitress, and in the process of ordering another bottle of wine I tuned out of the discussion. Besides, it was not a subject over which I have ever lost sleep.

The argument petered out, as such pointless arguments must, just about the time I was beginning to hear the siren song of my Saturday afternoon nap. I signalled for the check, but not before Douglas and Richard were off and running once again over whether Bach keyboard suites ought to be performed on the piano, the fortepiano, or the harpsichord. They both argued as if winning the point depended on the amount of energy expended in making it. I have never seen Richard so animated, while Douglas came close to losing his campus cool.

Because Charles was seated directly across the table from me, not to one side, it proved impossible to start a satellite conversation. Nor did I feel up to exchanging remarks across the combat zone. Having dispatched the apple strudel I urged him to have, Charles put down his fork and announced he had once heard the Fifth French Suite played on comb and tissue paper, and a rousing rendition it had been, especially the gigue. Both Richard and Douglas looked at him with the impatient hauteur of people frivolously interrupted in the midst of making a telling point. I seized upon the interruption to point out that we were the last people in the restaurant and perhaps we should think of moving on.

In the street I waved off thanks, said I would see them all in a matter of hours, and set off on the brief walk back to my apartment. As I paused for the traffic light at the corner I glanced down the street to see Richard and Douglas deep in discussion, with Charles trudging along behind. Were I given to envy I could have felt it over the prodigal energy of youth, that superabundance of vitality which can waste itself arguing over issues that have no ultimate solution. A long time has passed since I burned up calories trying to separate black from white. Now I let them bleed together into a comfortable grey, not a colour one bothers to defend.

I had been struck once again by how much Richard reminded me of my own father, even though I have always mistrusted that bit of lore about genes jumping generations. But in Richard I caught glimpses of my father, the visual equivalent of echoes or overtones. It was less a similarity of bone structure or sameness of colouring than a recollection of gesture, the angle Richard held his head when listening, the way he looked me straight in the eye when he spoke. He had my father's hands, large and shapely, and almost computer-designed for the keyboard.

Poor old Pop. I sometimes wonder how he would have felt had he known that not only his son but his only grandson had gone tripping down the garden path and over the stile into the alternate lifestyle. Oddly enough, I think he would have minded less than other men of his generation, just so long as we minded our manners and did not make others uncomfortable.

I had found myself thinking of Father from time to time during these past weeks. I suppose it was only natural, mired as I was in this wedding, such a family affair. Even now I caught myself remembering the last time we were alone together, the day we buried Susan and my daughter.

The Mount Royal Cemetery stretched bleak and desolate on that blustery March day. A handful of hardy mourners, who had left the warm church for the cold graveside, shivered through the short ceremony, then hurried back to the limousines. I had still failed to make the connection between Susan, the baby, and the trench hacked into the frozen ground.

By way of cheering me up, Father took me to lunch at his club, away from the women. After a couple of stiff drinks at the walnut and brass bar, we headed upstairs to the oak and damask dining room for Melton Mowbray pie and a bottle of claret. I could see Father trying to strike the right balance between solicitude and common sense. "I suggest," he began, breaking a roll, "that you pack up the baby's things and store them in the basement for the time being. And you're welcome to move back into your old room for a few days, or to stay as long as you like."

Suddenly, for the first time since the accident, tears welled up. I pushed away from the table and ran sobbing downstairs to the cloakroom. As I struggled to regain control, the door opened quietly and Father came in. Without a word he handed me the spotless white handkerchief he always carried neatly folded in his breast pocket. Then he put an arm around me and drew me close. I wept onto his shoulder, his solid, warm, reassuring presence only pushing the flood gates wider open instead of grinding them shut.

The door opened a second time to admit one of those WASPy Nigel Bruce types, who stood bug-eyed at the spectacle of two grown men embracing beside a rack of coat hangers. I raised my head, angry and embarrassed to be caught in a display of emotion. Even under stress I always had a mouth. "He's my father, not my date!" I snarled. Huffing, the man retreated.

Father led the way back upstairs, and without further ado we finished our lunch.

It is the portrait of the way he looked that day at lunch that hangs in my memory. What a beautiful man he was, even though back then we did not refer to men as beautiful. I can only hope he knew how much I loved him. Yet to have told him, as one grown man to another, that I did love him would probably have made him uneasy. Displays of strong feelings made his generation uncomfortable, and men, even married ones, did not admit to loving one another. The admission would have made them shy. And I would probably have stumbled over the words.

XIII

Patrick arrived on the dot of six wearing a loud tweed sports jacket, which made him look like a tourist. "I think I called the wrong escort service," I observed as he removed his overcoat. "Do you glow in the dark?"

"I'm supposed to be a friend from out of town. Would you have packed a three-piece blue suit for an all-stops-out weekend in Montreal?"

"Yes. But I have always counted on neutrality rather than disguise for protective colouring. Would you like a drink before we leave?"

"I'll pass. I'm not averse to enjoying myself this evening, but I think I'll start off easy."

"No drinking on the job?"

"I'll drink, don't worry. From what you told me about our hostess, there won't be any shortage of liquor. Did you move your car?"

"Yes, it's parked over at Mother's. Did you bring yours?"

"No, I didn't. It's snowing quite heavily, and there is what is laughingly called a weather warning on the radio. I thought we'd take a cab."

"No difficulty from this end. But if, as you say, it's a bad night we may have trouble getting a taxi all the way up at Mayfair Crescent."

"We'll manage. Wear overshoes. In a pinch we can walk

down the hill to Boulevard and flag something. Maybe someone will give us a lift. Or, better still – " Patrick winked a broad
wink – "maybe we can get the chauffeur to bring us home."

"With a pit stop before he goes back up the hill? What the
hell! If we're going to drink we shouldn't drive anyway."

I folded the cuffs of my trousers and tucked them into a pair
of rubber galoshes that zipped closed. They'll never be featured in
Gentlemen's Quarterly, but they do keep feet and trouser cuffs dry.

Sure enough, as we pushed into the street a blast of wind
saturated with fine, sharp snow stung my face. I tucked my scarf
more snugly around my neck and wondered whether I should
pull on the toque I had taken the precaution of tucking into my
overcoat pocket. Patrick wore a sensible nylon ski cap with ear
flaps that could be pulled down. Snow had already drifted
across the sidewalks, so we waded into the freshly salted road.
As luck would have it, a taxi pulled up about half a block away,
and three passengers climbed out. With one accord we broke
into a lumbering run and managed to catch the vehicle before
it pulled away.

I explained my destination to the driver in English, then
again in French. He replied in joual, the Gallic equivalent of
impenetrable cockney dialect. True joual is heavily seasoned
with references to the Catholic Church and its rituals. Blas-
phemous in French, they sound curiously watered down when
translated into English.

"Hostie!" he replied. (*Host!*) Une nuit de même! (*On a night
like this!*) C'est pas un cadeau! (*Just what I need!*) Calice! (*Chalice!*)

I assured him in fluent but stilted French that he would be
well tipped for his trouble. The cab smelled of stale cigar smoke
and the floor of the back seat was covered in soggy newspapers

to sop up the slush. But, as Mother used to say, beggars can't be choosers. Following the path of the salt trucks, the cab made its tortuous way up the hill and drew to a stop in front of Number 15. I tipped the driver generously, but obviously not generously enough. "Baptême!" he muttered.

"Bonsoir," I replied, turning the other cheek.

With lights blazing in every window under a snow-covered roof, Lois Fullerton's house had the fake Currier and Ives cheeriness of glossy magazine ads aimed at new money. The driveway had been cleared of the wedge of snow pushed up by the plough. Patrick and I made the small detour to the front walk, which lay under eight centimetres of white powder in spite of having been recently shovelled. If anything, the snow was increasing in intensity, and I did not tarry in ringing the bell and stepping smartly inside.

Extra staff had been hired for the evening. A young woman, who had the look of a moonlighting college student, took our coats and gave us each a fresh plastic shopping bag in which to put our overshoes. She then wrote our names on a slip of paper clipped to the collar of each garment. Already it was evident that nothing had been left to chance. I had only time to glimpse an enormous fan-shaped arrangement of calla lilies and birds-of-paradise before Lois bore down upon us, rippling across the floor in a gown of royal blue jersey almost liquid as she moved. The overall effect was Grecian, although the engineering involved suggested the age of Leonardo da Vinci rather than of Pericles. It was the kind of gown the wearer stepped into wearing only her step-ins, the contour controls all artfully built in. It was a gown for the stage, for a soprano about to sing arias from *Alcestis* or *Medea*. It was not the gown I would have chosen to wear to an engagement party, not even my own; but then, royal blue has never been my colour.

Her greeting, polite but perfunctory, told me she was pre-occupied. I shook hands and gave her a social peck on both cheeks. I have to admit she smelled good, obviously something French instead of the outrageously packaged and priced varnish remover pedalled on Rodeo Drive. I introduced Patrick Fitzgerald. Lois smiled a conditioned-reflex smile, proffered an automated hand to shake, and parroted how delighted she was he could come. She did not check him out, to my surprise. Even in that horsey Harris tweed, Patrick was a striking man. That she did not zap him with those big blue orbs demonstrated her mind was elsewhere.

"Of all the nights to be having a party! I've already had five couples telephone regrets because of the blizzard. I insisted it was only a snowstorm. I even offered to send the chauffeur, but they wouldn't be swayed. I was furious."

"Don't worry, Lois," I said in my most reassuring voice. "There seems to be a goodly number of people here already, and there will be just that much more food and drink for the rest of us."

The doorbell rang. Pausing only long enough to insist I see that Patrick got a drink, Lois melted away to greet the arrivals.

Even though it was early the party had managed to sub-divide itself into camps. Those who drank had gravitated to the library, where a long bar had been set up in front of the fire-place with two bartenders on the jump so nobody would have to wait. People who have been served but remain at the bar, talking and blocking access to others, ought to be ticketed, like jaywalkers. I shouldered my way past two men discussing poli-tics, the corners of their mouths pulled down to indicate seriousness, then snagged a pair of scotches and moved to where Patrick stood taking in the scene.

If the drinkers had graduated towards the library, the sippers – the sherry-Campari-Perrier set who seek to avoid the feeling of heightened awareness that liqior and being in a roomful of people can bring – had taken over the drawing room. Patrick whispered that he would catch me later and slipped away, just as Audrey Crawford, dressed in claret challis and the tan newly acquired on a cruise to South America, zeroed in on me like a heat-sensitive missile.

"Geoffry, pet!" She embraced me in that effusive way some people adopt when aware others are looking. "I thought you'd never get here. What an awful shame about Mildred and that beastly flu. Having to miss her own daughter's engagement party." She reached up, ostensibly to toy with her pearls but in reality to adjust a shoulder strap. Dropping her voice to a stage whisper, she leaned forward. "Actually, if I had known Mildred wasn't coming I would have begged off. I wouldn't put the dog out on a night like this, but I have to brave it myself. Hartland drove me over; he has some sort of athletic dinner on tonight. But I suppose I'll have to snowshoe home. How did you manage to get here?"

"I lassoed a cab."

"Was the driver Haitian?"

"No."

"Thank goodness for that. Which is to say if you had landed a Haitian driver you wouldn't be here but in the middle of an accident, with lots of shouting and arm waving and not a police car within miles. At least you're not a woman. Do you know, I once had a Haitian driver make a play for me? I could hardly believe my ears. He actually suggested we go back to his squalid walk-up for coffee – and you can guess what else."

"Tell me honestly, Audrey, can you blame him? With this love goddess palpitating in the back seat? Reflected in the rear view mirror? Sort of like the Lady of Shalott, but in reverse."

Pleased with the compliment, Audrey bridled archly. "Oh, Geoffry, you really are too much. But I still wonder how I'm going to get home."

"Perhaps the chauffeur will drive you."

"Heaven forbid! I'll end up in a snowbank with my throat cut. Have you seen him? He looks like a hit man."

The observation did not please me.

"Have you seen our hostess?" Audrey inquired after taking a sip of her vodka and something. "We can overlook the double chignon, which nobody has seen since 'Saturday Night at the Movies.' We can try to forgive the industrial-strength makeup. But we cannot forgive the gown: The Phantom of the Parthenon. All she needs is a large earthenware jug of water on her shoulder."

In spite of myself I laughed. A day without malice, and so forth. Then, as if to make amends for my laughter, I came to Lois's defence.

"I think she looks pretty good. The gown is very high sewing, as the French would say. A bit theatrical, perhaps, but that's her style. And she knows how to organize a party. Every detail has been worked out."

Right on cue, a moonlighting maid appeared at my elbow carrying a platter of smoked salmon hors d'oeuvres, topped with thinly sliced onion and capers. The maid's cap clung uneasily to her frizzed hair. Absent-mindedly, I took the cocktail napkin she handed me, "Jennifer and Douglas" embossed across one corner in silver script, and tucked it into my jacket pocket.

"She can throw a party, all right. She doesn't have anything else to do. I've approached her any number of times to serve on volunteer organizations: jobs for battered women, clothing for immigrants, daycare for unwed mothers. All she ever does is send a cheque, but she never does any real work."

"At least she sends the cash. That's already more than most." I wondered how Audrey would react to the idea that Lois would rather throw a leg over the chauffeur than scrounge second-hand clothing and furniture for illegal immigrants.

"True, and she'll work on a committee if it's a glamour job, a ball for the museum or a gala for the symphony. But nothing that will bring her into contact with the underprivileged."

Many years have passed since I read the *Boy Scout Handbook*. I don't remember a section on cocktail parties, but I am certain the spirit of that slender volume would argue against bad-mouthing the hostess whose Scotch you are drinking and whose dinner you are about to eat. I knew Audrey Crawford was a worthy woman, diligent and caring in her work with society's unfortunates. Yet she was afflicted with the arrogance that comes with the awareness of one's own goodness, if not quite holier-than-thou, at least more-deserving-of-a-pat-on-the-back-than-thou.

"Where's the bride-to-be?" I asked to change the subject. "I caught a glimpse of the groom, but he lives here."

"I suppose she encountered the same difficulties getting here as the rest of us." Audrey's eyes flickered over my shoulder. We had exchanged our ritual cocktail chatter, and it was time for her to move on. "If you'll excuse me, pet, there's someone I really must say hello to. I'll see you at supper." She moved away.

I couldn't see Patrick anywhere, so I squeezed my way up to the bar for a refill, quite literally bumping into Charles in the process. Even in a dark blue suit he still looked convex. He had just ordered a rum and coke.

I spoke first. "You know why Cubans and Central Americans and Brazilians do all those energetic dances, don't you? It's because rum goes straight to the hips."

Charles raised his hands to make a cross of his forefingers. "Out damned spot! And that doesn't look like seltzer to me."

I assumed my best mock-Hungarian accent. " 'I never drink – wine.' But I suppose you're far too young to remember Bela Lugosi."

"Any relation to Bela Bartok?"

"I doubt it."

Charles dropped his voice. "I have a guilty secret. But to you I'll tell. Maybe we can find a quiet moment during dinner. I should warn you. As soon as Jennifer gets here there's going to be an Ave Maria hour. I overheard Lois on the phone. You know, toasts and speeches, the blushing bride and till death do us part."

"Mierda! All that prenuptial cant?"

"The works." He began to move away with the drink he had ordered for someone else. "Remember, we must confer."

Things were beginning to look up. I had not initially held out high hopes for this party, but I hadn't even finished my second drink and already I had a secret rendezvous. On top of which, Patrick was snooping around and trying to uncover the identity of my anonymous nemesis.

A flurry of activity in the front hall announced the arrival of Jennifer, flushed with the cold, beads of moisture dotting her hair. I thought she looked quite lovely, an impression some-what modified when she shed her coat and boots to reveal the déjà vu long black skirt topped by a white blouse with ruffles cascading down the front under a tailored plaid jacket. Perhaps I should have been relieved that her hair had not been bril-liantined into spikes, nor her fingernails painted green, but she did bring to mind a tourist brochure for the Edinburgh Festival. To watch Lois ripple out of the dining room to greet the guest of honour, her future daughter-in-law, was to see the two extre-mities of Europe come together as if in pantomime.

Temporarily overwhelmed by the number of strangers, most of them my age, Jennifer crossed to say hello to me, the reas-suring, familiar face.

"Uncle Geoffry."

"Niece and bride." We embraced briefly. "You look as though you came straight from the bonnie, bonnie banks of Loch Lomond. What's the tartan?"

"I don't know, I'm afraid. The jacket was a present from Mother."

"I see." It was a relief to know that Jennifer had not volun-tarily lifted the garment off the rack and asked the sales woman to wrap it up. And it bore Mildred's unmistakable stamp, good, sensible clothing untouched by fashion.

With a proprietary smile, Lois came to usurp Jennifer and lead her away to be introduced. I could almost have felt sorry for my niece. Her engagement party had turned out to be no more than a gathering of Lois Fullerton's friends, those people to whom Lois owed hospitality or whom she wanted to culti-vate. The few friends of Douglas's age group who had been invited clustered in a small, tight circle in a far corner of the library, same race, different tribe. Not surprisingly, Richard had joined the younger group. He glanced at me across the room and smiled a greeting. I hoped he did not regret having come all the way from New York for this party, in this weather. I would, if I were he.

All other engagement parties I have attended are soon infected by wedding fever, a highly contagious, ultimately harmless affliction that knocks out the antibodies of irony and cynicism and allows the virus of happily-ever-after to invade the system. The visible symptoms are a glazed, sappy expression and a marked tendency to ask any single man how much longer he is going to postpone getting married. This party, however, had been successfully inoculated. It seemed more like a gathering to celebrate a merger, one between two corporations rather than two people. Granted, the noise level had begun to rise, the guests sounding not unlike a *National Geographic* special on seabird colonies; but that could be blamed on alcohol, not merriment. An air of solemnity hung over the occasion. Men in suits clustered in knots, talking in that humourless way men do when dragged unwillingly to parties by determined wives.

The men had taken over the library, the wives by now having congregated in the drawing room. More animated than the men, they too clustered in groups, standing about in those careless attitudes calculated to show off their clothes. I studied them without seeming to, struck by the way they all looked more or less the same: lightened hair, good bones, crepey chins, gaunt figures, all walking endorsements for strict diet, fitness classes, facials, three weeks south in February, and the occasional lover.

Unless I am at a party heavily populated by people I would enjoy talking to at some point or other, I do my best to remain a moving target, never standing in any one place for long. That way I can more easily avoid those aggressively friendly people who strike up conversations, usually beginning with "so." So what brings you here tonight? So what do you do for a living? Once having placed a foot firmly in the door of your attention, this congenial soul will go on to give you an encapsulated version of his *curriculum vitae*.

There are other pitfalls at parties, for instance people who expect to be recognized even though thirty years have passed since you last spoke.

"Chadwick, Geoff Chadwick," said an unfamiliar voice, just as I was about to enter the library. I turned to confront a tall, bald, heavy-set man who looked as though his weekend hobby was a quart of bourbon smuggled in from Vermont. Beside him a short, elaborately coiffed woman teetered on Minnie Mouse pumps. He grabbed my hand as if it were a bargain at a rummage sale.

No matter how hard I pressed the buttons, I could retrieve nothing from my memory bank. I smiled a big empty smile and allowed the handshake to play itself out, buying time by the diversion of physical activity. But I was to be thrown no life preserver.

"Come on, Geoff, I can't have changed that much."

Only ex-tricks or people who have known me since college days call me Geoff. Having dismissed the first possibility, I jumped backwards about thirty years. Like a police illustrator who translates verbal descriptions into portraits, I mentally redrew the figure, subtracting weight, pruning chins, adding hair.

But the remaining portrait was too generalized to be of any help.

"Still not a clue, eh, guy?" He laughed, a shade too heartily.

I decided to follow Mother's advice and take the bear by the horns. "Are we going to play twenty questions, or are you going to 'fess up?" (Never apologize; never explain.)

"Victor, Victor McPherson. We were in first-year law school together at McGill. Then I transferred to Osgoode Hall. This is my wife, Carol."

"How do you do, Carol," I said, offering her my hand. She took it as though I had a wad of chewing gum stuck to my palm.

"Of course I remember you now," I continued, smiling disarmingly at Victor. "I find, though, with encroaching age, I have difficulty recalling people out of context. No doubt the condition will get worse before it gets better. Have you returned to Montreal to live, or did you come down for the party?"

As I spoke, glibly, to camouflage my memory lapse, I managed to summon up a dim recollection of a student, tall and graceful, whose soft brown hair fell in waves over his forehead and whose eyes had not retreated into pouches. Kind of humpy, if I remember correctly, though the ghost of remembered desire was soon exorcised by the florid presence now confronting me.

"Are you still in law?" he asked.

"Yes."

"I got out. Went into business for myself. Window coverings, shades, Venetian blinds. You may have seen our slogan: Our Love Is Blinds."

"Of course!" I lied. "Never realized it was you. Will you be coming to the wedding? I have to be there. The bride is my niece and I'm giving her away."

"Then you must be Mildred Carson's brother, Mr. Chadwick,"

said Carol. "Her husband was a cousin of mine, actually a second cousin, on my mother's side." She sounded like a woman born in Ontario trying very hard to pretend she wasn't.

I looked at her in frank astonishment. So what's with this Mr. Chadwick bullshit? The race is not to the swift, nor the battle to the strong. Nor dignity to the dumpy. "I think we might move on to a first-name basis, don't you?"

She smiled one of those tight little smiles, which made her mouth look like a contracting sphincter. But now that we were on a first-name basis, what could I possibly find to say to this woman who, in spite of black brocade and hair lacquered into complete submission, looked incomplete without a shopping bag?

I was saved by the bell. In truth, I had only half believed Charles when he spoke darkly of a ceremony with toasts and speeches. I thought we might raise a glass of champagne to the bride after dessert. But no. There stood Lois at the foot of the staircase energetically ringing the silver dinner bell she used to summon the maid. Whatever the reason for commanding our attention, her timing was perfect.

"I think we are being summoned," I observed, and ducked over to the bar for a quick, comforting refill, a sort of liquid security blanket.

The wives obeyed the summons at once. Whether from curiosity, a wish for diversion, or simple female solidarity, they made their way out of the drawing room and into the front hall to face the staircase. Showtime at the Palace. Strike up the band. Send in the clowns.

Not so with the men, who stood immobilized as though they had put down roots. Nor could I really blame them. Who would willingly distance himself from the bar and interrupt the dank pleasure of thumping the government in order to stand cheek to jowl listening to the bride-and-groom party line? But they had not reckoned with our Lois. Realizing that they had collectively ignored the bell, Lois marched into the library and rounded them up, a cowperson riding herd on a gaggle of maverick steers. Making noises not unlike those of penned cattle, the men shuffled, awkwardly and reluctantly, into the front hall to take up positions behind the women.

Meanwhile, the hired maids circulated with trays of champagne cocktails, a drink that brings to mind the songs of Cole Porter, the drawings of Peter Arno, the clothes of Chanel. As most of the guests were already holding a drink, and several a cigarette as well, the champagne cocktails posed difficulties. There were mutterings, stubbings, shifting of handbags as the staff, politely but firmly, waited for each guest to take a glass.

After escaping from the McPhersons, I had gone to stand by the door to the vestibule, as far from the stage as it was possible to get. The large entrance hall made a natural amphitheatre, with all eyes on Lois, who stood on the third step, flanked by Jennifer and Douglas standing on the first. From my vantage point Lois's gown became a robe. I am certain that Mrs. Siddons, Eleonora Duse, Minnie Maddern Fiske could not have commanded an audience with half the ease of our hostess. For a moment I was almost relieved that Mildred wasn't here. The evening would probably have ended with a body, that of the hostess, on the library floor.

A small commotion began in the vestibule behind me. I heard the front door shut, followed by the sound of people removing boots in muted whispers. The inside door opened on silent hinges, and I found myself once more looking into the obsidian eyes of the chauffeur, who had obviously ferried the latecomers to the party. For just an instant that well-remembered look of intense malevolence distorted his remarkable features, but this time I was ready. My eyes bored back into his. Anyone who spent as much of his salad days cruising as I did knows how to apply an eyelock.

We would probably still be standing there playing chicken had not the late-arriving couple crossed between us on tiptoe into the hall with those gestures of exaggerated self-effacement that are one hundred percent guaranteed to draw attention. I moved aside to make room. Their punishment for arriving late was to endure Lois's little ceremony without a drink, not even a champagne cocktail.

"Ladies and gentlemen, may I have your attention, please?" began Lois, her vowels as smooth as ball bearings. "It is now an open secret that this party is for Jennifer" – here Lois extended an arm, the hand following gracefully behind in a gesture bringing to mind the Swan Queen – "and Douglas." Out went the second hand to turn her arms into parentheses enclosing the hugely self-conscious young couple. "But I am merely the mother of the groom. Like it or not, this is a man's world. Consequently, it is not for me to make the congratulatory speech and offer the toast. For that I must turn to a male member of our wedding party. And I now call on Geoffry Chadwick, uncle of the bride, who will be giving her away. Geoffry, if you please?"

Had I been sporting a Florida tan I am certain I would have gone pale beneath it. Another cute little Lois manoeuvre. All my good humour, every vestige of single malt euphoria I had been cultivating, went up in smoke, leaving me almost shaking with anger. I may not be as bad as Sir William Van Horne, reputedly reduced to near silence at the prospect of making a speech, but I truly detest being the centre of attention. It is one thing to address a board of directors, the bare presentation of facts, quite another to improvise on a subject where the clichés are so solidly built in that one can stand on them.

But I was trapped. All heads had turned in my direction; an expectant hush had fallen; even a path had cleared itself to the foot of the staircase. Short of setting my tie on fire or bolting through the front door into the blizzard, I had nowhere to go but forward. As I reached the bottom step I tried to replicate the dirty look the chauffeur had just laid on me, but pale blue eyes convey irony, not dislike. Besides, Lois was far too busy being hostess of the year to see me as anything more than a spear carrier. We exchanged places, I mounting two steps, she descending graciously to ground level. With my natural height, I towered above the crowd. Simeon Stylites on top of his pillar. In a small gesture of defiance, I refused the proffered champagne cocktail and clung to my Scotch.

"Ladies and gentlemen," I began in tribute to my high school English teacher, who taught the class always to address the audience first, "you see before you a man who has all the inner calm of a heroin addict looking for his last needle in a haystack. Not only am I unaccustomed to public speaking, I am terrified of it. Furthermore, asking me to toast the engaged couple is not unlike asking Scrooge to trim the Christmas tree."

I could see a few mouths almost relax into smiles.

"The easy way out would be to turn off my mind and let the wedding clichés take over: the blushing bride, the handsome groom, hand in hand down the road of life, all that Ken and Barbie cant which is so egregious and phoney. Let me rather use

some of these clichés as a point of departure. It has been observed, more than once, that familiarity breeds contempt. My
experience has been that familiarity breeds, or used to. Nowadays, thanks to the pill, the stork arrives by invitation only. I
refer of course to the pill the bride takes, not the one she sleeps
with."

There was a faint, almost inaudible ripple of laughter. (We
bombed in New Haven.)

"Another, less elegant, cliché concerns the Niagara Falls
honeymoon and the bride finding the falls a disappointment by
association. But today the honeymoon comes early in the relationship, often on the first date. With that hurdle out of the
way the couple is at liberty to examine those values which will
make living together for a lifetime even remotely possible.

"The last cliché I would like to dispose of is the one that
says: Marriage is not a word, it's a sentence. That might have
been true in our parents' day, when married people simply resigned themselves to a third-rate situation and operated around
it. Not any longer. It is comforting to imagine relationships will
last. Most of the time they don't, and it is a sign of progress that
couples who separate no longer have to wear a scarlet 'D' for
divorce sewn to the front of their blouse or shirt. The time will
no doubt come when the father of the bride or the best man
will raise his glass and drink to this, the first of many happy
marriages."

Another faint murmur of laughter. (I'll have to do some
more work on this act before I take it to Vegas.)

"What I propose, therefore, is to toast Jennifer and Douglas, not as the happy couple, but as autonomous beings who
have chosen to live their lives together. May these lives be

stimulating, useful, and productive. Should they be fortunate enough to discover these directions, then happiness will come as a by-product."

"Ladies and gentlemen, to Jennifer and Douglas."

I drained my glass, kissed Jennifer lightly on the mouth, shook hands with Douglas, and elbowed my way back to the bar. All the time I was wondering how I could get my hands on some of Lois's hair or nail clippings for the voodoo dolly I intended to make the second I got home. I had a set of shish-kebab skewers, another failed present from Mildred, which for the first time I could put to good use.

XIV

Now that the happy couple had been toasted, Lois climbed two steps to announce that if anyone felt like eating there was food in the dining room. Many of us were not in the least interested in dinner, appetites having been blunted by an unobtrusive but steady stream of platters and trays handed around: tiny sandwiches, shorn of crusts, endless smoked salmon, cheese twists, and crudités to be dipped in low-cal mustard-flavoured sauce. Hot *hors d'oeuvres* arrived, almost too warm to pick up: pigs in blankets, mini pizzas, toy quiches, diminutive portions of deep fried chicken, and, yes, chicken livers wrapped in bacon. The breast pocket of my jacket bristled with discarded toothpicks.

Most men my age would rather drink than eat, especially when the liquor is free. The male half of the party returned to the library with the slow but inexorable flow of a large glacier. Those still young enough to eat from hunger rather than habit fell upon the foodstuffs, followed by several of the nondrinking wives, who picked at the sumptuous buffet as though it were tainted. I could see Lois was a tireless organizer. Not simply content to provide food and drink and then let the guests entertain themselves, she manipulated and reorganized, moving people around in groups, breaking into conversational circles to make introductions, insisting the diners try some of this, a little of that. She had turned 15 Mayfair Crescent into an adult daycare centre. If only someone would drag her downstairs and chain her to the furnace.

Charles appeared at my elbow. "Are you starving, or can we talk?"

"We can talk. What's on your mind?"

"Not here. Let's go upstairs."

"That's the best offer I've had today. It's the *only* offer I've had today. But I still think you've been reading too many spy stories."

I followed Charles up the staircase. From the landing I glanced around the ground floor. Patrick was still nowhere in sight. I continued on up, past the white bedroom where the ladies could freshen up. Beyond the master bedroom lay a guest bedroom furnished in Quebec colonial pine, Laura Ashley co-ordinates, and an infinity of flounces. Charles led the way into a small-*d* den, the kind of room that howls its understatement. A large Chippendale console with folding doors concealed a television set. Prints of racehorses, spaced with geometric precision, circled the walls. A pair of striped wing chairs with matching footstools faced the console, on either side of which two indirectly lit alcoves with glass shelves held Lois's collection of antique decoy ducks.

I sat. "I'm listening."

"Okay, but first let me say I thought your toast was cool. Not the usual happiness crap. You never mentioned the speech at lunch."

"I didn't know about the speech at lunch. I didn't know about it until Lois spoke my name. The toast was the quint-essence of spontaneity."

"The Sugar Plum Fairy strikes again?"

"She's more of a not-so-sweet nutcracker." Even as I spoke I knew I had betrayed a member of my generation to someone of a different age group. Them and Us. But I no longer cared. "Now what's this cloak and dagger meeting all about?"

"You won't think me a crank?"

"Yes, I think you're a crank. I've thought so from day one. I repeat, what's it all about?"

"Remember that talk we had in Toronto, about why I didn't think Douglas should get married?"

"Clearly."

"Well, I was right. I said it was only a matter of time before he learned the truth about himself."

"Has he?"

"Yes, but he doesn't know it yet."

I looked down at Charles, perched on the edge of the other wing chair, and screwed my face into an expression of scepticism.

"You've lost me. Your turn of phrase is decidedly Irish. Please clarify."

In spite of his intense seriousness, Charles broke into a giggle. "Sit down, Geoffry, I have something to tell you."

Unable to resist the magnetic pull of the soap opera situation, I put my hand to my throat. "I am sitting down – Charles."

"Okay. Douglas has been really turned on – probably for the first time in his life – by your nephew. As far as I can tell, the feeling is mutual."

"Charles, not only have you been reading too many espionage novels, you obviously watch too much daytime TV."

"Stop condescending to me, you prick! There, I stopped you. Sorry, Geoffry, I don't wish to be rude, but you were just doing another of your easy G. Chadwick putdowns. I have been living in the house with them. You haven't. Nor am I a total moron, even if I do have the colossal misfortune to be young. Use your own eyes. When I first met Richard I thought he was a real stick, the kind who watches TV only for the commercials. Now, have you ever seen him as animated as he was at lunch?"

"Come to think of it, no."

"In all the years I have known Douglas I have never seen him so turned on. I thought he was going to jump right out of his skin. All those asshole arguments they were having. And they carried on that way for the rest of the afternoon. They were still at it while Douglas shaved and Richard took a shower. They haven't made it in the sack yet, only because I happened to be in the picture. I watched the way Doug greeted Jennifer, like she was about to serve him a summons. Now, what are we going to do about it?"

"We are going to do nothing at all," I replied, looking sadly at the melting ice cubes at the bottom of my glass. The bar seemed light years away. "It's none of my business. In spite of your crack about age, I still consider you an adult, as are Douglas, Richard, and Jennifer. They will have to work things out for themselves. I am not about to go downstairs and make another toast to Douglas and Richard. What will we do with all those embossed napkins and matchbooks? Correct them with a ballpoint pen? Finally, I have to confess, I would feel very foolish walking down the aisle wearing a morning coat with Richard on my arm."

"You know something? For an intelligent man you can be an awful jerk."

"For an intelligent young man you can be an awful pain in the neck. What astonishes me is how deeply conservative you really are. You don't think Douglas should get married because he may be gay or at least bisexual. I can't begin to tell you how many marriages I have encountered where the husband has a wandering eye, and not for girls. Are you certain how Jennifer feels about the situation? You are presuming to make judgements on and for other people. And if you're not careful you're going to turn out just like Lois."

"Holy shit!"

Suddenly we were both laughing, my previous good humour entirely restored. I had to admit this engagement party was breaking new ground.

"Seriously, Charles, what can we do? Outfit Richard with a chastity belt? Threaten Douglas with the stocks? For my part, if any of them seeks me out I shall hear him out, or her as the case may be. If advice ought to be forthcoming I shall offer it, to the best of my ability. I suggest you try to be as good a friend to Douglas as you can. If what you say is true he's going to need one. I wouldn't want to be in his Guccis when Lois finds out. Now it's time for me to get a drink." I stood and went to the door.

"Geoffry?" I stopped. "Is the man you came with, the va-va-voom jacket – is he the competition?"

I looked directly at Charles. "No, he's not. When I told you there was no one, I was not being coy. It's time to get back to the party and turn on the charm."

I left the den and went downstairs, Charles following. Patrick stood at the bar, waiting for a drink. I joined him.

"Do you come and go in a giant bubble, like Glinda the Good Witch of the North? I haven't seen you since we arrived."

"Good. I hope no one else has." He spoke low. "I sneaked off to use the toilet and kept right on going. Got lost in the servants' quarters, as it were. The maid and the cook live in a wing behind the kitchen, but the chauffeur has a room and bath in the basement. I checked it out. Very monastic. Nothing at all to suggest he does anything more than drive the car."

We moved from the bar to stand close to a group of men arguing noisily, the volume of their conversation a sound-screen for our own.

"It makes sense," Patrick continued. "If you have someone coming in to do out your room, make the bed, change the towels, and so forth, you would leave nothing telling to be accidentally discovered."

"Did you check the garage?"

"Yes. Fortunately, the door leading in from the basement is unlocked. But again nothing. It figures, though. Anybody can have access to the garage – gardeners, garbage men, the household staff."

"What is it exactly that you hope to find? Scissors? Paste? A magazine with pages missing?"

"I'm not fully certain. Most likely drugs, more specifically cocaine. If there is any to be found, I suspect it will be a large amount."

The volume beside us continued to screen our conversation. "Patrick, I am reminded of an Edgar Allan Poe story in which a critically important letter was effectively concealed by altering its appearance and leaving it out in full sight. If I was the chauffeur and I wanted to hide a package, I would tuck it away somewhere in that vulgar limousine. Nobody has any real access to the vehicle but he. Passengers simply get in and out of the back seat. And whatever he might be concealing would be under constant scrutiny."

"We think alike. Only the car is in constant use tonight because of the weather. And even if the limo is in the garage, he will still be on call."

From the corner of my eye I could see Victor and Carol McPherson edging in my direction. "Let's hang loose and hope something will turn up. I must find the terl."

I ducked out of the library and around the staircase to the powder room, the one I had been prevented from using on my first visit to the house. How did I know, with absolute certainty, that the small room would be done in the foil wallpaper so beloved of decorators who favour sectional furniture? It was like taking a pee in a decompression chamber, but for those few precious seconds I was safe from Victor and Carol. I was glad to see someone else had used the guest soap, shaped like a rosebud, and had crumpled one of the carefully ironed towels. I washed my hands; I always do after shaking hands with a lot of people, even though I am quite willing to believe Lois Fullerton's guest list is relatively germ free.

I stepped out of the shiny loo and almost collided with Audrey Crawford, who claimed to be looking for me so I could escort her around the buffet table. I was not hungry, nor did I wish to dull the Glenlivet edge I had been working on since I arrived. Furthermore, it is difficult to be a moving target while holding a dinner plate, particularly one that would cost about two hundred and fifty bucks to replace if dropped.

Not surprisingly I lied. "I'd love to, Audrey, but Jennifer asked me to chow down with her. She wants to talk about something."

"Women of all ages at your feet," she replied haughtily.

"Oh, I hope not. Men who have women at their feet always

trip, sooner or later."

"Sure I can't change your mind?"

I knew perfectly well Audrey had worked the party, holding a series of five-to-eight minute conversations with everyone she knew, chats which began with "Darling, how wonderful to see you!" and ended with "Isn't that Priscilla (or Peter or Poppy) over there? I must go and say hello." Audrey Crawford was bored and wanted to go off in a corner and shaft the hostess.

"Jennifer is the guest of honour," I replied. "I must defer."

Audrey was peeved. "I suppose you're going to give her a shower?"

"As a matter of fact I am, a bathroom shower. Someone is bringing a bathtub, someone else a bidet. I'm giving her the shower, with adjustable nozzle. If you'll excuse me . . ." I began to back away, smiling my retreat, like royalty fading from a balcony, when I saw Jennifer coming down the stairs. Even making allowances for the fact that I was by now a little tight, I still thought she looked shell-shocked.

"Uncle Geoffry," she said quietly, "do you think I could have a word with you in private?"

Another last-minute reprieve!

"Certainly, but if you want to be private we had better go upstairs. You pay a price for being the star of the evening."

As if to underline my words, a woman bustled up to Jennifer, one of those kindly, motherly types men marry for security. She took Jennifer's hand, wished her well, and said how sorry she would be to miss the wedding but she had to be in Boston for her daughter's graduation. It was all well meant, but Jennifer failed to respond on any level beyond the purely automatic. It seemed odd.

I led the way upstairs, past the Snow White bedroom, past the terminal colonial guest room, into the *Field and Stream* den. The television set had been switched on, with the volume turned low. Probably someone had wanted to check the weather and get a report on the blizzard. Using the remote control, I switched it off.

"Would you like me to close the door?"

"Yes, please, Uncle Geoffry."

Shutting the door entailed moving one of the chairs. The latch failed to catch properly, but the position of the door would discourage casual entry. I sat in my customary wing chair and prepared to listen. For a moment I feared there might be tears, but I was spared. I am totally incapable of dealing with weeping women, of any age. My first reaction to a sobbing female is to push her head into a bucket of water, not a standard feature of the drawing rooms and restaurants where women usually cry at me. I fully realize women have been obliged to fight with whatever weapons they have at hand, but as a youth I was manipulated by tears once too often. Now the surest way to lose my attention is to permit that crystal tear to trickle down the alabaster cheek.

I was relieved to see Jennifer's eyes were dry. As I waited for her to begin, I noticed her toying with a long string of perfectly matched pearls, which I had not seen when she arrived. Perhaps they had been concealed by the ruffles on her blouse.

"That's an impressive string of pearls, Jennifer. Even from here they look as though a lot of cross oysters worked overtime."

"They're an engagement present. Mrs. Fullerton gave them to me on the stairs, after you finished your speech." She looked at the beads resting in the palm of her hand, then let them drop. "The gift was a bit premature. I mean – Douglas has just broken off the engagement."

My heart leaped up, even though I compressed my mouth into a straight line. "That's a big one, Jennifer. And I am naturally curious why and how."

"There's not much to tell. No sooner had you finished the toast to the happy couple than Douglas whispered he had to speak to me. We sneaked up to the top floor. To be honest, I was a bit reluctant. I mean, with the party going on downstairs . . ."

"You still thought it would be one in the eye for Lois."

She shrugged. "I guess you're right. But it turned out to be one in the eye for me."

"What did he say? He certainly has an impeccable sense of timing."

"I guess your speech really spooked him. It startled me. All of a sudden the engagement seemed so public, so official." She fell silent. "Anyhow, Douglas said he understood it was going to be difficult, but he didn't feel he was ready to settle down for good." She smiled, a wan smile but a smile nonetheless. "He asked me, did I really mind."

"Do you?"

"To be honest, Uncle Geoffry, I don't. That's the odd part. I suppose I should feel like the jilted woman. Isn't that the word I've read? But now that it's out in the open I feel nothing but relief. Stunned but relieved."

Jennifer could not have been more relieved than I. To think she would not be marrying that dipshit Douglas, with his secondhand opinions and ambivalent sexuality, not to mention that ten-miles-of-bad-road mother who came with the package. If Jennifer were out of this engagement, she was well out.

However, I knew young people were mercurial; they split up only to come together again like pond water creatures under a microscope. How many parents have bad-mouthed the discarded fiancé only to have egg on their faces when the couple reconciled and the wedding went ahead on schedule? It was advisable to proceed with caution.

"Did he give you a reason, other than he didn't feel ready to settle down?"

"No. Perhaps I should have asked him to be more specific. But all I could think of was that we'd come this far and how were we going to stop the machine. Mrs. Fullerton will have to be told. Mother" – Jennifer rolled her eyes – "will have to be told. That's going to be a treat."

"It's your life, Jennifer, not hers. Unless you and Douglas are both completely sold on the idea of marriage, you are far better advised to call it off. Don't allow yourselves to be pressured by family. What the neighbours may or may not think doesn't matter a damn. My opinion, for what it's worth, is that I'm delighted you are postponing the wedding, perhaps scrubbing it entirely. You both have some living to do before you settle into the slow lane."

"However." I paused for a sip of the drink I had been rationing so it would last me through the interview. "For the rest of the evening let's carry on as though it were business as usual. Let the engagement party run its course. Flaunt your pearls. Now is not the time to quell the enthusiasm. Go and find Douglas and tell him to behave as though you had not had your little talk. Tomorrow will be time enough for truth. Lois has put far too much time and thought and effort into this party to have it spoiled, even by her immaculate son."

I went to move my chair so I could open the door. To my surprise, Jennifer embraced me, wrapping her arms tightly around my neck. I responded in kind, holding her close and rocking her gently until she loosened her grip. It was perhaps the first time we had touched fondly rather than formally.

Jennifer went off in search of Douglas, and I followed her downstairs so I could touch base with Patrick. I caught sight of the jacket in the dining room.

"I'm grabbing a bite to eat," he confessed with a grin, "to keep my strength up. There's no chance of getting near that limo at the moment. Several of the guests are leaving because of the blizzard, and I overheard that all the cab companies have taken the phone off the hook. So the chauffeur is driving people home."

"In that case, relax and enjoy yourself. Take the rest of the night off, and I speak as your employer."

A mountain of shrimp having been reduced to a foothill, one of the maids carried in a freshly heaped platter. The size and quality of the buffet bordered on ostentation, protein at its least caloric and most expensive, set out around a low silver bowl where three lonesome gardenias floated in a vain attempt to suggest less is more. I looked at the tissue-thin slices of rare beef, the split lobsters carefully cleaned out and filled with lobster salad, the chafing dish fragrant with beef bourguignon, hesitated, almost weakened, then resolutely made my way back to the bar for at least one more dividend. There would still be food when I felt like eating; Lois did not stint. Best of all, she had avoided those old buffet standbys, slippery ham and tepid turkey. The easiest thing in the world to give up cold turkey is cold turkey.

By now the party was beginning to thin out. Since most of the guests were of sober age, they had begun to head home after eating. The storm continued to perform outside; one's own home seemed like a good place to be.

I pushed the subversive idea of leaving to the back of my mind. By now the bartender reached for my glass without speaking. A tall, handsome young man came to stand beside me.

"Geoffry, I haven't had a chance to talk to you this evening. I looked for you, but you keep disappearing."

"Well, Richard, here I am, large as life and twice as real." Struck by an idea, I turned to my nephew. "Let's have a talk right now. There's an upstairs den where we can be private."

I turned and led the way. I had been up the stairs so many times this evening I felt like a twenty-buck hooker. Without hesitating I headed into the den, where I had almost filed a claim. Moreover, I had the added security of a fresh drink, which prudence dictated I sip slowly. I had not deliberately set out this evening to tie one on, but it seemed to be happening nonetheless. I am not an obvious drunk. I do not lurch about and slur my speech like a fourth-rate comic miming a drunk on stage; my voice does not go up in volume; I do not interrupt constantly and bray with mirth at my own bad jokes. Outwardly I remain much the same.

But alcohol allows me to take risks, to leave the middle-of-the-road Geoffry Chadwick stuck in the middle of the road and veer off across the shoulder, under the barrier, across the ditch, and into the wild country beyond. When I was younger, liquor led to sexual escapades. Now that I am older, my *faux pas* tend to be social. Sometimes I ignore the party line at parties and speak the truth, if not the ultimate truth then reality as filtered through my consciousness. This tendency has greatly reduced the number of invitations I now receive, no great loss I am the first to admit, as most of the time I am invited in my capacity as single man, not because of my winning ways. Perhaps one of the surest signs of middle age is to realize you are far less interested in tailoring yourself to other people's expectations than in trying to live up to those you have set for yourself.

I sat in one of the wing chairs; Richard took the other, but only after he had shed the jacket of the dark suit, worn stiffly for the occasion.

"I am not going to ask you about how things are going at Julliard. I got the impression over lunch that work is progressing well. I am curious to know what you think of Douglas. After all, he is slated to become your brother-in-law, and as such a member of the family. As you no doubt know, I am to give Jennifer away, which involves me in the wedding, more deeply perhaps than I would have wished."

Richard hesitated. "I like him fine, just fine. I only wonder if he is the right man for Jennifer."

"What makes you say that?" I made the question sound as neutral as I possibly could. "He is socially acceptable, physically very presentable, and he can read and write and do sums."

My nephew moved in his chair, less of a shrug than a squirm. "He's a bit young, for one thing. He's younger than I am, and I certainly don't feel ready to settle down."

In spite of the liquor I was treading softly. "Understandably, but your situation is not the same as his."

"Less so than you might think, Geoffry." (I had in the past asked Richard to drop the "Uncle" but to use my full name.) "Nowadays gays are far more nesty than they used to be.

There's a lot more refinishing furniture and making bathroom curtains than going out to bars. I am reluctant to settle down because I don't know where my life is going at the moment."

"What you say makes sense, but Douglas strikes me as a fairly conservative young man. And I seriously doubt Jennifer will dye her hair magenta and ride around on a motorcycle. My principal reservation is that they are perhaps a bit inexperienced to embark on marriage, although for that unexciting institution perhaps inexperience can be an asset. Anyhow, he seems like a pleasant young man."

"Geoffry – perhaps I shouldn't be telling you this, but I think they plan to break off the engagement."

For just an instant I thought of feigning astonishment, but the Scotch stepped in. "So you know. Good. Jennifer just told me, so you and I can stop shadowboxing. What I would like to know is why really they are breaking it off."

"You mean to say you don't already know?"

"If I already knew I wouldn't be asking," I fibbed. "When Jennifer spoke to me she was both brief and vague."

"You don't know that Douglas is gay?"

"Why should I? And is he? I've met the young man twice before this evening. He does not swing from vine to vine, but then again vines in this community grow up the sides of houses. Not to be macho does not necessarily mean gay."

As I had sneakily anticipated, Richard could not resist the temptation to one-up his "sophisticated" uncle. "Perhaps things have changed a bit since you were my age, Geoffry. People send out different signals than they once did." (I quelled the impulse to correct his usage.) "Take my word for it, Douglas is gay."

"And how have you found out with such dispatch?" I

inquired, springing the trap I had baited with my apparent naiveté. "You were invited up for the engagement party to meet your sister's fiancé, not to bring him out of the closet. Now before you waste both our time with indignant denials, let me assure you my spies are everywhere. I know everything. I had Douglas pegged even before I met him. I wanted to find out how much you knew. And I have. My next question is why you have been fooling around with your sister's fiancé?"

Anger brought colour to Richard's normally pale skin. "I have not been fooling around, in spite of what that lard-arse Charles may have told you."

"By 'fooling around' I do not mean you have been bumping your uglies. But you have been indiscreet, or candid, or direct, or honest, or whatever the trendy buzzword is for coming on to someone. In my time – remember, I span the plasticine, the epicene, and the obscene geological ages – we called it making a pass. But it amounts to the same thing: letting the other party know you are both knowing and willing. Now, let me ask you one more question: When did you learn the engagement was to be broken off?"

Again I could see Richard hesitate, obviously aware that to answer the question honestly would be incriminating.

"Richard," I said, nailing him with a look, "we have been honest with one another so far, not only tonight but previously. Please do not tart up the truth to put yourself in a better light. When did Douglas tell you he planned to break off the engagement?"

"This afternoon, after we got in from lunch."

"I see. He told Jennifer only minutes after I had toasted the engaged couple. I give him D minus for tact. It is, to say the least, a bit humiliating to be told at your engagement party that the engagement is off. And that is why we are having this little talk. It is one thing to learn your fiancé does not want to go through with the wedding. It is another to discover the other woman is her own brother. Under the circs, were I Jennifer, and were I to learn what I know now, I would come after you with a meat cleaver and go happily to prison. Douglas is as he is, just like you and me. The leopard and his spots, et cetera, et cetera. I would not expect rational and civilized behaviour from the leopard. But I expect – more than expect, I demand it of you."

I raised my hand. "Don't interrupt. I'm on a roll. Jennifer's ego has just been dealt a major blow. She can cope with it, I have no doubt. But she must never learn that you were the real reason behind the rupture."

"But don't you see? I'm not."

"Okay, let me rephrase that. You were not the cause but the catalyst. Is that better? You did not lead Douglas down the garden path; you just stood there under the lilac bush with your butterfly net until he went past. If you and Douglas have fallen for one another, or been turned on, or whatever happens to young people today, it has happened. I offer neither blame nor praise. *Le coeur a ses raisons que la raison ne connaît pas.* Now listen carefully to what I am going to say. If you and Douglas are going to become lovers, you will wait until the broken engagement has shaken down. A great many other people will be affected: Lois Fullerton, your mother, your grandmother, who has reached the age when members of the family outnumber her friends. At least Mildred won't be able to gripe too much. She will still have Douglas for a son-in-law, of sorts."

My remark managed to raise a weak smile.

"I suppose what I am trying to say in a roundabout manner is that if you and Douglas have the hots for one another, that is your business. But you will have to postpone the magic moment. A stiff prick has no conscience. Do not allow crotch fog to obscure your judgement and drive you to spend five minutes doing something you may regret for a long time to come."

I paused for a swallow of my drink.

"And now, Richard, lest you think I am being totally biblical and boring, let me say, in strict confidence naturally, that I am pleased this wedding is being postponed. Douglas's orientation aside, Jennifer is too young in too many ways for marriage. One day I hope she will find Mr. Almost-All-Right. By then she will understand the compromises involved. As for you yourself, if you are thinking of an ongoing relationship, I could think of many young men less desirable than Douglas. You have much in common, things that will still matter after sex has cooled down: background, intelligence, an awareness of pursuits outside of sex, politics, sports, and money. Be on guard. Don't forget how expediently he dumped Jennifer. Don't be astonished if he unloads you one day. Perhaps he won't. In any case, I happen to think he is getting the better deal, but I confess to prejudice."

Richard smiled, this time with more conviction.

"I think we understand one another," I said, wrapping things up. "I know this is strange advice for a cold and stormy night, but cool it."

"Okay, Geoffry, if you say so."

"I say so. Will I see you again before you return to New York?"

"Probably not. I'm taking the noon bus."

"Possibly just as well. Absence may make the heart grow

fonder; it also removes temptation from the immediate path. I have to get down to New York sometime in April. I'll call you and we'll have dinner, maybe see a show."

I stood and offered my hand. It was not a handshake of goodbye, but of two men sealing an agreement. The most masculine of gestures to seal a most un-macho bargain, but who's counting?

"And now perhaps I'll go downstairs and have something to eat." I still wasn't properly hungry, but the common sense I had been dispensing so liberally dictated I sober up, at least partially. The evening was still not over.

Poor old Charles, how he would smart to be called a lard-arse. A Crisco arse? Not much of an improvement. Those full, round bottoms are a tailor's terror when it comes to making trousers hang properly, but they are very comfortable in bed.

XV

As I entered the dining room I was reminded once again how much I dislike buffet feeding. I dislike it in inverse proportion to the way I like hot *hors d'oeuvres*, those delicious bite-sized portions brought to where you are standing and eaten in one mouthful, without fuss or fanfare. Another reason I try to avoid buffet tables, aside from the cafeteria overtones, is that by the time I get myself organized to eat, the food has been pretty thoroughly picked over. I end up with the ends: the heel of the ham, sticky with glaze and bristling with cloves; the bottom of the sliced tomato, one half covered in skin and impossible to cut with a fork. Like the poor children in cautionary tales, I have to make do with a crust of bread. The green salads have wilted from boredom, and what remains of the kidney bean salad lies submerged in its own dressing. Only the staunch potato salad never runs out, mealy, dense, viscous with mayonnaise from a jar.

It was therefore with a mixture of pleasure and admiration that I found the table as fresh and inviting as when the hostess had first announced guests could eat. Even though Lois Fullerton stood second on my shit list (number one being my mystery caller), I had to admit that she knew how to pull off a buffet. The secret lies in hard work, an unlimited budget, and all the kitchen help one can get.

I picked absently at a little roast beef, some shrimp, a few

slices of avocado. I decided against undertaking one of the half
lobsters. They have to be God's homeliest creation, edging out
even the iguana and the alligator as creatures you would never
want for a pet.

Something about holding a plate of food compels me to sit
down. The dining-room chairs had been pulled away from the
table and placed against the walls. I sat, resting the plate on
knees pressed together like those of a convent-school girl on her
first date. By sitting I also managed to avoid being drawn into
a small group that had formed itself around a French couple,
late arrivals. They were from Paris, and never let you forget the
fact for a second. In Westmount they are what passes for cultivated people, largely self-proclaimed, although their *soi-disant*
sophistication seems to rest on a taste for Cartesian tragedy,
Impressionist painting, Spanish wines, Corsica in the summer,
and lesbian movies.

My chair afforded a view of the hall, and I could see Lois
coming down the stairs. Gone was her habitual air of assurance;
she did not command the staircase. Her descent was less regal
than precipitous, and for a moment I feared she might trip over
her hem. Spotting me through the archway, she marched up
and spoke without preamble.

"Geoffry, I must speak to you at once, upstairs. Bring your
plate with you. Take some more if you like. What are you drinking? I'll get it for you."

"Scotch," I mumbled around a mouthful of beef, ever mind-
ful of the childhood injunction never to talk with my mouth
full. ("Full of what?" I had once asked, to be met with stony,
disapproving silence.)

Lois turned on her heel and strode to the bar. In seconds

she had returned to stand over my chair. "If you'd be good enough to follow me. What we have to discuss is private."

She headed towards the stairs. For a handful of rebellious seconds I thought of staying put and finishing my food in peace and the hell with her. But if and when I had a confrontation with Lois Fullerton it would be over an issue more compelling than a plate of cold cuts. I stood, forked a couple of slices of beef onto my plate, spooned up some more shrimp, reached for a salad roll, and followed her up the stairs.

She was already past the landing. So conditioned was I by now that I walked right past the bedroom towards the den.

"Geoffry? In here!" she called, and for the second time I entered the white bedroom.

She had already placed a white occasional table adjacent to one of the white brocade armchairs and set my drink on a white ashtray so as not to leave a ring. By the time I sat, put down my plate, pulled up my trouser legs, and spread the double damask dinner napkin in my lap, Lois had shut the bedroom door and crossed to perch rather than sit on the edge of the matching armchair.

I took a long swallow of the extra-strong whisky Lois had carried upstairs. It tasted like carefully aged nitroglycerine. At the same time I was trying to decide whether I felt like someone on a promotional tour, with interviews back to back, or like a spectator at the college production of a Greek tragedy, where messengers come on stage and tell about the juicy disasters that have just taken place offstage right.

"Geoffry," began Lois urgently, "we have a problem." By strategic use of a simple pronoun she had already involved me in whatever it was.

"As long as *we* are implicated, perhaps you had better tell me what it is."

Her hands gripped one another as they rested on knees clamped together. No longer the siren on the rock, she seemed more like Hecuba dealing with the cleaning staff on the morning after the fall of Troy.

"I've just had a talk with Douglas. He was in tears."

"Big boys don't cry."

She ignored the comment. "He told me that Jennifer has just broken off the engagement."

"He's a goddamned liar!" As I spoke I moved my dinner plate from lap to table and dropped the napkin onto the carpet, clearing the decks for action.

"He is my son." Lois tried to appear glacial, but agitation made her sound merely short of breath.

"I know. And that is the problem you said *we* had a moment ago. Only it's your problem, not mine. I repeat: he's a goddamned liar and a manipulative little sonofabitch to boot, no disrespect intended."

The blast of adrenaline that first flush of anger had sent galloping through my veins made me realize I was well and truly drunk. Although I was still in control of the physical plant, my social censors had just been bound, gagged, and locked in a closet.

"How dare you speak of my son that way! You scarcely even know him."

"True, but I know a couple of things about him you don't — or else refuse to acknowledge. To begin with, if he uses the facts of any given situation to serve his own ends, I think I know where he learned how. That was really cute, the way you blackmailed me into making a speech before a roomful of people, without even a hint of a warning."

"You are standing in as father of the bride. I took for granted you knew you would be expected to make the toast."

"You take a great deal for granted. But that's water over the God Damn. What I am more interested in at the moment is why Douglas terminated the engagement, unilaterally I happen to know, and why it is better for everyone that he did – most of all for Jennifer."

"I'm sure I don't know what you are talking about."

"Don't you, now. Well, dearie, let me spell it out. Douglas told Jennifer the engagement is off. I repeat: Douglas broke off the engagement because he is gay, or what people of our age used to call queer, light on his feet, a pansy. He wants to bed boys, not girls! And – much as I realize you love stage clichés – please do not tell me I have taken leave of my senses."

Lois did her imitation of Queen Victoria in middle age. "And how, may I ask, do you presume to say you know?"

"How the hell do you think I know? Why do you suppose your carefully staged seduction scenarios ended in a draw? Or – again as people of our generation used to say – it takes one to know one."

Under her foundation Lois's face flushed. "You have the nerve to sit there and accuse my son of being homosexual and claim to know because you are one too?"

"You've got it. Lois, I don't know how much you have kept abreast of the women's movement, but it's time you raised your consciousness above the waist. Still, I am convinced you know, or suspect, far more than you are prepared to admit, even to yourself. Otherwise, why are you trying so hard to hustle Douglas into this marriage? Believe me, it won't change a thing. It will only make two young people unhappy. For Douglas I don't much care. That little shit could use a good dose of misery; it might turn him into a human being. But I care very much about Jennifer. And I will not allow her to be sacrificed on the altar of your absurd, lower-middle-class notion of respectability."

"I will overlook the insult, Geoffry. Nor am I going to rush to Douglas's defence, even if you do grossly underestimate him. Once he is married he will make an excellent husband. I could almost feel sorry for Jennifer because she will never know. A man is not automatically gay because he is sensitive. Anyhow, perhaps Jennifer will come to her senses and realize she has made a foolish mistake."

"You still refuse to believe he broke off the engagement, just as you persist in believing he will marry one day. Maybe he will, but he shouldn't. Being exposed to heterosexuality will not make a homosexual do an about face. Marriage will not inoculate him from, or build up antibodies against, other men. One of the sillier heterosexual myths is that all a homosexual needs is one good lay from a member of the opposite sex and, like a vampire, he will turn into a slavering straight."

"You seem quite the authority," Lois spoke down her nose. Her attempt at hauteur went flat. She needed to be taller, thinner, with more prominent cheekbones for that kind of grandeur.

"I am. And I also know the root of Douglas's problem. He has not yet learned to be honest with himself, so how can he be honest with other people? And for that he owes no small debt to you."

Lois stood abruptly. "I'm sorry I'm not a man. I'd show you a thing or two."

"I'm sure you would. And no one is sorrier that you are not a man than I. But we are getting off the subject. Jennifer did not axe the engagement; Douglas did. Jennifer told me only a few minutes ago. My nephew, the ex-head usher, also told me that Douglas told him this afternoon that he intended to call the whole thing off. Not surprising when you consider Douglas has been putting the make on Richard, or trying to, ever since Richard got off the bus." I too was slanting my facts, but I wanted to stick it to her.

"You really are vile."

"I don't have what is known as a way with children, if that's what you mean. In fact, I'm just truthful, with perhaps more vinegar than oil. Next time you are putting on your eyeliner, pause for a moment, study your reflection in the mirror, and ask yourself, 'Where did I go wrong? Why did I fail as a mother?' Someone ought to take that young man into an alley and slap him bowlegged."

Lois laughed a brittle stage laugh. "Do I perhaps hear the voice of wounded vanity? Did you by any chance make a pass at Douglas yourself, only to be rejected because he doesn't like old fairies?"

"Not fairy, Lois, homosexual. If I were a fairy you wouldn't have tried so hard to put the make on me. But you are barking up the wrong shins. When the mother is breathing hard down my neck, I do have the taste to keep my hands off the son."

Lois started towards my chair. I could tell she intended to slap my face. I stood and raised my arm in front of me. Her hand hit the side of it. With my other hand I pushed hard against her shoulder. She executed an involuntary buck and wing across the white carpet to land with a soft plop on the bed."

"What I fail to understand, Lois, is why you would waste time on a burnt-out case like me when you are screwing the chauffeur, twenty years younger and finger-lickin' good."

"You sonofabitch!" Lois struggled to her feet, like someone treading water.

"Just remember, Lois my sweet, every cloud has a silver lining, tarnished at times, but silver none the less. With a gay son you won't have any telltale grandchildren to pinpoint your age. You can go on being forty-five for the next twenty years."

A knock sounded at the door. Lois stamped across the carpet and wrenched it open.

"Some guests are leavin'," sang the maid. "They want to say goodnight."

"To be continued," I said as Lois patted herself into repair. "Don't forget to smile."

"Bastard!" she hissed as she stalked out.

I stood, irresolute, as Lois followed the maid downstairs. An interrupted fight is more frustrating than an interrupted fuck, mainly, I suppose, because good fights are scarcer than good fucks. First-rate fights and fucks start slow, build gradually to a screaming climax, then taper off into detumescence or détente. Best of all is a no-holds-barred fight followed by an all-stops-out fuck, but I doubted that was to be the scenario this evening. Anyway, hyperventilation is better than no breath at all.

Faute de mieux, I sat in the white chair and resumed eating. After the tense exhilaration of truth seasoned with malice, I could no longer face polite party chatter. At least alone I could continue the fight in my head, reviewing all the things I didn't have time to say and luxuriating in regret for my *esprit d'escalier*.

My reverie of aggression was to be short-lived. Patrick

ducked into the room.

"I've been looking all over for you. Can you give me a hand?"

"Two, if necessary."

"The street is being ploughed and the limo is in the garage. The chauffeur's in the kitchen having something to eat. Could you cover me while I sneak into the garage, stall him if necessary?"

"As the French would say, I'll do my possible. But really, Patrick, I think you should be paying me."

He smiled a quick smile. "Remember, tonight is on the house."

We made our way unobserved to the basement. At the far end of the large space stood a glossy furnace, which looked as though it had just arrived, gift-wrapped, from Birks. On the wall between us and the furnace, a door covered in sheet metal led into the garage. Patrick slipped through the door, leaving me on guard.

The basement walls had been refinished in knotty pine, that psychedelic panelling which brought to mind the forties, when self-reliant homeowners turned basement areas into recreational rooms. How many teenaged evenings did I spend in rec rooms, complete with ping-pong tables, automatic record players that dropped records down a spindle with a clank, camp cots covered in burlap with bolsters along the back to simulate couches, and Air France travel posters taped to the walls?

Feet started down the stairs. I hoped they belonged to one of the maids, or the cook, but well-pressed trousers and shiny oxfords announced the presence of a man. Could it possibly be one of the bartenders looking for the basement bathroom he had no doubt been instructed to use? But the bottom of the jacket matched the trousers, and the bartenders were wearing maroon pea jackets.

Even though technically drunk, I had a sudden flash of apprehension, a realization that Patrick and I might be in grave danger. Were the supposed chauffeur truly involved in narcotics, large amounts as Patrick suspected, then he wouldn't fool around. He would no doubt be armed, with a knife, if not a gun. And there was no question in my mind that he would not hesitate to use either.

It also occurred to me that in our haste to scurry down to the basement, the frolicking mice taking advantage of the cat's absence, we had not mapped out what precisely I was to do should our adversary suddenly loom. It was one of those situations that is infinitely more amusing in the movies than in real life, like a man in a chicken suit having to pee.

The shoes continued resolutely down the stairs, finally bringing the entire man into view. Obviously unprepared to find me standing alone in the basement, the chauffeur paused at the foot of the stairwell. But not for nothing had I read all those fatuous self-help articles on "How to Succeed in Business," each of which tells you to grab the initiative on first meeting a prospective client. I seized on that brief moment of hesitation and walked up to him. "I've been waiting for you."

He studied me suspiciously. "Would you like me to drive you home, sir?" Even in that straightforward question I caught an echo of the voice on the telephone.

"No, at least not yet." I did not feel in the least amused, but I still managed to smile. "I was wondering if the two of us could get together some time, perhaps on your day off."

He stared at me blankly as he tried to fathom my meaning.

"Excuse me?"

"Come on now, Melvin. You know what I mean. Every time we meet we look at one another. Just the way we looked at each other upstairs, earlier this evening. Are you trying to tell me you don't know what that kind of look means?"

I could see understanding beginning to dawn, comprehension blocked by disbelief.

"Do I have to spell it out?" I continued, lowering my voice in a strangulated attempt to make it sexy. I had manoeuvered myself to face the furnace, thereby obliging the chauffeur to stand with his back to the door of the garage. "You're a good-looking guy, young, strong. I like Latin types. I'll bet you're dynamite in bed."

Even as I spoke I could see the garage door open a crack. Patrick pointed at the furnace. Whatever that crazed detective was up to, I had to keep the chauffeur's attention fixed on me. I reached out and squeezed his upper arm. Solid muscle, should he decide to take a swing. Physical contact has always been an attention grabber; to be touched by someone you are trying to avoid compels attention.

"Look," I began, "I'm not an unreasonable man." I could see Patrick slip through the door, push it to, and move on silent feet to crouch behind the furnace. If my heart was not in my mouth it was only because my well-tied tongue did not leave it room. "I realize you are from the Caribbean." Tension made me stumble over the *b*'s, but I carried on. "You're probably sending money home each month to your family. I'm quite prepared to pay for a service, provided the service is satisfactory." I half closed my eyes and took a short step forward. Involuntarily, the chauffeur took a corresponding step backwards.

"So you see," I continued, "you don't have to warn me away from Mrs. Fullerton. It's not her I'm interested in, but you. Now, how about driving me home and coming up to my apartment for a while." I was doing a bad imitation of Mae West. "You can say you got stuck in a snowbank. You might even let me have the first one on the house, in exchange for the tire you ruined. Come on now, what do you say?"

I moved in close. At the same time I partially opened my mouth and ran my tongue suggestively over my dry-from-nervousness lips. This time there could be no mistake; my message came through loud and clear. I watched the man draw in on himself, as though he were being sprayed with a noxious chemical, every fibre of his machismo vibrating with outrage. For just a second I thought he might strike me. Then again, I was only a drunken guest coming on to the help.

"Maricòn!" he muttered. I knew it was not a compliment.

"Think it over," I said, still doing my bargain-basement Mae West. "You know where to find me if you change your mind. I'll make it worth your while – any way you say."

I was certain he wanted to spit in my face. Instead he moved sideways out of my odious aura and ducked into the garage. At once Patrick came around the furnace and made for the stairs, which he took two at a time. I followed, one at a time. The coast lay clear through the butler's pantry.

"Back to the bedroom," he whispered and led the way up the back staircase to the second floor, where we ducked into Lois's bedroom.

"Close the door."

I did as ordered. From under his jacket Patrick took a parcel the size of a loaf of bread and wrapped in brown paper.

Carefully he peeled away the wrapper to discover a plastic bag that contained a white, powdery substance.

"Looks just like icing sugar, doesn't it?" he said.

"How should I know? I never bake. Is it what I think it is?"

"What else? If it were cornstarch, why would it be hidden with the spare tire? There must be two kilos here." Patrick glanced around the room, then slid the package under the bed. "Do you suppose there's a phone up here?"

"If you can find the thing. It's probably white."

A telltale cord led us to the night table, whose bottom drawer pulled out to reveal a white princess phone.

"This is a matter for the police," said Patrick as he dialled.

I did not have a chance to overhear the conversation. His terse, urgent message was interrupted by Lois barging through the door.

"Don't bother to knock," I said, crossing to pick up the drink I had abandoned. By now the ice had melted, diluting the Scotch.

"I believe this is my bedroom," she replied, surprised to see Patrick.

He put down the receiver. "Please close the door, Lois. And listen carefully to what I have to say. Are you aware that your chauffeur is dealing drugs?"

Lois had obviously intended to pick up where she and I had left off, and the question stopped her short. "What do you mean, dealing drugs? He's a Cuban refugee who drives my car."

"Lois," I began, "this is no time for bullshit. Not to mince words, you had better cover your ass. Patrick is a private investigator whom I hired because I had reason to believe I was being threatened by your chauffeur. He has a record. Patrick has just found a package hidden in your limousine, which we suspect is cocaine. The police are on the way. We have pretty good evidence that Melvin is, or has been, your lover. For your own sake, if you know anything, anything at all, now is the time to tell us."

"Geoffry's right," added Patrick. "You could be in trouble, or at least in the papers, which often amounts to the same thing."

Lois Fullerton was a wilful woman, but not a stupid one. "I may have been indiscreet, once or twice, a woman alone. I'm sure you understand." She made the quintessentially feminine gesture of touching her hair. "But I know nothing whatsoever about any drug dealings."

Lawyers and investigators develop a gut instinct for the truth. I believed Lois, and I could see Patrick did too.

"Your driver has been using this job as cover," he explained. "It was perfect. He had a false identity and a car at his legitimate disposal. He must have thought that if you took up with Geoffry you would discard him, perhaps dismiss him, just at a time when he couldn't afford to give up this job, not with something big just about to happen. He threatened Geoffry, phone calls, notes, a slashed tire."

"Why did you never mention it to me?" demanded Lois.

"I couldn't be certain it was he. That's why I hired Patrick. Then when we learned what he was probably up to, we didn't want to frighten him off."

Further explanations were interrupted by the bedroom door opening quickly. The chauffeur stepped neatly inside and shut the door behind him."

"All right, junior detectives, game's over. Hand me the package, and now. I'm with the RCMP," he said, reaching into his inside jacket pocket. He pulled out a wallet and flashed a badge.

"Better check it out, Patrick," I suggested. "It could be from a novelty shop.

"It's the real thing," said the chauffeur quietly. In spite of his colloquial English, he still sounded as though his first language was Spanish. "And if the badge won't convince you, perhaps this will."

From a side pocket he produced a small but very business-like pistol. "Now, I don't have time to argue. Give me the package."

"What package?" replied Patrick, bluffing for time. "I don't know what you're talking about."

"The one you took while Mr. Chadwick headed me off. Hand it over. Now!"

As Patrick had uncovered the cocaine, I figured it was his party. Up to this moment I was prepared to let him call the shots, but I am allergic to bullets.

"Patrick," I said quietly.

"You bastard!" Lois spoke low, but with venom. Ignoring the pistol, she marched up to her former lover and slapped him hard across the face. I guess it was the slap originally intended for me. Talk about more guts than brains.

The butterflies in my stomach were the size of pterodactyls.

Placing his large hand on a bust that was hard to miss, the chauffeur gave Lois a sharp, hard push. She took a few steps backwards, like someone executing a tricky dance routine, and landed spreadeagled on the bed one more time. She was taking more pratfalls than a second banana.

It takes more than a tumble on her back to down a tough broad like Lois Fullerton. She crawled to the end of the bed and levered herself upright, quite obviously unharmed, even though her chignons had taken a beating.

"For the last time – the package."

My immense relief at seeing Patrick reach down and slide the incriminating parcel from under the white satin peplum could not be expressed. I didn't give a tinker's fart about that damn cocaine, but I cared a good deal about Patrick's not being shot, not to mention what bloodstains would do to that white carpet.

Moving slowly, Patrick crossed the room to relinquish the package. A knock sounded at the door. Lois went quickly over and pulled it open. A worried maid stood in the hallway. "Excuse me, Ma'am, but some officers are here. Shall I show them to the buffet?"

A burly man in a brown tweed suit shouldered his way past the maid, followed by a second man who lingered in the doorway.

"Ronalds, ma'am, RCMP," he announced, proffering a badge that looked just like the one the chauffeur carried. "Sanchez!" he almost shouted at the chauffeur. "Where the hell have you been!"

"Why don't you ask these two boy scouts?"

"We caught him in possession of cocaine," said Patrick. "That's it, in the parcel."

"Cocaine we provided so he could nail our local dealer."

"You mean he really is one of your agents?"

"Go to the head of the class," barked Ronalds. "And he's supposed to be in the east end of the city in ten minutes. He may still be able to make it. Ma'am, we'll have to take your car. Don't worry; if there's any damage we'll pay. He must show up in his uniform driving the limousine. Now let's move it. We have no time to lose. Sanchez, as fast as you can. Let's hope they think you've been delayed by the storm. I'll explain later, ma'am."

The two officers took off, followed by the chauffeur carrying the troublesome package. I went to the window and opened the curtain to see a plain dark car idling in the street. Patrick and Lois came to stand beside me. In short order the limousine pulled out of the garage and headed down the crescent, the second car following.

"Well and well and well," I said, letting the curtain fall closed, "that's a tough act to follow. What do you have planned now, Lois? A magician, a folk singer, someone who blows up balloons and twists them into animals?"

A woman who obviously had her priorities in order, Lois crossed to her dressing table and began to repair her hair. "Why don't you two gentlemen wait for me downstairs."

Dismissed out of hand, we left the bedroom and walked to the stairs. On the landing I raised my arm, a signal to stop. "Patrick, what about all the stuff you uncovered about Manuel Alvarez, the supposed flight to Cuba, his being dumped in the U.S., the Miami Beach miniseries?"

"I probably found out what I was supposed to have found out, or what anyone investigating the man would have uncovered. He has been very carefully stage managed."

"You were right; something big was going down. Only the bad guy turned out to be one of the good guys in disguise. And in our zeal we almost blew the whole operation."

"Maybe we did, although nobody expected the blizzard: blocked streets, cars left in garages, the driver working overtime."

"I suppose he was just leaving to conclude the deal when we waylaid him in the basement."

"The only thing missing was a laugh track."

I could not repress a smile. "Who could have anticipated that a grand single gentleman would take arms against a sea of troubles and engage a gung-ho private eye who would upset the apple cart? Block that metaphor."

Patrick grinned. "I guess there's a bit of egg on everyone's face."

"Which a Scotch and water will help to dissolve. I must say, I'm very relieved you didn't get shot."

Patrick dropped his hand lightly onto my shoulder. Ordinarily I shrink from being touched, but this time around I didn't mind in the least. The two of us went downstairs to the library.

By now most of the guests had gone home. Only one bartender remained on duty. He reached for the whisky bottle as I came through the door. Glancing into the hallway, I saw Jennifer with her coat on, apparently searching for someone.

"You're on your way?"

"There you are, Uncle Geoffry. I was just looking for you. Richard's going to take me home. He's gone upstairs to collect his things. He says he can sleep on the lounge chair in the TV room at Gran's, and leave for the bus after breakfast and a visit with her."

"Good. Are you aware that Douglas spilled the beans to his mum?"

"Yes. I didn't catch him in time. He believes in being honest. But that kind of honesty is a form of cowardice, lacking the courage to keep a confidence."

"You're no dummy, Jennifer. I am delighted things have

worked out this way. Another plus is that you won't have to deal with those monogrammed napkin rings. And when the right man comes along – which I hope he does at least half a dozen times – I'll be glad to walk you down the aisle. Now, I'll be in Toronto next month. Let's have dinner out, sans Mildred."

"I'd like that." She reached for my hand. "Here comes Richard."

"Do you suppose we should find Mrs. Fullerton?" he asked.

"I'd just as soon not," replied Jennifer. "What am I supposed to say? 'Thank you for the lovely engagement party?' By the way." She reached up and lifted the string of pearls from around her neck. "Would you please return these. Under the circumstances . . . And please don't tell Mother I gave them back."

"Scout's honour." I put the pearls into my jacket pocket. "How will you get to your grandmother's? I know for a fact the chauffeur is off duty for the night."

"We'll walk," she replied. "I wore boots and carried my shoes. And the storm has died down."

I walked with my niece and nephew to the front door. Sure enough the wind had fallen and with it the blowing snow.

"If I were to ask my sixth grade class to describe this night," said Jennifer, "they would all write: 'The snow lay on the ground like a blanket, glistening like diamonds.' "

"Well, it does," said her brother.

"Stick to music," said his sister.

I stood in the warmth of the porch, the front door still open, watching them walk away. At the foot of the path they turned. Richard waved; Jennifer blew a kiss. I waved back. A perfect exit.

I was about to close the front door when a car drove up the crescent, blue, with white letters on the door. It braked to a stop and two uniformed officers jumped out and hurried up the walk.

"You called?"

"It wasn't me – I, officer. There has been a misunderstanding. Would you please come inside?"

Carefully wiping their feet, the two officers stepped gingerly into the front hall.

"This may take a minute," I said. "I don't suppose being on duty you'd like a drink. But come and have something to eat, and some coffee, and I'll explain what happened."

I ushered them into the dining room and handed them each a plate. "Just help yourselves. I'll go and get the man who actually made the call." I crossed to the library. Patrick got me into this; let him mollify the officers he had summoned.

I gave him the signal to follow me, and we headed back to the dining room. Lois intercepted us at the foot of the staircase.

"Geoffry, there are two policemen at the buffet. Did you invite them in?"

"Yes, I did. They heard about the wedding and they want to be ushers. Truth time, Patrick, and make it good."

While Patrick was telling the police officers a somewhat edited version of recent events, Lois excused herself to see the last guests out the door. This meant that ad hoc staff could be dismissed, while the resident staff cleared away the buffet. The two police officers ate voraciously, far more interested in the lobster than in asking questions. Such faint curiosity as they may have felt was soon quelled by suggesting a second helping. With obvious reluctance they pulled themselves away from the food, the coffee urn, the warmth, to head out into snowy streets.

That left Patrick, Lois, and me, "in calm of mind, all passion spent."

"Richard took Jennifer back to my mother's, where he will stay the night. She really didn't feel up to a cheery goodnight." I felt Lois deserved that much explanation.

"That's a relief," she said. "Neither do I. Charles has got Douglas calmed down. They're watching a Sherlock Holmes movie on television."

"I can't think of a better thing to do after trashing a party, or what once was a party."

Abandoned plates, orphaned glasses, crumpled napkins, and ashtrays filled with toothpicks bore evidence of a celebration whose *raison d'être* had vanished like the beef and shrimp.

"What do you say, Chadwick. Time to hitch up the dogs and sled home?"

"I guess you're right, Fitzgerald. If we get into a postmortem over tonight's events we'll be here until Wednesday. I suppose we'll have to tramp down the hill and hope to flag a cab."

"I'll drive you," volunteered Lois. "I'll get the Buick."

"That's way beyond the call of hostess duty," I remonstrated. "You've had to cope with more crises tonight than the Red Cross. At least spare yourself driving through that winter wonderland."

Lois laughed spontaneously. "No arguments. I'm so far up I feel I'm never going to sleep again. A drive is just what I need. Give me three minutes to change."

"He's right," added Patrick. "You probably don't believe it, but we can find our own way home – provided you pin our mittens to our sleeves.

But Lois was already going up the stairs. I confess I had been genuinely surprised by her offer of a lift. During our recent tête-à-tête in her bedroom I had not pulled any punches. Nor had she, for that matter. But the fight was over and done with; she seemed to harbour no resentment. Neither did I, but I had delivered far more zingers than she. I must say I admire people who can slug it out, then carry on as before. Grudges take energy; they must be fed and watered like house plants. But the entire evening had been so bizarre that it was almost impossible to apply any conventional standard for judging it. I decided to play the rest by ear.

Our coats and boots had been brought into the front hall. Patrick and I dressed to go out. In the dining room the white-uniformed cook dealt with the leftover food, while the maid collected dead drinks. The party was officially over.

Lois came down the stairs wearing an oversized black wool turtleneck and black slacks. She filled them out generously but well. She pulled on her boots, slung on her mink, and led the way down to the basement and into the garage.

Patrick hopped into the back seat. Lois started the car, flicked a control to open the automatic door, and we pulled out onto the crescent. By now major streets were being cleared. Logic dictated we drop Patrick first at the corner of his still unploughed street, from where he had to wade half a block to his apartment.

"Thanks, Lois. Sorry about the false pretenses. But under the circumstances . . ."

"Please! Don't apologize. I'll be dining out on this evening for the rest of the year."

"Goodnight likewise to you, Chadwick. I'll be in touch."

He shut the door. Walking through deep snow is one of life's more undignified activities, even for the young and spry. But snow-covered countries don't have tarantulas or killer bees or malarial mosquitoes. I guess the occasional blizzard is a fair tradeoff.

Lois drove me to my apartment building, whose front door faced a street that merited early ploughing.

"The party's over," I said.

"The candles flicker and dim."

"I guess this is not au revoir; it is goodbye. I shall go upstairs and put my morning coat into mothballs."

"Geoffry," Lois began tentatively, "could we have lunch some day? My treat. If I am to deal intelligently with Douglas I'm sure to have some questions."

"Sure. Why not? He's going to need some dealing with. But he is your son, and you may as well get as much mileage out of him as you can. Accepting him for what he is seems like a good start. I thought he handled tonight as badly as was humanly possible. But he is still young; he can grow. Just don't stand in his way."

"Yes, sir, Mr. Chadwick. Remember: I'm going to have my hands full being forty-five for the next twenty years."

We both began to laugh.

"Do you suppose we will ever be friends?" she asked after a minute.

"I don't know. It's too soon to tell. At least hostilities appear to have ceased, and that's a step in the right direction. Thanks for the lift, Lois. You needn't have, but I'm awfully glad you did."

Almost as a reflex gesture, Lois leaned sideways, offering her cheek to be kissed. Then, abruptly, she jerked her head back and pulled the glove from her right hand. "Goodnight, Geoffry."

I shook the hand she offered. "Goodnight, Lois." Just about to get out of the car, I remembered something. "Jennifer asked me to return these," I said, handing her the necklace.

Lois held her hand up, not out. "I really would like her to have them, if you can persuade her."

"I'll try," I said as I swung myself out of the car. On the sidewalk I turned and waved. She gave a brief toot on the horn and pulled away.

In my apartment, still wide awake, I changed into a bathrobe. I poured myself a glass of club soda, sat in my Eames chair, and switched on the television set. Sherlock Holmes, complete with pipe and profile, was explaining something to a disbelieving Watson.

Perhaps I should have spoken to Charles before leaving, but I was all talked out. Also, saying goodnight to Charles would have meant speaking to Douglas, and I did not feel like being civil to that poison ivy leaguer. I would have been hard pressed not to bounce him off the walls. Small matter; the wedding file could now be stamped CLOSED. I put my tumbler onto the floor beside my chair and fell instantly asleep.

XVI

There are no happy endings, but sometimes events manage to steer themselves into channels that make us glad. The cocaine caper went off without a hitch. Melvin Abrams, a.k.a. Manuel Alvarez, a.k.a. Daniel Sanchez drove, as Mother would have said, like a bat out of hell, using the weight, power, and sheer presence of the limousine to break through drifts, bring snowploughs to a skidding halt, and send those adventurous souls on skis and snowmobiles dashing for cover. It was, as Officer Reynolds was later to admit in hushed, almost reverential tones, a triumph of the chauffeur's art.

Sanchez parked outside the seedy row of triplexes, climbed the unshovelled outdoor circular staircase in slippery oxfords, pushed his way into the squalid flat, and handed over the much travelled parcel in exchange for a sports bag full of money. (At least it wasn't in a briefcase.) Hot on his half-rubber, half-leather heels, the RCMP, led by Officer Reynolds, moved in to make arrests. Escape through the drifts was out of the question; besides, the element of surprise turned out to be complete. Nobody even fired a shot, and Lois's limousine was returned without a scratch, a nick, or even a bullet hole through the windshield. Not a single incident in the entire operation could have been incorporated into a film for Pay-TV, so smoothly did the enterprise wrap itself up.

The chauffeur, whose name really was Daniel Sanchez, turned out to be an agent from Colombia working with the RCMP to intercept a huge shipment of cocaine so pure it made 24 carat gold seem positively adulterated. The cocaine in our package finally ended up flushed down a toilet, not laid out in neat rows on the lid, and the shipment itself went up in a sheet of highly euphoric flame.

Now that he had become a sort of local hero, almost better-looking in photographs than in person, Daniel Sanchez doffed his chauffeur's livery and hopped into Lois's large white bed for a steamy reconciliation, or so I was able to gather from the hints she dropped over the pricey lunch she bought me the following Thursday. From undercover, Daniel Sanchez had gone under the covers, and Lois positively glowed. The subject of Douglas never even came up.

It has been observed that the way to a man's heart is through his stomach, a saw I have always doubted, certainly for someone as uninterested in food as I. By the same token, the way to a woman's heart may not necessarily lie through multiple orgasms, but they are a pretty good substitute until the real thing comes along. Now that Daniel Sanchez had turned from chauffeur into officer of the law – a less radical metamorphosis, granted, than from frog into prince – Lois realized she had grown quite attached to this taciturn man who was merely tall, dark, well built, drop-dead handsome, and a ten in the kip.

Unfortunately, now that his mission had been accomplished, there was nothing to keep him from returning to Colombia, of which country he was a citizen. However, our Señor Sanchez was reluctant to return to his home and native land, not surprising when one remembers that the leading cause of death for men under forty-five there is murder. Furthermore, his role in the drug bust had given him a certain profile, one that could make a return home hazardous to his health. As a result, he found that Canada, even buried in snow and a search for national identity, seemed a haven.

"Marry him, Lois," I heard myself saying over an excellent Bordeaux. "You're a Canadian citizen. By marrying you he could remain, without all the hassle of returning home and trying to emigrate, providing he isn't shot before he is issued his papers."

"I don't know whether I could. He's so much younger. I know perfectly well what people will think."

"They won't think, Lois; they'll know – that you are being well and truly laid. And they'll be green, but what do you care. You'll probably be saving his life. And remember: screwing well is the best revenge. Also, with a young, healthy husband, you will not spend the golden years as a widow."

Lois fell silent, but I could tell she was thinking furiously.

"I understand the second time around you are not supposed to wear white," I suggested, "at least according to Amelia Gates. You have a perfect house for a wedding. You've even broken in the temporary staff."

Lois tapped a crimson nail against her front teeth. "Would you give me away?"

"Why not? I'm all revved up for a wedding, doesn't much matter whose. Just so long as there is no video."

"Heaven forbid. A camera always adds ten pounds. Oh my goodness, Geoffry. I'll have to think this over carefully."

"Just let me know the date," I replied.

Mildred took the news of the broken engagement with less fuss than Jennifer had expected. I was not as surprised as my niece, having known my sister a lot longer. Mildred is a woman of intense but brief enthusiasms. Three months is generally the amount of time she will spend on any one project before moving on to the next. By now her excitement for the wedding had begun to wane, to be replaced by high indignation over the way refugees were being treated by our surly immigration officials. She opened her house to a family from Sri Lanka. In fact, no sooner had Jennifer moved out to share an apartment with the friend who was to have been her maid of honour, a move I heartily approved, than her vacant bedroom was filled by an immigrant student, whom Mildred tried to wean onto wholesome Canadian food. I sometimes wondered whether, faced daily by Mildred's fascist christianity, those former boat people were not, on occasion, filled with nostalgia for the boat. But they were warm and well fed, and Mildred had her hands way too full to bother me. Why argue with success?

It took one five-day visit from Douglas to New York to convince my nephew that this particular love was transient rather than true. Gone were the obstacles so dear to the homosexual young, for whom love must be doomed from the start in order to be any fun. Having to den-mother Douglas through his coming-out period, while having to prepare for his Ph.D. orals, had led Richard to utter that deathless line, "Let's just be friends." After being granted his own Ph.D., Douglas went off to teach at an agricultural college in Ontario. Perhaps it was a dirty trick for Quebec to play on a sister province, but Douglas

Fullerton moved out of my vision, my thoughts, my life.

Meanwhile, back in Toronto, Charles met a chubby, cheerful French Canadian named Claude, who adored food. They fell calorically in love, and opened their own business: Double C Catering, Ltd. It sounded more like a ranch than a cottage industry, but it soon flourished into a booming business, especially in catering corporate functions. Charles calls me once a month, and we talk like old, old friends, which one day we may become.

The happiest ending of all, as far as I was concerned, was the unconventional one. To have grown up on novels celebrating marriage as women's ultimate achievement caused me to smile as I thought how pleased I was that Jennifer was not going to marry Douglas. Whatever their respective destinies, they were both better off alone searching for the pot of fool's gold at the end of the neon rainbow. Regardless of my own satisfaction at the turn of events, I still had to tread softly with Mother, who took a few days to absorb the full impact of the idea that there really was to be no wedding. The Sunday following the party I went to lunch.

"I had so looked forward to seeing Jennifer come down the aisle on your arm," she began over vodka. "You in your tailcoat, she in her Regency gown, while the organ played Wagner's march from *Siegfried*."

"That's how it goes, Mother. We'll never get to hear the soprano soloist sing 'I know that my Redeemer spendeth.' "

"Now I probably won't live to see any of my grandchildren married." She paused for a swallow of vodka that would have shortened the life of an elephant. "I had so looked forward to seeing Jennifer married, even though I don't have a thing to wear."

"I know, Mother, but Jennifer came to realize that Douglas wasn't the right man for her, fortunately before she married him. I am quite certain you wouldn't want any of your grandchildren to marry unless you knew for certain they would be as happy as you were with Father."

"You know, dear, you're absolutely right." She brightened perceptibly. "Nobody could have had a happier marriage than Craig and I. Poor Craig."

I knew I was shamelessly manipulating Mother's memory, but I thought the end justified the means. She and Father had undergone the marriage of their generation, a chaste courtship followed by the compromises of conjugal life: two children followed in time by two bedrooms, a courteous, almost formal relationship, with no real intimacy at the core. But it was their marriage, and it would never have occurred to either of them not to see it through to the end.

After Father died, Mother slid gently into drink and nostalgia. Glimpsing backwards through a rose-coloured telescopic lens, Mother remembers her marriage as the paragon of unions. Who am I to disabuse her of this reassuring fantasy?

She took a swallow of her drink. "Something this morning, I can't for the life of me remember what it was, reminded me of the time Craig and I took the train to Niagara Falls. Mildred was about two, so it wasn't a honeymoon trip, you may be sure. Did I ever tell you the story?"

"No, I don't believe so," I fibbed. "But before you begin, why don't I get us both another little drink?"

"Well, perhaps a small one."

I returned to the living room carrying two belts of vodka and settled myself for the now familiar story. I knew that Mother was never more content than when reminiscing about Father, reliving what for her had become the Golden Age, which ended the year Father died. But as she related the well-told tale, she forgot her disappointment over Jennifer's broken engagement. What the hell! I had a fresh drink, and Madame had made tourtière for lunch.

"Didn't you stop over in Brockville to see Cousin Celeste?" I asked.

"You're right. I had forgotten. But, Geoffry, you must have heard this all before."

"So long ago I've forgotten the details."

"You're right. We did stop over in Brockville to see Cousin Celeste. She came down to the station wearing the most dreadful hat you have ever seen . . ."

Predictably, Lois married the man, in a small private ceremony at 15 Mayfair Crescent. She came down the grand staircase on my arm, wearing knee-length café-au-lait chiffon with matching picture hat. Off the record, the wedding gown was the one she had originally intended to wear to Douglas's wedding. Her dressmaker had pruned the skirt (hemming chiffon must be hell on earth) and added a little something to the neckline to make it a touch more demure. Lois carried a huge spray of white orchids, and I had to admit she looked splendid. I looked pretty good myself, as Lois had asked me to wear my thrift-shop morning coat. Fortunately, my grey hair and deep lines prevented me from looking like a chorus boy in a 1930s musical comedy.

In *Fifteen Steps to a Lovelier Wedding*, Amelia Gates says the keynote of a second ceremony must be simplicity. Lois decided against potted palms and a striped awning, and compromised on baskets of long-stemmed white roses on each of the steps leading down from the landing. We paused briefly on the landing, just long enough for the guests to admire her legs, then came slowly down the stairs, carefully avoiding the roses, which were to be delivered after the ceremony to a palliative care hospital. For some mysterious reason the terminally ill are supposed to love fresh flowers.

The groom wore a double-breasted blazer and flannels, no doubt because a blue suit was too reminiscent of the chauffeur's livery. He had turned out to be quiet, courteous, and dazzling when he smiled, an expression I had not heretofore seen. He was full of apologies for his hostile behaviour, and arranged for me to be reimbursed for the ruined tire.

And who should be standing in as best man but Patrick, carrying the wedding ring Douglas had designed. When it came to assembling the cast for the small ceremony, it turned out that Daniel Sanchez had no Canadian friends. Working as an undercover agent does not lead to male bonding. Even Officer Reynolds was in Winnipeg on a case, and Lois did not want Douglas, the ambivalent stepson, standing in as best man. (By apparent mutual consent, Douglas and I avoided each other during the reception. I may not wear my heart on my sleeve, but I have been known to carry my spleen on my shoulder. He picked up the unspoken message and kept his distance.)

I volunteered Patrick, knowing he would be happy to undertake the job if only for the wedding meal to follow, another buffet, this one featuring king crab and oysters, mercifully disengaged from their shells. By prior agreement, I toasted the bride.

"To Lois, who learned there is more to Colombia than coffee, and to Daniel, who found his good luck in mukluks. May they drive happily into the future."

It was pretty corny, but I had popped a couple of Glenlivets before the ceremony, "a couple" meaning quite a few. Drinking and toasting don't mix.

There remains to explain why I had presumed to volunteer Patrick as best man. The wedding took place on a Saturday afternoon, and Patrick and I were now spending weekends together.

Let me return to the night of the engagement party. After dozing off in my chair, I awoke just long enough to pop a couple of aspirins and stumble into bed. I slept until after ten the next morning, late for me. I felt a good deal better than I had any right to feel, although I was fully aware that last night had taken place. Coffee helped to get me going. I thought of going out for the Sunday papers, but the idea of all that snow made me stay put and risk an attack of news withdrawal.

I was just about to mix a Bloody Mary, only to take the taste of toothpaste out of my mouth, when the phone rang.

"Geoffry, it's Patrick, a.k.a. Inspector Clouseau. We have a little business to transact. May I come over?"

"If you hurry you'll be in time for the first Bloody Mary. Do you have any tomato juice on the premises?"

"Shall I bring it along?"

"Please, on the double."

"Fifteen minutes or so, depends on the snow."

Seventeen minutes and some seconds later the porter rang up. I gave the requisite clearance and opened the door of my apartment. Patrick stepped off the elevator heavily burdened. In one hand he carried a shopping bag, in the other an irregularly shaped package which could have been flowers, had I not known better. After that true north ritual of peeling off gloves, pulling off boots, tucking the scarf into the sleeve of the overcoat, and blowing his nose, he crossed to the coffee table on which he laid the large package and a red plush box in the shape of a heart he had taken from the shopping bag.

"Candy and flowers for the host."

"La, sir, I'm all pretty confusion." I tore off the protective paper to discover the oddest-looking roses I had ever seen. It took me a minute to realize they were plastic.

"I'm sorry they're a bit dusty," he apologized, "but they've been in my basement locker for some months now, waiting for the right person. Unfortunately, my dishwasher is on the fritz, and a dishwasher is the only way to clean plastic flowers."

"Is that right. Live and learn."

"Open the box."

"It says 'Be My Valentine,' but we're in March. Can I think it over and let you know next Feb. fourteen?"

"Open it."

"Let's have a drink first. Ah's so dry Ah's spittin' cotton. Let's forget all those harmful additives and go for straight vodka and vitamin C."

"Sounds good."

I returned with two tumblers and confronted the large crimson box, whose curves suggested something vaguely obscene.

Teasing off the lid, I found a piece of paper torn in four. On closer inspection the pieces fitted together to form a blank invoice with the heading *Patrick Fitzgerald Associates, Inc.*

"I may be dense, Patrick, but I fail to make the connection."

"It means no charge for services rendered."

"No, no! That won't do at all. I engaged you to uncover and to discourage the person who was bothering me. And that you have done. I insist on paying."

"And I insist it's on the house. After last night's episode of the Keystone Kops I couldn't in all conscience accept a dime. But there's more. You are aware, I am sure, of the significance of candy and flowers?"

"A courting gesture?"

"Correct. I make it a strict rule to keep relations with clients purely professional. But as of now you are no longer a client."

"What am I, then?"

"I think the rest of the day will answer that."

"God almighty! Now I'm being hassled by the detective." But my flip remark could not stifle the surge of euphoria that swept through me like a powerful drug. "Do you want to finish your drink first?"

"Not really."

"This way for a good time," I called over my shoulder as I walked into the bedroom, "although I have to confess it's so long since I've had sex I've forgotten who gets tied up."

Turning back the covers, I found myself laughing out loud. Candy and flowers: a hideous valentine box and ghastly plastic roses, their awful tastelessness the result of far more thought and consideration than mere hothouse flowers and designer chocolates. And I found myself oddly, unexpectedly touched. Candy and flowers indeed!

But isn't it true that love makes the world go square.